THE CHURCH

CELIA AARON

The Church
Celia Aaron
Copyright © 2018 Celia Aaron

Copy Editing by Spell Bound

CONTENTS

CHAPTER 1

GRACE

I spit the come out of my mouth and stand, using the sleeve of my habit to wipe the remnants from my lips.

"You spit?" The guard frowns at me then zips up. "I figured you Spinners would be old-school swallowers."

"Can I go now?" I stand and edge around him.

He grabs my arm and squeezes until it hurts. "Five minutes. That's it."

"Okay."

"Go." He shoves me, and I almost fall, but the gravel is forgiving, my flats skating over the surface as I gain my feet.

Brushing the dust from my black skirt, I hurry into the punishment circle. It's eleven-thirty, and the Prophet is in the middle of his sermon. I won't be missed if I make this quick and get back before he's done.

The three crosses beckon, the center one heavier than the others. Adam hangs there, his head drooping and his body limp. My throat closes, a sob threatening, but I bite it back. I'm good at that.

I hurry to the cross. "Adam."

He opens his eyes.

"Adam, it's me."

"I know who it is. What do you want?" His voice is still gruff, but scratchier now. Raw.

I say the first words that come to mind. "I'm sorry."

"Always with the sorry." He shifts his feet on the tiny scrap of wood beneath him, doing his best to support himself.

Blood still oozes from the wounds in his hands, and I know they'll scar horribly. I'm deeply familiar with flesh —how easily it's marred, how quickly it can bleed, and how long-lasting the damage can be.

I'm fascinated by the rips in him, the man I used to think was invincible.

"Well?"

I look him in the eye again. "Your mother is working to get you down as soon as possible."

He smirks, his personality still intact even if his body is bruised and broken. "What's her plan? Murder another innocent and ask the Father of Fire to intervene? No thanks."

"No." I reach out and touch the cold wood, the texture rough and ugly under my fingertips. "She's going to speak to your father."

"Because that works so well." He grimaces and shifts his feet again.

So much pain. That's what this entire place is—pain. Given and taken. I'm a walking testament to it. But I play my part, like I always have. I bide my time. I hurt whoever gets in my way, and I won't stop until Adam is by my side and the Prophet is buried in a shallow grave.

"She can do more than you think. But I need you to trust her. To trust *me*." My voice shakes as I speak the deepest desire of my heart—to mend the trust I broke, to bring back that spark of love that I extinguished with my foolish devotion to the Prophet.

He spits on the ground next to me. "Never."

"Adam, please." I reach up toward him, but he's so far away—just like he's always been since … Since *she* died.

"How can I trust you? *You?*" He shakes his head and winces. "I can't."

"You can." I grip the cross so hard my knuckles crack. "I can show you."

3

"How, Jenny? How?"

He uses my name. My *real* name, and some small piece of me is reborn.

"I'll ..." I lean my forehead on the wood. "I can maybe ..."

"Delilah," he grinds out her name.

I recoil. "What about that whore?"

"You take care of her, and I'll trust you."

"What?" I want her dead, not under my wing. The moment she came to the Cloister, the moment she touched *my* Adam, she's been a never-ending source of trouble. I've been pushing for the senator to take her as soon as possible. Delilah is nothing more than another harlot who thinks she can tempt Adam. I'll be damned if I do anything to save her from her well-deserved fate with Senator Roberts. "Why would I ever do anything for her? She's the reason you're here. She led you down the wrong path with her virgin pussy and freakish looks. If it weren't for her, you'd—"

"Jenny!" He struggles to stand, more blood spilling from his palms. "You heard me. You protect her, keep her away from that senator. If you can do that—if you can *show* me that you're capable of doing what I ask in that regard—then, *and only then*, will I trust you." He ends on a harsh breath, as if it's his last.

I walk around the cross, as if playing a harmless game of "Ring Around the Rosie," as I think about what he's said.

Do I feel threatened? No. Of course not. I laugh the thought away. Delilah is nothing, no one. She doesn't have the history that Adam and I have. Once she's gone, he won't even give her another moment of his time. He's mine. He's always been mine, and one Maiden with a shitty attitude can't change that.

"Well?" he grates.

I stop in front of him and peer up at the man who owns half of my soul and all of my heart. "If I keep her away from the senator, then you'll take me back?"

"Keep her *safe*, which includes keeping her away from that dickwad. If you can do that, I'll trust you again."

Trust. Adam used to be big on that. Maybe he still is. To me, it's just a word that can be used to control people, to bend them to your will. But for him, it's something bigger. I don't understand it, but I want it all the same. That and so much more.

The idea of helping Delilah burns like acid in my veins, but it doesn't have to be all bad. After all, I'm the one on the ground, the one with leverage. Adam can't call the shots from the cross. Not really.

"Here's the deal." I fold my arms over my chest. "I'll keep her safe. You have my word. But when this is over and you're the new Prophet, you will cast her out and marry me."

His mouth hardens into a line. "Jenny, I can't—"

5

I turn on my heel and walk away.

"Jenny!" he calls, his worn voice breaking.

I stop and face him. "What's your answer?" My heart forgets to beat, hanging on whatever words spill from his battered mouth next.

He sags, pain twisting his face into an ugly mask. "It's a deal."

CHAPTER 2

DELILAH

*W*arm water runs over me, though I can barely feel it.

Ruth, the apparent leader of the women in the Cathedral, stands behind me and asks, "Too hot?"

I shake my head and wrap my arms around myself. "I don't know what to do." My thoughts are fractured, but that one flows out with utter clarity. I'm lost. Adam is crucified. And no one can help either of us.

"You can't do much. Not when you're in here." She leans against the white tile wall, just out of reach of the spray. "And not when you're nearly frozen through."

"I have to save him. He can't stay up there like that." I can see him so clearly, the anguish pouring out of him and painting everything in a desperate black.

7

"The Prophet will take him down." She hands me a bottle of body wash. "Eventually."

"When?" I just stare at the soap she's offering.

"We have to wait."

"Wait?" I take the body wash, my movements more mechanical than human. "That's the only thing you've told me since I got here."

She proffers a baby-blue bath sponge. "When you're locked in, surrounded by armed guards, and scrutinized at all times, that's all you can do." She shakes the sponge.

I grab it.

A bell rings somewhere outside the wide, white bathroom.

She sighs. "I'm going to service. You'll stay here, most likely. I doubt you'll be allowed out of the Cathedral. I'd play sick and stay for you, but it's one of the few times I get to see my son Ezekiel. Just stay put and warm up. I'll lay out some clothes for you on my bed, okay?"

"Why?"

"Why what?"

"Why are you being kind to me?" I glance around at the wide expanse of empty shower stalls. None of the other women have come near me in the short time I've been at the Cathedral. And even though I know Ruth is part of whatever Chastity has bubbling on the compound, that doesn't mean it's smart for her to take such an obvious interest in me. After all, I'm a problem.

"Sometimes that's all we have left. Being kind." She turns, her dark braid flowing down her back. "I'll be back after service. Maybe I'll know more. But don't count on it." She disappears into the tile labyrinth, and I'm left alone with my unwieldy thoughts and the hiss of the water.

I lean against the wall, and the vision of Adam nailed to the cross invades my mind and brings me to my knees. My heart is twisted and punctured, and I wonder if I can survive this? Can Adam? The tears don't come. I must have shed them all at Adam's feet.

My tears meant nothing to the Prophet, who oozed satisfaction as Adam suffered. *"Let this be a lesson to any here who would think to defy me. I am the Lord's Prophet, and I will punish the unjust!"*

No one helped him. Not even Noah, his own brother. The man just stood stone-faced and stared. But maybe that fits. If he killed Georgia, what's a little more suffering to him? Nothing. He was probably just glad it wasn't him up there, naked and beaten. Something sparks beneath my despair, lighting it on fire with slow blue flames. Adam didn't deserve his fate. But there are plenty of people here that do.

The same rage that fueled me to find Georgia's killer begins to percolate in my veins, all of it directed at the

Prophet. Any man who would torture his own son deserves a slow death. I drop the sponge and turn my palms over. Water trickles down my skin, and I feel every minute movement. Could I use these hands to kill someone? *Yes.*

The truth whispers through my mind. When I came here, I wanted answers and vengeance. Now—after seeing what the Prophet is capable of—I've changed. How could I not? Violence and terror are harsh mistresses that mar everything they touch. Including me.

I'm not after closure anymore. I'm after blood.

I should be shocked at my thoughts, afraid of what I intend to do. But I'm not. I pull myself up to my feet and lean my head back, embracing the flowing water instead of hiding from it.

I'm done being a Maiden, done pretending to believe in the Prophet. I will fight and claw and kill if I have to. I don't know how just yet, but I'll find a way.

Heavenly will burn. I smile. It's a real one that reaches all the way down to my roots. Pure delight prickles along my skin at the thought of the Prophet hung on that same cross, his lifeblood pouring out of him.

"Fuck me."

I startle and open my eyes.

Evan Roberts stands outside my shower stall, his gaze roving over my naked body.

I drape one arm across my breasts and cross my legs.

"It's already in here." He taps his temple. "Not to mention what I've got on my phone."

"What are you doing here?" I dart forward and grab the towel from the hook. "I'm tainted goods, remember?"

He smiles as I wrap myself up and flip off the water. "You aren't pure anymore, that's true." Stepping to the side, he blocks my way out of the shower. "But I blew off some steam last night and saw a beautiful sight this morning."

I glare.

"Oh, not you, darling, though I enjoyed the show." He smirks. "Adam on the cross—it was the best way imaginable to start my day. Dropped by to get a good look before I came here. He wouldn't speak to me. But I told him a few things—mostly about what I intend to do to you. How I'm going to fuck every one of your holes till you bleed. And then I might share you. I haven't decided on that part yet. And, because I want to show that I'm still a good sport, even though he stole something from me, I promised him I'd send him the video."

My knees threaten to give, but I straighten my back. I won't show any weakness in front of him. Never again.

I step forward with feigned strength. "I can still feel him inside me. Did you know that?" A thrill pulses through me when his smirk dies. "Maybe I'll always feel him since he was my first." I close my eyes and make an mmm

11

sound. "God, what I wouldn't give for another time with him. Just one more—"

He grabs me by my throat and slams me against the tile. "Shut your mouth!"

I keep my smile intact despite the pain in the back of my head. "He was so thick, filled me until I thought I'd burst." I bite my lip. "I wanted it from him. All of him. He made me bleed, then kept fucking me until I came. No one can take his place."

His grip tightens, his face only inches from mine. "Is that what you want? To be fucked until you bleed?"

"Yes." I lick my lips. "But only by Adam."

Squeezing harder, he blocks my breath. "You fucking tease." He slides his other hand between my thighs. "You want me riled up?" He cups my sex, his fingers seeking to punish, not please. "You got it."

Someone clears their throat, and a man's voice echoes through the empty shower room. "I'm sorry, Senator. But you can't touch the Maiden until you've—"

"Bought her. I know. I fucking *know*." He removes his hands and steps back. Letting out a labored breath, he burns me with his harsh gaze, the psychopath inside blazing through.

I swallow and tamp down the well-hidden panic. Maybe I can't stop my fear, but I can refuse to give in to it.

"I'll never stop talking about him, thinking about him, wanting him instead of you." I tighten my towel around me. "Never."

He clears the way for me to walk by, but I stay put. All my trust belongs to Adam, no one else.

He puts his hands up, palms out, and backs up another step. "If you think your smart mouth is going to stop me, you don't know me at all."

"I don't want to know you, and you don't want to know me." I hurry past him. "I will fight you, hurt you, do everything I can to kill you."

"Maiden!" The guard glowers. "Watch your mouth, and know your place."

I stride past him. "I know my place. It's beneath Adam Monroe."

The guard grabs me by my hair and wheels me around to face Evan. "Apologize to the senator."

"No." I grit my teeth.

He yanks harder as Evan approaches, hunger in his eyes. "I said apologize, bitch."

Despite the flaring pain in my scalp, I glue my lips together.

Evan grabs the front of my towel and rips it away.

I will not cower. No matter what he does.

He licks his lips as the guard presses a cold barrel against my temple. "Apologize."

"Don't move. Either of you." Evan pulls his phone from his pocket and holds it up.

"Sick fuck." I want to smash his goddamn camera.

"You have no idea." After a few camera clicks, he grins, pockets his phone, then motions to the guard. "Now put that away."

"She needs to—"

"I said put that away!" His yell is like a shot.

The barrel disappears as does the grip on my hair. I scoop my towel off the floor and dart past the guard and into the large dormitory with the baby-blue carpet.

Evan follows me to Ruth's alcove. "I'll be back for you, Delilah."

I edge away from her bed, though I eye the clothes she's laid out. I won't let Evan catch me off guard. "I'll kill you." It's not a threat. Just a fact.

"Do you have any idea how hard that makes me?" He runs the heel of his palm over his crotch.

"I'm not playing some power game with you." I shake my head at him. "This isn't foreplay or some sort of lure. This is me telling you that I want you dead. I don't know how to make myself any clearer—I will fucking kill you if you touch me."

The guard moves up, his glower verging on a death mask.

"Oh, I believe you'll try. Probably several times until I break you." Evan straightens his tie and runs a hand through his too-perfect hair. "But I *will* break you."

"I hope you like the taste of your own blood." I don't know how to fight, but I will do whatever it takes. Desperation can turn anyone into a gladiator.

"I'll enjoy the taste of yours more." He gives me a smug grin. "But I won't be paying full price for you. Not anymore. I'll head up to the church and do some horse-trading. After that, you'll be mine."

"I'll *never* be yours." I put every ounce of venom I have into my words.

His smugness increases ten-fold as he turns and walks away. "Oh darling, I love it when you underestimate me."

CHAPTER 3

NOAH

"*R*at me out. See if I give a fuck." I stagger past the guard on the road leading to the punishment circle. Or maybe there are two roads? It's fuzzy at the moment.

"The Prophet said—"

"Fuck off!" I keep walking.

He gives up.

I kind of wish he'd put his hands on me so I could stomp the shit out of him. *Damn.* I'm thinking like Adam. Not good. Especially considering where thinking like Adam got Adam. I chuckle and burp, but somehow manage to keep walking.

The day is chilly though the sun is high and bright. The morning service ended an hour ago. I had to attend, waiting in the wings. But I took two bottles with me, drinking up as my father preached about the new year and the new future for Heavenly.

All I can think about is the numbing liquor and Adam. I can still hear his screams. They echo through my mind whenever things get too quiet. So I drink to keep the noise going, the slosh of my mind roaring in my ears.

Adam doesn't move as I approach. For a moment, I fear he's as dead as Christ on the cross. But Adam won't get a second chance to come back. If they roll the stone away from his crypt, they'll only find rot and death, not a fresh new savior.

"Shut up," I berate myself and continue walking toward him until I'm standing beneath the cross. "Adam?"

His eyes open, and he shifts his feet on the narrow plank. "Afternoon." His hoarse voice hides the pain that I can see all too well in the bright sun. Bloodied hands, each one with a nail through it. His skin is already chafing at the edges of the leather straps that hold his upper arms to the wood.

My eyes water. The pain isn't gone. The liquor didn't dull it enough. Fuck. My knees go weak, and I drop to the cold ground. Great, heaving sobs that aren't fit for a man like me—they come anyway, rolling through my body.

It's all so fucked, and there's nothing I can do. I can't take Adam down. I can't stop my father's madness. I can't even fucking drink myself to sleep like a decent alcoholic. I weep until my nose is running and I can barely breathe.

"Noah." His voice scratches its way through to me.

"I'm sorry." The words hurtle out as I gaze up at him.

"Not your fault." He winces and changes position again, his legs shaking from the effort.

"I can't do anything." I shake my head.

"I know." He lets his weight go for a moment, allowing the leather straps to hold him up and give his legs some relief. A low wail rips from him, and his hands bleed more, crimson drops plopping to the barren ground.

"Oh, God." I swipe at my eyes and stand. "I have to get you down."

"No." He flexes his legs again, standing. "Don't."

"You'll die." I'm wearing a light jacket, but I can feel the cool air seeping through. "When it gets dark, for sure. You'll die of exposure."

"Maybe." He peers down at me, constant pain etched into his face. "But you can't interfere. You don't want to be up here with me."

If I wasn't such a coward, that's exactly where I would be. I should have listened to him, taken some chances. Instead, here I am, drunk, useless, and a fucking disgrace. "I can't let him kill you."

"He won't."

"How do you know?"

19

"If he wanted to kill me, he would have done it already. With more show. And probably with fire or some sort of over-the-top crazy shit."

"You're just guessing." The cross seems pretty fucking over-the-top crazy to me.

"Maybe." He shakes his head a little. "But I'm not what's important. I need you to help Delilah. Save her. Don't let that senator take her."

"How?"

"I don't know, and I can't do anything about it at the moment." He lets out a raspy laugh. "A bit tied up. Really nailed." He winces, his false bravado cracking under his own weight.

"How did we get here?" I dig my palms into my eye sockets, trying to rub away the image of my brother, naked, nailed to a fucking cross. It doesn't go anywhere. Will it ever leave?

He doesn't offer an answer.

I look up again, the sacrilege and horror melding into a desperate need to vomit that I force down. My panic rises instead. "I can get you. I just need—I don't know—a ladder or something."

"You can't." His hoarse voice drops to a whisper. "You can't save me, Noah."

"When it gets dark, the temperature will plummet. You won't last up there." Will Dad let him die like this? No matter what Adam says, I don't know the answer, and that scares the shit out of me.

He lets his head hang. Maybe he's only been holding it up this whole time out of pride, or worse—to show me that he can take it. He can't. No one can.

"Leave it, Noah. I told you. I can't have you up here next to me. Look after Delilah. Keep an eye on Dad. Don't let on about Mom. And ... talk to Grace. See if you can work with her to help Delilah."

"Grace?" I must be hearing things. Thanks, liquor.

"Yes. She will want to keep Delilah safe."

"Did I just enter some other, I don't know, reality or something?"

"Just trust me. But not her all the way. Or Mom."

"Mom. Right." The booze still forms a film over my thoughts, but she cuts through it. "Maybe she can do something."

"She won't tip her hand. Not yet. Not until she's ready to take over." He narrows his eyes, my shrewd brother still alive inside his aching shell. "Don't believe anything she tells you. Not really. She's a snake. Don't show her your weaknesses. Spin lies with your truth. If you're honest with her, she'll use that information to gut you when the time's right."

21

"How do you know?"

"Because that's how I'd play it." His brow furrows. "I need you to go."

"What? Why?"

"I can't hold on much longer. My legs. They're already worn out. I have to let go again. But when I do ..."

"Fuck." I step toward the cross. Maybe I can scale it and give him some sort of relief.

"Don't." He tenses. "Can't risk it. Please. Go."

I want to roar and tear the fucking cross out of the ground. But I got him here. My actions—or, really, my inaction. Because I wouldn't back him, he's here. My eyes tingle. *Fuck.*

"I'm sorry." I won't cry. Not again. Not ever. I don't deserve it. "I'm so sorry."

"None of this is your fault. You were so young when this all started." His scratchy voice softens. "You didn't have a chance, Noah. Not at all."

"Don't make excuses for me."

"They're not excuses. Just the truth. You can't help it. I forgive you. I'll always forgive you."

Just hearing him say it knocks the breath out of me.

"Please." His voice breaks. "Go before I can't—" His words cut off on a wretched groan as his toes slip off the edge. "Please," he gasps.

"Fuck!" I'm desperate to climb up and help.

"Go." It's not a request, he's begging me. I've never heard him beg, not like this, not broken to the point that I see the boy inside the man—the same scared kid that I was when our father started Heavenly and tore us away from everything we knew. The same scared kid I *am*.

Against every instinct I have, I turn and stride away, my steps still wobbly but with renewed purpose.

I'm barely out of the punishment circle before his searing cry tears through the chilled air, cutting through bone and straight to my heart.

CHAPTER 4

DELILAH

One Year Ago

The white plastic chair creaks beneath me as I take my seat toward the back. Several other women file into the room, purple worship binders in their hands. The church service ended with the Prophet asking that any women interested in joining the Cloister meet in one of the fellowship rooms.

I wait as the room fills, at least two-dozen women taking seats, some whispering amongst themselves. In my time at Heavenly, I've been polite and spoken to people who've approached me, but I haven't made any friends. That's not what I'm here for. So I sit alone, empty seats on either side that only become occupied when there is nowhere else left.

A young woman, maybe eighteen, with strawberry blonde hair sits to my right and holds her binder to her chest. "Hi,

I'm Sabrina." Her voice is small, the squeak of a mouse, but she's friendly.

"Nice to meet you. I'm Emily." We don't shake, but a soft layer of comfort falls between us like a light snow.

"I hope I get picked." She turns to look at me, her eyes big and green.

I swallow my real thoughts, tucking them away, and say, "So do I."

"We could be Maidens together. Do the Lord's work." She smiles. "Bring glory to the Prophet."

My devout persona chafes the real me, but I return her smile. "Wouldn't that be a blessing?"

"The highest." She nods and turns away, likely lost in thoughts of how great the Cloister must be.

I know better, but revealing it now—even if it would help these girls—isn't part of the plan. So I stay quiet and wait.

When the Prophet walks in, he beams at us, his charm a fountain that never runs out. The chatter stops, and we all focus on the one man who claims to know God's plan for our lives.

"Ladies." He stands at a wooden lectern at the front, and someone closes the door with a faint metallic click. "I'm so glad to see you all here. Thank you for coming."

Some women murmur "thank you" in response.

"I know there's a lot of talk about what the Cloister is, especially when people see the Maidens in their white dresses and veils. But here, at this informational meeting, I'm going to tell you what it is and what it isn't."

I know what it is.

"The Cloister is a place of safety. Somewhere young women can go and live and learn for one year. There, you will be taken care of and treated as holy. Every need you have will be taken care of, and you will want for nothing. There is only one requirement that you must meet in order to be considered." His gaze sweeps the room. "And I'm certain you young ladies won't have a problem getting over this hurdle. In order to be sacred to the Lord, you must be pure of heart, mind, and body. I won't go into details and shock your finer sensibilities, but if you aren't sure what I mean, please feel free to ask one of your sisters here or, if you see a Spinner, she can guide you with the knowledge. The Spinners are holy servants, and serve me and the Maidens with equal parts love and devotion."

I glance around. A few of the women fidget, their fingers clasped in front of them. Others keep their eyes on the Prophet. I would guess that maybe a third of them just got disqualified. They have no idea how lucky they are.

"We have a questionnaire for each of you to fill out. Basic questions about your heritage, education, interests—things like that. We wouldn't want to pry, of course, but we need truthful answers." He motions toward the door. It opens,

27

and a Spinner walks in with a sheaf of papers. She passes them out, and I pull a pen from my handbag and start filling it out as the Prophet continues telling us all the benefits of becoming a Maiden.

Name: *Emily Lanier*

I print my address, birthdate, and social security number. They'll use this information to erase me, to change me into whatever new persona the Prophet creates for me at the Cloister. I discovered the way they erase the victims when I was searching for records on Georgia. Her name had legally been changed to Mary, her taxes filed for her. They even claimed government benefits in her name—food stamps and welfare checks delivered to a Heavenly address. The Prophet's scheme covers every angle, keeps the Maidens dependent on him, and changes them at an almost cellular level into whatever he wants them to be. By filling this out, I'm offering myself up to be destroyed. But I do what I have to do for my sister, for justice.

I fill out every blank space, determined to seem as transparent as possible. I have to get in.

When I come to the final question on the first page, I hesitate.

Reason for Wanting to Become a Maiden:

"The need to know what you bastards did to Georgia and why"—that would be the most accurate, closely followed by "revenge." I write down neither of those and steal a

glance at Sabrina's page. In a neat cursive hand, she's answered the question with "So I can serve the Prophet."

I know a similar answer is the key I need to unlock the Cloister. With a deep breath, I press my pen to the page.

CHAPTER 5

DELILAH

*R*uth never returns to the Cathedral, even though the rest of the women, or "wives" as they call themselves, arrive shortly after the end of church service. When they open the main door, scents of food waft through the air, and my stomach twists. I can't remember the last time I ate.

The wives mill around for a few minutes, none of them meeting my gaze.

"Where's Ruth?" I approach the pregnant one whom I'd encountered briefly the night before, when I first arrived.

She shakes her head.

"Tell me." I grab her elbow.

"Not here." She shakes her arm free. "Now lay off or you'll get me in trouble."

I approach another woman, this one with demure braids and large, expressive eyes. "Why didn't Ruth come back?"

She doesn't reply, but the ghost of an emotion—maybe pity—flickers across her face before dying. "I can't help you." Her small voice matches her steps as she backs away from me slowly. "I'm sorry."

More than hunger eats away at my insides. Something happened to Ruth. It seems like every crutch I'm given falls away the second I put the slightest bit of weight on it. I'm the common thread in all of it. Maybe that's why she's gone. Maybe they saw her talking to me.

Some of the women change clothes and others use the bathroom. I watch them from a perch on one of the couches, though none of them dare approach me. *Wait*, Ruth had said to me so many times. I see why. Nothing here is under my control, and I'm at the mercy of the clock—always waiting for something to happen instead of making it happen myself. I grind my teeth and consider approaching another one of the wives. Surely, one of them will break free and say something helpful, or at least tell me what happened to Ruth.

I rise from the couch, resolve firmly in place, when a low, dull electronic bell rings three times, and the women line up at the doors, a tingle of electric excitement running through them like a current.

"What's happening?" I step to the back of the line, trying to blend in with the wives as the row starts moving forward.

"Lunch," the brunette in front of me whispers.

My stomach clenches again, and my mouth waters as the scent of freshly-baked bread dances around me like a wispy dream. It's odd how specific your sense of smell becomes when you're hungry—I mean the "haven't eaten in days" hungry, not the "I'm jonesing for my next meal" hungry. I can even pick out the notes of browned butter and the unwelcome odor of baked broccoli.

We're led down the main corridor, the guard paying me no attention. But I'm not fooled. I have no doubt that he knows exactly who I am. Whatever I'm doing, it's being allowed by the Prophet.

The sense of nervous excitement grows as the women walk quickly out of the dormitory area. We file through the nursery corridor, some of the women cooing at the babies, then through the hall with children's rooms on either side. They're empty now, the dark rooms with their childish décor eerie and silent.

When we enter the dining area near the front door, the women walk quickly toward the tables, and I can see why. Children are seated at intervals, as if they've been assigned tables, and some of them amble around playing chase with their friends. The kids beam as the women— their mothers, I assume—rush to them and pepper them with kisses. The sweet tinkle of children's laughter and the warm hum of mothers' voices fills the room.

I follow a line of women who aim for a long table against the back wall. No children welcome them, and some of them glance with open envy at the mothers who hug their excited little ones.

The brunette who was in front of me sits near the end of the long table, and I take a seat next to her.

"No kids?" I ask gently.

"The Prophet has blessed me with his seed, but ..." Her cheeks flush, and she clamps her mouth shut.

"I'm sorry." The words are out before I realize it's an odd thing to say. But it's a reflex. I apologize because I've hurt her. Even though the horror of it all isn't lost on me—she's upset because she hasn't become pregnant by her rapist, the Prophet. No matter how willing she may think she is, she's not. The Prophet's lies brought her here, and his armed guards and locked doors keep her.

She straightens up and laces her hands together on the table. "I will be blessed soon. The Prophet has told me so."

So many replies dart across my mind—most of them involving the words "lying monster"—but I keep my thoughts to myself. None of this is her fault, and there's no point railing against the Prophet to a true believer. It makes me wonder if I'll ever be able to shake the wives free of their delusions, or if they'll be like birds that have been caged for far too long—once you let them out, they *can* fly, but they don't know it and never try.

Still, even if they refuse to believe the truth, I'm going to show it to them. Bringing this place down physically is one part, but breaking down the myth of the Prophet is the other. I don't know how I'm going to do it, but I've resolved myself that I will die trying. Hearing Adam's anguished cries from the cross cemented that future for me.

Adam. I close my eyes and see him again, hanging there helpless, a pinned butterfly in a display case. My heartbeat moves to my throat and thunders there, making it hard for me to breathe. The Prophet has to have let him down by now. He wouldn't leave his eldest son there to die. It's the only reassurance I can give myself.

"I heard it was lunchtime!" The Prophet strides in, his arms open wide as several children rush to him. Wearing a white button-down and khaki pants, you'd think he was just a normal middle-aged man, one that doted on his grandchildren and fell asleep watching football on lazy weekend afternoons. The illusion almost holds, shimmers, then shatters. That's not who he is at all.

The children don't yell "Daddy" but there can be no mistaking their lineage. He scoops up one little girl with blonde braids and kisses her on the cheek. "And how's my Mary doing today?"

She giggles and throws her arms around his neck, hugging the monster tightly. His camouflage works perfectly on the children, all of them exuding happiness at nothing more than his presence.

Grace walks in behind him, her dark habit at odds with the pervasive baby blue of the walls and the sunlight streaming in through the high, barred windows just under the eaves. Head bowed, she still shoots her gaze around the room. When she catches me in her sights, she stops, her attention a laser beam.

He picks up another child and swings him in the air, the little boy squealing with delight as the rest of the children follow the Prophet to the center dining table. "I'm so glad to see you all on this Lord's day." He sits the little boy in his lap and pats the nearest child on the head. "So many blessings all in one place."

Grace sits to his right, her back stiff.

Flicking his eyes up, he casts me a glance, then lets his gaze rove over the rest of the women, a king purveying his harem.

The women seem to hold their collective breath.

"Esther, Anna, Eve, and Judith." He rattles off a list, and the handful of women respond, standing and walking to his table. They seem to have a jaunt to their steps, and one of them casts a smug look to some of the other women as she goes.

Disappointment flows in a river through the rest of the room, the other wives instantly deflated. The double doors to the kitchen open and Spinners march in with trays of food and drink. I can't stop my mouth from watering.

"Father," one of the wives calls out.

The room stills, all eyes turning to the woman who spoke. Her round face reddens, but she continues, "Father, there's one more seat at your table. Who—"

"Leah." The Prophet holds up a hand. "The Bible says that 'a person's wisdom yields patience.'" His tone is like a shallow stream running over hard, sharp rocks. "Were you aware of that passage in the Psalms?"

She swallows. "No, Father."

"Do you find that you are exhibiting patience?"

She clasps her hands in front of her. "No, Father."

"Do you need correction so that you may learn the ways of patience?"

Her wince telegraphs through the room, and my palms begin to sweat.

"I ..." She blinks hard.

Say no, say no, say no. Nobody moves, everyone's concentration hanging from her lips.

After another moment's hesitation, she says, "Yes, Father."

His mouth turns up in a smile, the cold kind that never really warms anyone or anything. "You shall have it. Come."

She rises, her cheeks even redder than before, her steps steady though her chest rises and falls with rapid breaths.

The Prophet scoots his chair back, and Leah bends over him, her movements awkward as she settles across his thighs. No one speaks or makes a move as he lifts her long denim skirt and drapes it across her back, then rips her white panties down to her ankles.

The urge to grab the children and run snakes through me, but they watch along with everyone else. When one of the girls tries to speak to another child nearby, her mother hushes her and turns her attention to the Prophet.

The Prophet lifts his hand. "'Prudence is a fountain of life to the prudent, but folly brings punishment to fools,' so sayeth the Lord." He brings his palm down hard on her ass. She barely moves as he strikes her again and again, the loud slaps echoing around the room as everyone watches Leah's humiliation.

My hands turn to fists, every bit of rage inside me crystallizing into a hate so real that it's almost corporeal, a ghost of my anger that I can see and touch.

She doesn't yell, doesn't do anything but take the recurring hits until the Prophet's face is tinged with pink, his front locks of hair falling across his forehead, and his breath coming in gulps. He gets off on this. And the way all the women stare—maybe they do, too.

He finally stays his hand and yanks her panties back into place, then shoves her skirt down. "Now go in the light of my love, and with the wisdom to be patient." His voice is breathless, the hellish light in his eyes still bright.

She turns, tears streaking down her blotchy face, and retreats to her seat. I can feel her shame like a punch in my gut. And the scornful looks of the other women heap more of it on her head. The children seem unfazed, their little minds already full of abuse and torment—their mothers nothing more than objects for the Prophet to play with and set aside as he sees fit. I tell myself they're salvageable, that time away from here will reverse whatever damage has been done. Children are resilient; adults are the ones who can't change.

"Now." He waves at the Spinners who begin serving plates of food as if the brief interlude was nothing more than someone pressing pause on a movie, inconsequential and temporary. So callous to the abuse, they would likely stand still and watch even if the Prophet murdered Leah before their eyes. After all, they did just that when Sarah —no. I can't think about Sarah right now. Letting grief derail my rage isn't an option.

The Prophet scoots to the table as a Spinner places his plate before him and drapes his napkin across his lap. With a sharp glare, he turns his eyes on me. "Delilah, would you please join me?"

Ice shoots down my spine, and openly envious gazes turn toward me from every corner of the room. The woman next to me elbows my side.

I rise and sidestep the nearest Spinner, her sharp eyes watching me as I ease toward the center table. Throwing a glance to the door, I find a guard there. Not that I'd have any chance of escaping this place. The Prophet keeps a tightly closed fist around the Cathedral, an even tighter hold than he has on the Cloister. Lowering myself into the seat next to him, I keep my eyes down, examining the plate of food before me—roast chicken, green beans, mashed potatoes and gravy, and a small roll. My stomach gives another ugly twist.

"Bow your heads." He holds a hand out toward me.

Revulsion courses through me, and I have to bite back an avalanche of hatred as I take his hand. But it's either do it or face the same punishment as Leah. Or maybe worse. He takes my clammy hand in his dry one, and I clasp palms with the wife to my right. A prayer ensues, one that I don't listen to. Instead, I think about Adam, about his plans for us to escape. They're all burned away now, ash just like the cinders from the winter solstice bonfire. Then I picture Georgia, her warm smile. She is burned away, too, destroyed by the Prophet one way or another, even if his son Noah was the one who struck the final blow.

"Amen." The word reverberates through the room, and I pull my hand away from the woman to my right. The Prophet, though, won't let go. His fingers clamp around me, my bones grinding against each other. "So happy to have you here, my dear." He pulls my hand to his mouth and brushes his lips against my knuckles.

I clench my teeth together, only taking a breath when he releases me. Wiping my hand on my skirt, I drop my gaze to my plate again. I want to ask about Adam, but I know that won't get me anywhere. The Prophet wants me here for a reason, but he's a snake that only slithers when he feels the time is right. *Wait.* Ruth's word again. Ruth. Where is she?

"Eat." Grace points her knife at my plate. "Don't be rude."

Insane laughter careens around my thoughts. *Don't be rude.* God, that's so fucking rich coming from her, and in this place. Still, I need to bide my time, so I pick up my silverware and scoop a bit of mashed potatoes into my mouth. I swallow them far more quickly than I intended, their buttery softness so delicious.

The room falls into a quiet hum of chat broken by the raucous sounds of children here and there. Our table is silent, perhaps waiting on the Prophet to speak.

I eat a bite of roast chicken, and then another, unable to resist my simplest need. But I glance at the Prophet. He eats slowly, methodically, only one thing at a time. His chicken is first, and he makes square cuts to the meat, forking cubes into his mouth and chewing slowly. If I didn't already know what a pyscho he was, his surgical manner of eating would have been a dead giveaway.

The silence lasts a few more minutes, and I almost finish the food on my plate. It's nothing spectacular, but it's so much better than what I'm used to at the Cloister that I feel as if I'm eating a five-star meal.

When the Prophet clears his throat, I still.

"Delilah, I have good news for you." He sets his knife and fork at perfect angles on the edges of his white plate.

I can't imagine what news he has for me that could ever be good.

"Senator Roberts has agreed to acquire you, despite your unfortunate situation."

My food threatens to make a reappearance.

Grace clangs her fork down on her plate. "Sir, that's the reason I asked for some time with you. I need to—"

He turns toward her with a quick twist of his head. "I wasn't finished."

"Apologies." She pins her lips together and stares into my eyes, as if turning her scolding into hatred meant only for me.

"As I was saying," the Prophet continues, "he has agreed to take you on and to marry you as soon as possible. I expect him to take delivery within the week."

No. The word is on repeat in my mind. But my voice seems to have deserted me. I grip the knife harder. It's a simple butter knife—dull and curved. How much force would I need to shove it into his neck and twist?

"I believe this is the part where you thank me, Delilah." He grins, his eyes narrowing with a snakelike quality. "After all, I have delivered you to a bright future despite your damage and worthlessness."

The room takes on that eerie quiet once again, the women looking at me as their children prattle on, oblivious.

My palm is slick with sweat, but if I can generate enough force, that won't matter. The knife will plunge deep, severing something important. A child behind me giggles. Can I murder their father right in front of them? The thought cools my fire. I can't damage them. Not like that. I won't turn into the monster, won't hurt them like that. Even if they are his blood, they are innocent.

"Well?" His voice carries an edge far sharper than that of my butter knife.

I loosen my grip. "Thank you." The words burn, singeing their way from my lungs. I promised myself I wouldn't cower, but that doesn't mean I shouldn't be smart. When the moment is right, I will strike, and I will not falter. This is not that moment. Not yet.

"That's better." The Prophet returns to his food.

The room seems to relax, the women returning to their food. I've completed the subservient dance, bent to the Prophet's will, and now everything is as it should be. No discipline need be meted out, and the Cathedral will continue running smoothly. Their world is safe. Like cattle waiting to be slaughtered, the wives breathe and eat and ignore the reality of their surroundings—will they even protest when the saw comes down on their necks?

After a few moments, Grace says quietly, "May I?"

"Go on." The Prophet draws off a square of potatoes and scoops it up.

"Delilah is not ready, especially not for an assignment of this magnitude." She dabs at the corners of her mouth with her starched white napkin.

The Prophet swallows and turns to her, his eyebrows inching up his forehead. "You want her to stay?"

"No," she responds quickly, then tempers her words. "But, if she is to serve and further your glory, she needs more time."

He shakes his head, his confusion wafting over the table and making the nearest wives look up from their food with worried eyes. "You've wanted her gone, Grace. I know what's in your heart. Your jealousy and hatred."

Grace's face blanches, but she continues. "I am fallen, a woman descended from Eve, and cursed like all women to be self-centered and foolish."

He nods, her self-loathing perfectly in line with his misogynistic teachings. If I had the ability to pity Grace, I would have done it right then. But she lost any chance at my pity the moment she broke my finger, or likely before that.

She folds her hands in front of her, the picture of contrition. "But Prophet, you have inspired my better nature. And I know, without a doubt, that Delilah cannot perform her duties in a way that will glorify you. She is not ready. Just this morning, she threatened to kill the senator when he visited her in the Cathedral. I was watching the video, ensuring that she acted in accordance with the Cloister's teachings on her place."

The Prophet looks at me, his dark eyes accusing. I tilt my chin up just a smidge, even though my insides are going cold, and I feel the ghost tap of water on my forehead. Will my behavior get me sent back to the Rectory?

"What did she say to Senator Roberts?"

Grace lifts her hand and waves at the guard near the door— the same one who accompanied the senator this morning.

The tips of my ears go cold.

"Please tell us what Delilah did this morning." Grace looks up at him, her expression expectant, hungry.

"I took the senator into the dormitory like you asked me, Prophet. This one was in the shower." He gestures at me. "She threatened to kill him. Told him she wouldn't do what he said, would fight him, try to escape, and then said again that she'd kill him."

"Why didn't you report this to me earlier?" The Prophet pulls his napkin from his lap and throws it down onto the table.

"I-I—" the guard stammers.

The Prophet makes a sharp chopping motion with his hand, dismissing the guard. He turns to me. "You led Adam astray, and now you think you're free to threaten the man I've chosen for you? You think you know better than your Prophet?"

"You aren't my Prophet." The words spill out, the truth emblazoned on the air.

The wives gasp, and Grace reaches for her baton.

"No." The Prophet holds a hand out toward Grace. "This is my cross to bear." He reaches over and grabs me by the hair, yanking me from my seat and dragging me through the tables and out into the hall.

I scratch at his hand and try to kick, but he doesn't let go. He's strong for his age, and despite the food, I'm still tired and weak.

"Let go!" I thrash as my scalp burns, and I fear he'll rip my hair all the way out.

He throws me on the floor in the adjacent living area, my hands sliding across the baby-blue rug and burning as they go.

"Hold her!" he bellows and yanks his belt free from its loops.

I struggle to stand, but Grace is on me, shoving me back down to the floor as the guard grabs my arm and holds me in place.

Grace rips up my linen skirt. I'm not wearing panties. Ruth didn't offer me any.

"Slut!" the Prophet yells.

My ass erupts in pain before I even hear the stroke of the belt. I buck, but Grace and the guard keep me still. He strikes me again, his fury arcing across my flesh like burning electricity.

"'I will punish the world for its evil, the wicked for their sins. I will put an end to the arrogance of the haughty and will humble the pride of the ruthless.'" He punctuates his words with ruthless strikes.

I scream, agony leaving my mouth in a torrent of cries, but he doesn't stop. His belt ravages my ass, the backs of my thighs. Again and again he hits me until my body is nothing more than a conduit for pain.

When the strikes stop and I'm nothing more than a sobbing heap on the too-soft carpet, the Prophet leans down, his red face darkened by his black eyes. "You *will* obey me. You *will* obey the senator. 'Slaves, submit your-selves to your masters with all respect, not only to the good and gentle but also to the cruel.' I don't care what he does to you. In fact—" he spits in my face, the wetness trailing across the bridge of my nose "—I hope he does far worse than anything you've ever imagined. You deserve it, filthy harlot, for what you did to my son." He grabs my hair again and wrenches my face to his. "You will submit to me, serve me, and be obedient, or I will string you up like the witch you are. But first I'll let every man on this compound have his fun with you." He shoves my head back down and stands.

I close my eyes and curl into a ball, my lower body ringing with agony, and my mind a torrent of hate and thwarted wrath.

"Grace, take her back with you. Teach her to be obedient. Once she's ready, send word, and I'll let the senator know."

"Yes, Prophet." The smugness in her voice is another wound.

"Now, children, come give me hugs and kisses. I must be on my way." His voice is so calm, warm even.

I have no doubt his children rush to him with love in their eyes.

Grace leans to my ear, her whisper more of a hiss. "Welcome back to the Cloister, whore."

CHAPTER 6

ADAM

The sun is going down, hiding behind the trees. I lick my dry, cracked lips. My skin prickles from sunburn, the cold air causing aching goosebumps to rise along my flesh.

No one has come to see me since Noah. I'm glad. I can't be strong anymore. My will is still intact, but my body has given up on me. I can't blame it. At least I can't feel my toes anymore. I shredded them on the edge of the small shelf when I was trying to hold myself up. Now I hang. And if I stay completely still, the pain in my hands is just a dull, never-ending ache. It's hard to breathe, but I keep pulling in air.

I'm going to die up here. I accepted that fact the moment my father left the punishment circle. When he turned his back on me, it was with finality. I've known him for far too long to misread his signals. He left me here to die. I was too chickenshit to tell Noah the truth, to tell him goodbye. Besides, if he knew, he'd try to save me. I won't let him kill himself for me. No matter how fucked up things are, I still hold onto hope that he has a chance. Somewhere outside of this fucked up prison, maybe he can have a life. He just needs to be strong enough to choose it for himself.

My Emily ghosts through the trees, her white dress at the edge of my vision. I blink hard. She's not there. A long day of blood loss, sun poisoning, and cold can do that to a person, I suppose.

My eyelids droop closed again, and I retreat to where I can find the real Emily. In my memory. Her gray eyes haunt me, and I hope they never stop. Did I ever tell her how soft her skin is? I can't remember. Doesn't seem like something I'd be forthcoming with, no matter how true. But it is—soft and warm and so real I can almost feel it under my blood-crusted fingertips.

Some scuffling in the woods draws my attention. I force my eyes open and stare into the deepening gloom. Nothing there. Except another hint of Emily's white dress.

White. I want to see her in another color—all the colors. I bet she shines so bright no matter what she wears. She certainly catches my attention naked. I try to imagine her in a sunny yellow dress, her hair flowing down her back. God, what a stunner. She smiles at me and takes a few steps into a green field. I follow. She moves farther away.

"Come back." I chase her, her skirt flying up and showing me her long pale legs. She laughs, the sound light and sweet, drizzled honey on my tongue.

More scuffling pulls me from my daze. The woods are dark now. When did the sun go all the way down? Something gleams in the darkness. Eyes. A deer walks into the punishment circle, its ears flickering as it sniffs the air. In the faint moonlight, it looks white, the shadows along its coat painted in shades of gray. No antlers. I'm pretty sure it's a doe.

It moves closer. *Am I dreaming?* I can't tell anymore.

Its tail twitches as it walks to me, then pauses beneath my cross. With snorts, it scuffs the dirt, the sounds verging on disapproval. Mad that I'm here or mad that I'm still alive?

Movement catches my eye—the guard is creeping closer into the circle, his gun raised. Nothing pure can survive here.

Not this time. I split my parched lips and let out a guttural yell. The deer startles, its white tail lifting straight up as it darts away, its hooves light on the cold earth as it disappears into the trees.

"Motherfucker." The guard marches over, gun still drawn.

"Going to shoot me and put me out of my misery?" I grin down at him.

It's Gray, his nose still bruised from the last time we had a run-in. He aims at my leg. "No. But putting a few more holes in you won't matter."

"Aim for my side. I want to get this look just right." I'd like to spit at him, but I barely have any moisture in my mouth. No need to be wasteful.

"Sacrilegious piece of shit." He moves the barrel up until he's pointing at my chest.

"Just playing the role I've been given." I try to put my feet down, but I can't feel the board beneath me anymore.

"The Prophet should have killed you straight up."

"Second-guessing the Almighty? Better watch out for the lightning bolt."

His eyes narrow, his finger closing on the trigger as the muzzle lifts even higher until he's aiming at my face.

"Do it, coward." I close my eyes and wait.

Maybe I'll see Faith again. I'd give anything to hold her one more time, to tell her how much I love her. Even with that happy thought of reunion, regret stings in my chest at what I'm about to lose. *Goodbye Emily.* Her white dress flutters away from me, gone beyond my reach.

A thunk and a groan pull me back into the now.

Gray lies face down on the hard earth, not moving.

A woman stands next to him, a pistol in her hand. "He's out, but he'll live." She's wearing a black mask, but her voice is familiar.

"I know you."

"No shit." She motions toward the trees and two more women—also in masks—run out with a wooden ladder.

"He'll kill you for this." I can't tell if this is real or I'm already dead. But if I were dead, wouldn't I be seeing Faith instead of these masked people?

They steady the ladder against the wood and the first one climbs up. She brandishes a hammer, the claw end pointed toward my right hand. "This is going to hurt."

"Pain? That's a new one. Changing it up a bit for me. I like your sty—" My words cut off on a yell as she hooks the nail in my hand and yanks it free.

"One down." She drops the nail to the ground and climbs another step, leaning out so she can reach my other hand.

"Don't." I can't see through the gloomy streaks in my vision.

"I have to. I'm sorry." She grips my wrist and uses the claw hammer again.

I can't breathe through the agony, and I don't understand why I'm still conscious. Bad luck.

She saws through the leather straps at my arms. I can't stand, can't even feel my feet. Maybe I'm floating, Jesus come back to earth on a trash heap of pain instead of a cloud of glory. That has to be it.

With a grunt, she leans my body against her. Everything hurts.

"I need help." Her words are strained. "He's like a bag of fucking bricks."

"Lower him." The other two women stand beneath me, their hands up.

I don't know how she manages not to drop me. Her muscles shake as she slides me down her body toward the women below. At the last moment, the ladder gives, sliding sideways. I fall, the women catching me roughly, my back scraping against the hard earth as I slip from their grasp.

"Fuck!" She leaps off the tumbling ladder and lands on her ass.

"You okay?" one of the women calls to her.

"Good. Just going to have a sore tail for a while."

"So, the usual." The third woman kneels in front of me and inspects my body. "Shit. Look at these toes."

"The Prophet will kill all of you." I turn and stare at the first woman, her eyes black dots in the holes of her ski mask, though I know from memory that her irises are a deep green. "This won't go unpunished. Why are you doing this?"

She huffs out a sigh, her breath a white plume in the cold night, then pulls off her mask. "I can assure you this wasn't my idea, but you're valuable." Jez rolls her eyes at me, no love lost between us. "Apparently."

CHAPTER 7

NOAH

I sit in my father's office even though my thoughts are about a mile away in the punishment circle where Adam remains. It's already dark, and Adam won't last long in the dropping temperatures. I have to talk Dad into bringing him down. Fuck, I want another drink, or maybe more than just one.

Castro sidles in, his rifle slung across his shoulder like he's some sort of GI Joe wannabe. I flex my fists. Taking him down wouldn't be hard if we were just man to man. But there's no point in me being pissed at him. He's just a tool in every sense of the word.

"Noah, I have business to attend to, so make it quick." Dad walks in, his steps unhurried despite his words.

"Adam."

He sits behind his desk and peers at me. "What about him?"

"He has to come down. Now."

"No." He pins me with a glare. "Adam made his choice, and now I've made mine."

"Dad." I lean forward, trying to find some connection between us. "Please. It's Adam. He'll die—"

"He knew the consequences of what he did with that Maiden." Dad speaks about killing his firstborn with an air of easy acceptance. "He has to pay for his sins, just like we all do."

I shake my head. "But, Dad—"

"He disobeyed his Prophet." He drums his fingers on the desk. "I am an emissary of the Lord, of the Father of Fire. To disobey me is to disobey them. That can't go unpunished."

"He's been punished!" I stand.

Castro fidgets on the couch, his hands going to the rifle.

"You've left him up there all day. He'll be lucky if he doesn't lose any fingers or toes to frostbite. Dad, please. He's had enough."

"Son." He lets the word hang, beats passing by as he stares up at me. His dark eyes are familiar. But they're so hard now, even more so than I remember. "I've made my judgment. Adam will remain on the cross."

"He'll die!" I step toward him, and Castro rises.

"And that's his own fault!" my father roars and slams his hand on the desk. "He ran headlong at this punishment, and I had to give him what he deserves. I am the Prophet, Noah! Not just a man, *not* your father, not anything except the direct emissary of the Almighty! My judgment is final." His chest heaves as he glowers at me.

My righteous anger recedes until all I'm left with is desperation. "Dad, please."

"Get out." He leans his head back and closes his eyes. "I have meetings."

"Dad, you—"

"You heard him." Castro steps toward me, his gun cradled in his arms like a baby. "Move."

I stare at Dad, but he doesn't look at me. I've been dismissed, and Adam's death warrant signed. There is no changing any of it.

"I do have one task for you." His voice is calm now, the mask back in place.

I don't respond, just stand outside his door and wait. Zion leans against the wall near the main staircase, his smug smile a punch to my gut. I hate that guy.

Dad continues, "Delilah needs a new Protector. She's returning to the Cloister. I'm assigning you."

More weight piles onto my back, but I don't care anymore. I'm about to make some mistakes, big ones—so a little extra bullshit from my father barely makes a dent.

"Go to her tonight. Use a firm hand. She's gotten out of control. Adam went too easy on her, and now she's a feral bitch. Get her back in line."

I walk away, my steps hollow in the gilded foyer.

"Don't fail me, son." His cold voice follows me. "There's always room for more on the cross."

I creep through the trees, my dark clothes warding off the cold and prying eyes. The icy wind reminds me that I need to hurry, to get to Adam as quickly as possible. But if I'm not careful, one of the guards will bust me, and then there'll be no saving anyone. So, instead of rushing toward the punishment circle, I ease through the underbrush, keeping my eyes and ears attuned to any noises. A few animals scuttle through the dry leaves, and the wind knocks some of the trees together. Other than that, the night is still.

The crosses finally come into view. I'm on the backside of them, and I squint into the dark to try and find Adam's figure on the middle cross. I can't see him. Must be the angle. I circle around a bit, edging nearer and peeking toward the road. The guard is out of view, but I know there's at least one stationed at the entrance to the punishment circle. Dad wouldn't leave Adam's death to chance. I swallow the thought; it scrapes down my throat like a tangle of thorns. For the hundredth time today, I think about how badly I need a drink.

Keep it together. You owe him that much.

I reach into my pocket and palm my pistol. Killing has never been something I've wanted. But now, I see no other way around it. If the guard catches me, I'll have no other option. I just hope that I can get Adam down without anyone seeing.

Easing closer, I hug the edge of the circle. The clouds strangle what little moonlight there is, leaving the ground shadowy. But I think I see a lump near the foot of the cross. I still haven't spotted Adam, which seems wrong. I'm far enough to the side to have a view of him, but ... maybe my eyes are deceiving me, because it seems like he isn't there. Did Dad change his mind?

I bury that little spark of hope and ease closer. But it isn't a trick. The cross is bare. No Adam. The lump on the ground groans and rolls over.

The fuck?

"Gray?" I take another step and turn my head to the cross. He's gone, and from the looks of Gray, it wasn't my father's decision to bring him down. I slide my pistol into my pocket and try to process what the hell is going on. Someone saved Adam before I even got here. Who?

Gray sits up and rubs the back of his head. "Shit." When he lifts his eyes to the empty cross, he spits a litany of curses, then turns to me. "Was it you?"

"Was it me what?" I smirk. "I just came out here to say my goodbyes and found your dumbass on the ground. Where's Adam?"

He scrambles to his feet and stares, slack jawed, at the cross. "Fuck. Fuck. Fuck!"

I laugh, unable to bottle my glee. "You lost him." My laughter invades the frosted air, out of place but so, so good. "You had one job, asshole. One job!"

"Shut up. I—" He stares around as if he'll find Adam just standing there waiting to be hammered back into place. "He has to be somewhere."

I pull my phone from my pocket. "I'll just call up Dad and let him know that you—"

"Wait!" He holds up his hands and eyes my phone like it's a live grenade. "Just wait."

I, of course, have zero intention of sounding the alarm. Not yet. I want Adam to have a chance to get as far away as possible before my father finds out. But relief is making me fuck with Gray more than I should.

"We have to tell him. You know that." I poise my thumb over the screen.

"Just give me a goddamn minute. Let me think. Let me think. It had just gotten dark." His voice shakes as he whirls and stares back at the road. "I saw a deer. That's right. And then I ... I was going to take it out. And then ... Adam scared it off so I couldn't shoot it."

That's the one thing I know about Adam that he doesn't even know about himself: he has a good heart buried underneath all the darkness and dirt.

"And so I—" He glances at me, his eyes shifty. "I walked over here and was talking to him."

"Just talking nicely, huh? After he scared off your deer." I grin. "Sure."

"And someone." He raises his hand to the back of his head. "Hit me."

"What did he look like?"

"Never saw him." His shoulders seem to slump even more. "Didn't even have a chance."

I clap him on the back. "Oh, I'm sure the Prophet won't hold it against you. Being distracted by the deer and then my brother, turning your back on your post—he won't be mad. Come on, let's go tell him." I take unnatural joy in the terror that fleets across his stupid face. Maybe I'm more like Adam than I like to think.

His eyes narrow. "It could have been you."

I shrug. "Could have. But wasn't. I was with my father at dusk, not over here cracking your skull like an egg." Elation like I've never felt ripples through me in waves. I don't know who took Adam, but whoever it was saved his life. "I'm sure everything will be fine. Come on, we can head back slow. Give you time to come up with what you're going to tell the Prophet."

When his lip quivers, I hold back a laugh.

He knows what my father does to people who disappoint him. And this? This is a disappointment so epic that I doubt Gray will come out of it alive.

CHAPTER 8

ADAM

*E*mily whispers around me, her dress brushing against my leg. I want to reach out for her, but I can't seem to move. My mouth forms her name, but no sound comes out. I try to blink and look around, but there's something covering my eyes.

"He's awake." It's not her. Who is it?

"Sort of. I only have one more syringe of the strong stuff. I almost got caught the last time I went to visit the doctor, so I'm low on supplies." An older woman. Her voice is familiar, but I can't place it.

"Well, he's going to need it. These two toes have to go. They'll rot and poison him if we don't cut them off."

My toes? I want to scream, "Don't touch my goddamn toes!" but only a weak exhalation of air makes it out.

Hands probe me, sliding along my aching skin until they press and prod along my sides. "He seems okay. What about his hands?" The older woman leans over me. I can sense her slow breaths.

"I did the best I could. He'll have permanent damage from the tendons they wrecked, but the bones seemed intact. I cleaned and stitched them."

"This thumb doesn't look so good. Frostbite got it, too, maybe?" The older woman squeezes my right thumb.

I try to move and get nowhere.

"Adam, just relax. We've got you tied down so you can't hurt yourself." I know her voice. It's Jez.

I rasp out her name.

She moves the blindfold away, and I blink against what seems like unbelievably bright light. "I need you quiet. Understand? We have customers on the premises. If one of them hears you, all this is over, and you'll be right back up there on that cross with me beside you."

Her green eyes finally come into focus. Leaves arch above me, exotic plants that don't belong on the compound. I realize I'm in the baptistry of the Chapel, hidden behind the wild garden that the Prophet allows Jez to keep in her quarters.

"Emily?" My throat is fire, though I'm not sure why. The cold air? The screaming? Maybe all of it has stolen my voice.

She rolls her eyes. "You mean Delilah? Always with that bright white fairy."

I glare at her.

"Fine. I heard she's going back to the Cloister. Word is that she's gone wild, threatened to kill that senator if he even thinks about touching her."

I smile, my dry lips cracking.

Jez recoils slightly. "Jesus, man. You look ... Anyway. She'll be here for a while longer. The Prophet wants her broken. All the way. So she can be the perfect wifey to Evan and the perfect slave to the Prophet."

"She won't break." My words come out like shattered glass.

"We all break." She blinks hard, her past written in the scars on her body and her mind. "Every one of us. Eventually."

"Not her. Not my Emily."

She smiles sadly and lies to me. "Sure. Not her." She scoots the blindfold back into place. "Just relax. We've got some work to do. But first we're going to knock your ass out."

Someone touches my foot. My toes.

Shit! "Wait, Jez, don't—" But I feel the sting in my arm, and then the world turns on its side, the darkness swirled with rainbow and a girl in a white dress. She runs away from me, and I chase her.

I'll always chase her.

CHAPTER 9

DELILAH

J lie on my stomach, my head turned on the pillow. No matter how far I think I can get, I always wind up back here. My room at the Cloister.

"They aren't as bad as some I've seen." Chastity smooths aloe across the belt marks on my ass and thighs.

I wince at the light, caring touch of her fingers.

"Do you want to talk about it?" She finishes her work and pulls my dress back down.

"I should have used the knife."

"What?" She leans closer, her voice a whisper.

"I had a butter knife." I can still feel the warm metal in my hand, see the vein pumping in the Prophet's throat as he sat and ate his lunch. "I should have used it."

"Don't talk like that. Not when they can hear you."

My gaze meets hers. "I didn't do it. You know why?"

She shakes her head. "Stop."

"Because I didn't want to do it in front of all his children. Because that would scar them." A dry laugh crackles out of me. "Because I didn't want to be the monster that haunts their dreams every night—the crazed women with the bloody butter knife."

"Shhh." She smooths her hand over my hair. "Don't do this to yourself."

"I should have used the knife." I turn back to my pillow, feeling the tears burn behind my eyes but not letting them fall.

"I have to go."

"I know." My voice is muffled.

"If I can come back, I will." The bed shifts as she stands.

"Adam." I turn toward her again, catching the swish of her skirt as she walks away. "Do you know anything about what happened to him? Did they take him down?"

Her back stiffens. "I ... He's still up there, as far as I know."

She knows more. I can feel it in the way she refuses to turn around and meet my eye. "Chastity, please—"

"I told you. He's there, *as far as I know*. I'm sorry." She hurries out of the room, the door clicking shut behind her.

My mind races with possibilities. Maybe he escaped? What if—I don't know—maybe Noah grew a pair and rescued him? I clench my eyes shut at the topsy turvy thought of being grateful to the man who killed my sister. *Breathe.* I'll deal with that when I come to it. Not before.

When I shift onto my side, slices of pain echo from the lash marks across my backside. But I've been hurt before. The marks will heal—even the few spots where he broke the skin.

My thoughts stray into darker territory. Will Adam be able to recover? And—the one place I don't want to go beckons—what if he's dead? What if Chastity knows it, but didn't want to tell me.

"Stop." I bite my lip. Thinking like that could break me. And I promised Adam that I wouldn't break for anyone but him.

The Prophet wants me here for more training, that's what Grace has convinced him I need. I'm a pawn in whatever game that bitch is playing. She wanted me out of here so badly that she practically threw me at Evan. But now she wants me to stay. Why?

Too many questions whip around inside me like a whirlwind. No answers join the maelstrom. It's all sound and violence and blood. I shift again, ignoring the ache, and hug my pillow. There is a way out of all this. I know in my bones that I can bring this place to its knees. The only thing I'm not sure of is whether I can do it without Adam.

If I've lost him, too, I don't know if I can find the will to go on.

A memory fires—the little girl at the bonfire, the one who looked up at me with hopeful eyes.

"Can I be a Maiden one day?" she'd asked.

Her mother replied, *"If you are faithful and obedient, you may be chosen by the Prophet."*

And there's my answer. Even without Adam, even if the pain of losing him rips my soul into a million pieces, I will fight to destroy Heavenly until my last breath. No more lambs to the slaughter, not if I can help it.

My door opens, the room deep in gloom this late at night.

"Who's there?" I peer through the darkness, the hairs on the back of my neck standing on end.

"Me."

I don't know the voice. "Touch me, and I'll scream. I'll claw your fucking eyes out." I try to sit up, but the pain in my backside has me balancing oddly on one hip as I ready for the attack.

"I'm not going to—" He steps closer. "I won't hurt you."

74

Noah, his voice a little smoother than Adam's, his stance a bit less aggressive. He eyes me warily and circles around the bed to stand at the foot.

Blood roars in my ears. Am I looking at my sister's killer?

"You shouldn't have come here." I stand, the lash lines stinging across my skin.

"Dad assigned me to be your new Protector."

I raise my fists, though I realize I probably look especially pathetic. I don't care. I'll do as much damage as I can before he overcomes me.

"In case you haven't noticed, I don't need protection." I follow his steps.

He holds up both hands. "I'm not here to hurt you. I swear!"

"So you won't hurt me? What about Georgia?" Just saying her name out loud frees some part of me—the one I've held back even from Adam.

"Georgia?" He blanches.

Guilt! My heart sings the word, triumph in the note. He looks guilty.

How long have I waited for this chance? Too long. Vengeance sings in my veins. I don't care about the camera or the microphone or the Spinner in the hall. All I care about is exacting my pound of flesh from the man who killed my sister. An exuberance fills me, lightens my steps. Judgment is here, and I am her sword.

"You know who I'm talking about, don't you?" I follow him until his back is against the wall.

He nods and keeps his hands out in front of him. "Mary. She was my Maiden."

"A confession?" I ease closer, staring up into his eyes that I once thought were guileless. I know better now. "I already know what you did to her. I read the police report. I know every cut, every gouge, every fucking bruise, even that the slice to her throat was just over four inches wide. Thorough. You made sure she didn't have a chance." Despite my rage, my voice is calm. So calm, like a placid lake with a razor-mouthed beast lurking just beneath the surface.

"I didn't—"

"You did." I'm directly in front of him now, our eyes locked, the faint hint of whiskey on his breath.

"I never would have hurt her. Never."

"Liar." I rear back and slap him. Hard.

"I'm not." He suffers the blow, then returns his gaze to mine. "I swear on my life that I never hurt her."

"I don't believe you." I slap him again. My palm rings with the reflection of his pain. It feels good.

"Delilah." He grabs my shoulders.

I fight, struggling out of his grip.

"Don't!" he yells as I swing, my fist hitting his cheek with a fleshy thunk. The impact radiates through my knuckles, a deep, jarring pain. But I swing again, on fire, ready to hurt him, to show him at least a tiny slice of the agony I live with each day since he took her away from me.

"Stop this!" He wraps his arms around me, pinning my hands in tight to his chest.

I kick and struggle, but he walks me to the bed and lays me down, my ass on fire, my hands desperate to rip him to pieces. He straddles me and pins my wrists next to my ears. I'm trapped, too weak to escape.

I spit in his face. "Do your fucking worst."

He lets out a low, frustrated noise, like a growl deep in his throat. "I need you to calm the fuck down."

I turn my head away, my chest heaving with each breath. At least I gave it all I could.

"Listen." He squeezes my wrists. "Or wait, no." He shakes his head. "Talk. How do you know Mar —Georgia?"

"Her name was Georgia, you piece of shit. Not Mary."

"Okay. Georgia." He seems to try and adopt a soothing tone. "How do you know her?"

I turn back to him, giving him my honesty like a knife through his worthless heart. "She was my sister."

77

He closes his eyes and hangs his head. "Fuck. She talked about you." His voice gentles, and I could swear that sadness rolls his shoulders forward a bit, tinges his words with grief. "You're her Firefly, aren't you?"

I swallow hard. That's the name she used to call me. Only Georgia.

"I'll find you!" Georgia's voice rockets across her father's wide garden, the stalks of corn tall in the dusky sunset.

I slink behind the wide oak with the trunk that looks almost like a face. Her swing—just a piece of throwaway wood situated between two lengths of rope, sways light in the evening breeze. The spring scent of honeysuckle tickles my nose and threatens to make me sneeze and give up my location. Not happening. Pressing myself against the warm bark, I rub my sleeve across my nose with a ruthless motion, killing any sneezy inclination with brute force.

The whisper of corn leaves pulls my attention to the right. I peek out, but don't see her past the stout wire rows of climbing cucumber vines. Eyeing the wooden fence that separates her backyard from her neighbors, I wonder if I can slip through the spot where the boards are loose without her seeing me. Then again, going into another yard is cheating. Crap. I should have run to the other side of the house.

"I know you're over here." Her sing-song voice is a threat laced with laughter, and I can't help my smile as I try to stay as still as possible.

Playing hide-and-seek is still one of her favorite games, even though we're almost teenagers. We play it every time I come to visit, times that are coming farther and farther apart ever since my mother ... No, I won't think about that now. I focus on where I think she is, maybe towards the back edge of the garden now, her Keds silent on the red dirt as she stalks me.

When I think she's about to break free of the rows of corn, I make a calculated decision to dart toward the opposite side of the garden.

I shriek when I collide with her, standing just around the tree, and we fall in a heap. A few crows lift from the branches above us, squawking away into the muggy twilight.

"Gotcha!" Her triumphant shout is all-too familiar, and I lay back on the grass and admit defeat.

"You're too good at this." Crossing my arms over my thin chest, I stare up through the new leaves on the dark branches. "There aren't enough hiding spots."

"Oh, don't be a sore loser. Pro tip—you need to stop picking the first good place you see to hide. Be a little more sneaky." She flops next to me and tucks her hands behind her head. "Besides, I'd be able to find you in the dark. You shine no matter where you are, Firefly."

"Delilah?" Noah wrinkles his forehead and peers into my eyes.

"Get off me." My temples are wet, though I didn't realize I'd been crying.

"No. Not until you stop swinging at me. You're going to hurt yourself."

"Or you." I spit back.

"That, too." He nods, and I notice he's been careful not to squeeze my wrists too hard or settle too much of his weight on my hips. He's holding back.

"You killed her." I lock eyes with him, daring him to look away with a lie.

"I did not." He holds my gaze, his voice steady and low. "I swear on my life that I never harmed your sister."

I can feel it niggling in the back of my mind, the tendril tickling—the thread of truth in his words. The tears flow more freely now, vengeance doused with the familiar bucket of disappointment and loss. I let go, my body going limp beneath him. The fight is gone. He didn't do it. I can see it in his eyes, and I hate the fact that I still haven't achieved the one thing I came here to do. *I'm sorry, Georgia.* I think it over and over again, sending my apology out into whatever world where Georgia still exists. *I'm so sorry I failed you again.*

"Fuck." He relents and scoots off me, sitting on the bed, his head in his hands.

I roll to my side, the ache in my backside forcing me to face away from Noah. Tears still flow, and I hate the weakness in me, the utter failure.

"She was my Maiden, but I never hurt her. Not like ... Not like the others. She was different." His voice is so low I have to lean toward him to hear it. "Something about her. I don't know. She would tell me things about her childhood. About you. I loved her stories about high school, her normal life. She sort of ..." He shakes his head. "She showed me all the things I missed out on. She made me doubt." He sighs. "She made me doubt everything. Adam had been trying to pull the curtain back for years. Hell, I already knew what was behind the curtain, but I believed anyway. But with her, she made everything seem so much brighter."

"She shined." I remember every moment of her sparkle.

"She did." He nods. "And I was so afraid I'd do something to dull it. I did what I had to do as her Protector, but I treated her differently than the others. Grace knew it." His tone turns hard. "She tried to use it against me. Threatened me with hurting M-Georgia. Sorry, Georgia."

"What did Grace want?" I can guess, but I want to hear it from Noah.

"Adam. She's always wanted him."

I flex the finger she broke. "Makes sense." Turning over, I groan and face Noah, though I have to crane my head up at an awkward angle to meet his eyes. "Tell me more about her." I'm starved for this information, for this glimpse at what my sister's life was like when she was beyond my reach.

"Not much to tell. The Cloister hasn't changed since then. Georgia kept her spirits up, helped the other girls and assured them that this life wasn't forever." He smiles, but it's wistful and sad. "I got in trouble for that, for giving her too much leash, Dad would say. The Maidens aren't supposed to be like her—" He blinks. "Like you. I don't know how I didn't see it before. You remind me of her."

"What happened to her?"

He turns away, his face shaded in darkness. "I thought she ran away. That's what we all thought."

"She didn't."

"She didn't." He sighs.

"Do you know who did it?" I hold my breath.

"No." He doesn't look at me.

"Noah." I force myself to sit and face him. "Tell me."

He stays silent for a long time, his eyes hidden from me. "Adam is off the cross."

"What?" I cover my hand to hold in a sob of relief, his words a blindside. "He is? Is he okay?"

"I don't know." He finally meets my gaze. "Someone knocked out the guard and took him down. The Prophet is turning the compound upside-down trying to find him."

I can barely believe what he's said. "Someone saved him?"

"Looks like it."

"Was it you?"

He shakes his head. "I was too late. Just like always."

"Everyone, out of your rooms. This is a search!" A masculine yell comes from the hallway.

I grab Noah's hand, urgency eating away at any time I may have had to think through what he'd just revealed about Adam. "Please, my sister. Please tell me who killed her. You know. I can tell you know who it was."

He rises. "I have to go."

"No." I stand and block his way around the bed. "Tell me now!"

With a sad shake of his head, he pushes past me. "You can't ask that of me."

I grab his arm and yank. "I'm not asking. Tell me!"

He pulls away, gently removing my hand from his arm. "I won't, and I never will."

My hands shake, and I want to hurt him, to make him feel the emptiness inside that I do whenever I think about what happened to Georgia.

"Coward!" I beat on his back as he walks to my door.

He opens the door as the rest of the Maidens pile into the hallway, men rushing this way and that, the sound of crashing furniture mixed with shouts of "not here!"

A Spinner stands just a few feet away, her eyes wide at the destruction.

"You're a goddamn coward," I hiss at Noah.

He turns to me, his head down. "I know." When he meets my eyes, I feel like a steely piece of Adam is looking out at me. "But that's about to change."

CHAPTER 10

ADAM

*S*ilence. The cloying kind that seems to invade every cell. I blink my eyes open and stare at nothing. Pitch black. A series of dull aches tear through me, the pain pulsing along with the beat of my heart. They come from everywhere, and my hands and feet feel as if they're tearing away, the skin gone, bones exposed, biting ants chewing through what flesh is left.

I try to sit up. My forehead knocks against wood. *What the fuck?* Spreading my arms, my elbows bump against more wood. I'm in a coffin. I shake my head, willing away the rising panic, but my breathing speeds up, my pain increasing with each tortured beat of my frantic heart.

Pressing my hand against the wood is a mistake. Agony snakes up my arm, and I have to gulp in a breath as sparks burst in the dark. Instead, I use my knee, lifting my right leg and bumping the top of the coffin. It's sturdy, barely moving despite my efforts. A bead of sweat rolls down my forehead to my temple, and I force myself to relax. Or at least I try to. *Think*. There has to be a way out of this—whatever *this* is.

How did I get here? I cast my thoughts back to the cross, to Jez. I put my hands together in the narrow space over my chest. Feeling around, I can tell they're both well-bandaged. Why go to the effort of fixing me up just to bury me alive? Maybe they were just playing some sick game. Maybe my father put them up to it.

More sweat beads along my skin, and I could swear the box closes in tighter around me. *Breathe. Breathe.* I press my bare feet down toward the bottom, feeling out the space. My left foot feels tight and hot, and I groan at the ripping pain that emanates from my toes. I use my right foot instead, stretching down until I feel the wood. A perfect enclosure, no way out.

Taking in a deep breath, I yell, my hoarse voice loud in my ears though I can tell it doesn't go much farther than the timber around me. Someone would have to be standing right next to me to even hear it. And if I'm underground ... I swallow hard, my mouth dry, my guts twisting in primal horror.

I yell again until my voice gives out and the stillness returns. Trapped. I clamp my eyes shut even though the darkness is absolute either way. She's there, Emily, her white dress fluttering as she watches me with intense gray eyes. I want to call out to her, but nothing passes my lips.

She moves closer, a slight smile tipping up the corners of her lips. "You're in quite the predicament."

God, is she teasing me while I'm buried alive? Naughty little lamb. "I'll get out of it."

"You sure?" She lies down next to me and turns her head.

We're so close, our noses almost touching.

"Piece of cake." I swear I can smell the scent of her hair.

"I hope you're right." She reaches up and raps on the wood with her knuckles. "Dying in here seems even worse than on the cross."

"Are you safe?" I try to scoot my hand over to touch her, but my fingers meet timber and my vision fades, returning me to the utter darkness. "Emily?"

Something thumps just outside, and then I can sense movement. The coffin is sliding sideways, first the bottom half, then the upper half. I'm jostled, and dust falls onto my face, sticking to my sweaty skin as I breathe out hard through my nose to clear it.

With a wrenching noise, the lid is pulled away. I blink against the light as hands grip my arms and help me to a sitting position.

"Jesus, you almost got us busted." Jez comes into focus, her anxiety drawing crow's feet next to her eyes. "You have any idea how close that was?"

I peer over her shoulder. We're in a narrow space under the baptistry. Bird shit coats a thin ledge behind her, and plants soar above us. One of her birds peers down, its head cocked to the side. I've never heard them sing, not in any of the years they've been here.

"Why did you put me in a coffin?" I try to swing my legs over the edge, but I can't do it.

Another woman I don't recognize grabs my legs and helps me up, Jez digging her shoulder under my arm and supporting my weight as they lower me to stand. I groan as the blood rushes to my feet.

"Maggie, put it all back and close it up." Jez jerks her chin at the wooden box I've just exited.

Maggie grabs some magazines, CDs, and other contraband from a pile in the floor and shoves it all into the box.

"It's our stash. Lucky for you, the space was just big enough to hide you." She pulls me up and out via the small staircase. Maggie follows and pulls a huge planter back into place, the fronds of an exotic tree hiding the narrow passage behind the garden. From any angle, it looks as if there is nothing but dirt and plants back here.

"Dad come looking?" I let Jez lead me to one of the chairs around the front of the garden.

"Yes. His asshole brigade trashed the place and would have found your noisy ass if some of my girls hadn't distracted them. But we still have to be careful. Eyes everywhere." She points up at the camera in the corner of the ceiling. "We've changed the angle on the cameras slowly—ridiculously slowly, a centimeter a day over the course of weeks—and they haven't noticed. My area back here is clear, but you can't leave this room or they'll see."

The room has been tossed, clothes strewn everywhere and the door to her private bedroom wide open, the mattress standing on one end.

I stretch my left leg out and stare at the fat wrapping that obscures the bottom half of my foot. "My toes?"

"You lost two of them, the little one and the one next to it." She shrugs and sits in another of the gaudy church chairs with gold cushions. "I talked Abigail out of taking the third. It's not the right color, but I think it'll survive. The tips of all your toes may come off eventually, but they'll grow back. At least, that's what Abigail says."

I've already lost so much of myself to this place, to my father, that a few toes should seem inconsequential. But they don't. I know he left me there to die. He didn't get his wish, but the fact that I've lost parts of my body tells me that I was right in my line of thinking—I have to take him out along with all his Protectors. He'll stop at nothing, and neither will I.

I rest my foot on the worn carpet. "Abigail from the Cloister? How did she even get in here?"

Jez smirks. "Oh, we have our ways." She points at my left foot. "You probably still have some of the numbing stuff working for you, but once that wears off, I imagine you'll be in a world of hurt."

Holding up my bandaged hands, I say, "I'm already there."

"Fair enough."

Even though I believe her when she says my toes are gone, I can still feel them, as if they're pressing up against the thick white gauze. Will I still be able to walk? I hobbled over to the chair fine—though, admittedly, I had help. But I'll need to be as close to one-hundred percent as I can get when the fight starts. And I have zero doubts that a fight is coming, and soon. "Is Emily okay?"

"This again? She's fine. Back at the Cloister." She glances through the stained glass behind me, as if she can see the Cloister from here. "Good news and bad news on that front."

"What do you mean?"

She shrugs. "It's good that she didn't have to go to the senator yet. Bad news that she got a new Protector."

I tense. "Who?"

"Noah."

My shoulders relax. Noah isn't a threat. She'll be safe. Jealousy, though, that roars through me like a freight train. If he touches her. If he ... *does* anything to her. My hands start to curl into fists, but the wretched burning pain has me stretching them out again. Noah wouldn't touch her. Right? I shake the thought away. He wouldn't. Especially now that he knows I'm still kicking. Word has to be all over the compound and even farther. The Prophet will stop at nothing to get me back up on that cross.

"I figured you'd react like that." Jez gives me a lopsided grin, her green eyes sparkling.

"So, I'm here." I look around. "What's the plan?"

"Plan?" She crosses her bare legs at the knee, her tiny black shorts barely covering the goods.

"You brought me here. I have to assume that was for a reason. What are we doing? Who's with you besides Abigail? What's the plan?" What I want to know is whether she's with my mother. But I don't want to play that card just yet. I'd rather have her tell me than reveal the extent of what I know.

"All you need to do is recover."

"That's not good enough."

She sighs, blowing out a big breath that lifts the stray strands of dark hair along her cheek. "Do me a favor and take a look at yourself. Your hands are fucked, your foot is fucked, you look like you just went twelve rounds with a meat grinder. Even if I have a plan, your part comes in later. A lot later."

I've known Jez for years, all the way back to when she was one of the first Maidens. She's always been stubborn and rough, and not even her time in the Cloister changed her. That's why she wound up here in the Chapel, an unwilling Madam to even more unwilling girls. When she tried to escape with Chastity, I was one of the men who found them. They didn't make it out of the compound. I had to sit through her punishment—the scars down her spine inflicted by my father one by one. She didn't shed a tear. It doesn't surprise me that she's taken the lead on whatever rebellion is brewing. All the same, she's going to need me to make it work. She just doesn't know it yet.

I lean my head back on the cushion. "Tell me what you've got cooking, and I'll tell you if you'll die fast at the start or slowly on the cross."

Her back stiffens. "I don't need the son of the Prophet mansplaining shit to me, got it?"

"You need someone who knows the ins and outs of the Prophet, what it's like at the highest level, the best way to get to him, and the way to bring it all down without collateral damage."

"Collateral damage?" She leans forward, her elbows on her thighs. "What would you consider that to be?"

I cock my head at her. "The Heavenly idiots. The sheep who believe the Prophet."

"Why would I save them?" Her eyes are granite now, her mouth a hard line. "What have they ever done for me, for the girls here, for the ones in the Cloister?"

I don't like the coldness in her voice, the way she dismisses all those lives—even children. They are stupid, sure. But that's not a capital offense. Unease crackles down my spine. "Jez, they haven't done anything to—"

"No." She stands. "They choose not to look, not to see. All they have to do is pull back the curtain, but they won't. They want to live in this fantasy where the Prophet is chosen by the invisible man in the sky. Innocent?" She tosses her hair over her shoulder. "You've got to be kidding me. They are at the root of all this, at its very core." She holds her palm up, as if the church sits there. Perusing it from all angles, she smirks. "This entire shit-show is built on them. Their money. Their belief. Their entitlement. Their selfish need to feel like they are chosen. That's what it's all about in the end. Every one of them that crosses the threshold, that follows the Prophet —they do it because they can't see past their own noses. They want to feel special. They fill that hole inside themselves with our misery." She crushes the imaginary church in her palm, her eyes blazing. "And now I intend to show them just what their devotion to a false idol is worth."

CHAPTER 11

DELILAH

race walks down the long hallway, her footsteps sure as I follow her past the training room where the other Maidens are. She fetched me from my room this morning, her manner somehow even more severe than usual. I'd spent the night drifting in and out of sleep, my thoughts returning to Adam over and over again. Is he safe? Who took him?

"Eyes down." Grace doesn't even turn around, but she somehow knows I'm staring at her thin back.

I drop my chin and watch my feet as we move farther down the corridor, then turn toward the Spinner's dorms. We keep going until we reach her office—the room where she'd broken my finger.

"Sit." She points to the same chair as she walks around her desk.

I choose the other one. The aching skin on my backside protests, but I don't let it show.

She raises a brow but doesn't say anything as I take my seat. The monitors are lit behind her, my room still visible on the center screen.

Sitting in her chair, she settles back and stares at me, her unblinking hatred like a laser beam.

I meet her gaze and hold it. She intimidated me from the moment I set foot on Cloister ground. But not anymore. She can still hurt me in any number of ways, but I'm not backing down.

After what has to be a minute of intense silence that feels like an hour, she says, "You know, when you first came here, I figured no one would want you, given your freakish looks."

I smile. It's the response that I know will irk her the most.

Her eyes glint. "But I was wrong. Being a freak made you more desirable. Being different is what these idiot men like about you. Even Adam. He was drawn to you because of your appearance. Nothing more."

"Keep telling yourself that." My smile stays in place.

A muscle next to her eye twitches, but she continues, "Maybe you think that just because you're a genetic disaster that you're truly special. That you have some-thing more to offer than a sideshow act." She shakes her head. "You're just like the others. Ass in the air for the enemas, eating the poisoned fruit whenever it's offered, sucking your Protector's cock the second you get a chance. You're no different than any other Maiden, no matter what you may think."

I study her, trying to discern the basis for her continued attacks. It has to be Adam. Her jealousy is the one emotion she ever lets show. For someone so skilled at playing mind games, she doesn't do a good job of guarding her defenses. I know just where to turn the screw. "I suppose you think you were the different one. The special Maiden set apart from the others. But then Adam tossed you aside, didn't he? Just like all the other Maidens."

She leans forward, her shoulders bunched with tension. "I *was* special. I still *am*. Adam is mine."

"Is he?" I reach between my legs and fake a wince. "Because I can still feel him inside me, even now."

"You fucking bitch!" She lurches across the desk and grabs for me, but I scoot back, her grasping hand barely missing me.

I stand and back away.

She straightens and reaches for her baton. I bring my hands up, ready for the fight.

Closing her eyes, she takes in a deep breath through her nose and blows it out her mouth.

I'm wary, back against the wall, just watching her.

Leaving her baton in its holster, she lowers herself into her chair. "Sit." She points at my seat.

"So you can jump me?" I've never seen her control herself like this. It's like she has a leash and she just pulled a hair too far. Now she's been jerked back to her owner, scolded, and made to fall in line.

"No, you little fool. So we can talk." She leans back, the picture of ease.

I edge up and pull my chair a few more feet from the desk, then sit. "About what?"

"Sadly, our darling *First Lady*—" I don't miss the venom in the words "—is busy in Montgomery and can't spend any more time on your training. Instead, I'm in charge of readying you for your marriage to Senator Roberts."

"I'll kill him." I keep my tone even, stark.

She tsks. "I'm afraid you don't understand how important this assignment is to the Prophet and to Heavenly. It's come to our attention that, after pulling a few strings, he's up for a seat on the Ways and Means Committee, which—"

"I don't care if he's running for president, if I get the chance, I'll kill him before I let him hurt me or anyone else ever again." I mean every word, and I think she knows it.

She keeps her tone even, continuing doggedly. "As I was saying, that seat would give him a broad amount of control over state funding. Projects that Heavenly would like a piece of, ways to funnel money into our godly coffers instead of to the heathens. All this is a high priority for the Prophet. Now, despite my efforts to talk Evan into a more appropriate bride, he's focused on you despite your diseased mind and body. So I have to do what I can with you. First, we're going to have to re-tread ground on obedience. You're sorely lacking in that area."

"You aren't listening to me." I lean forward, returning her stone glare with my own. "I will never marry him. I will fight and scratch and claw and do everything I have to do to end him."

"Oh, I've been listening. So has the Prophet. When I showed him your little tirade in the bathroom at the Cathedral, he was most displeased. But he's also a problem solver."

"I think you meant to say 'also a psychopath.'"

"Funny you mention that." She smiles, then reaches for the remote.

With the click of a button, the center screen goes dark, then flickers back to life. It's set on night vision, the scene in odd greens and shiny silver. But I don't miss the details. The woman strapped to the table, the shiny drop of water on her forehead. My stomach drops, my hands go clammy, and I think I might vomit.

Grace sets the remote down with a hard thunk. "I think you'll cooperate. Won't you?"

I can't look at her, can't tear my eyes away from the pitch black room in the Rectory where my mother is bound and suffering. "You can't do this."

"It's already done," she simpers.

"Someone will find out. They'll look for her. They'll know you took—"

"An addict?" She smiles, smug and full. "Who would miss a junkie? Maybe her dealer. Maybe the guys she blows for cash. But no one that matters. No one who would report her as missing. She's trash. Like mother, like daughter. I bet they won't even notice she's gone for weeks. Why would they?" She stands and moves around behind me. "If she wound up in the landfill or dead in the gutter, people would think 'she had it coming.' Even her own daughter abandoned her." Her words slither in my ear. "If you don't bother to tell her the truth or even keep up with where she's living or what's she's doing, why would anyone else?"

"Shut up." I blink through my tears but can't look away from the screen. Mom's arms are drawn out beside her, tied down just as I was. The drip flashes through the dark at the same interval, and I can feel the water drilling into my skull right along with hers. It broke me, but my mother is already shattered. What will this do to her? "Let her go."

"You don't give the orders around here, freak."

"I'll do what you want. Just let her go."

"Oh, the time for bargaining has passed." She circles back around to her desk and grabs the remote. "You will do as you're told when you're told. If you do, your mother will remain in the Rectory. Unharmed."

"Unharmed?" My voice rises on the tide of panic. "You call that unharmed?"

"I call that uncomfortable." She clicks the remote and the screen changes to a room with a handful of men sitting around playing cards. "I call this true punishment. These guards are off duty at the moment, but one call from me will have them on their way to the Rectory. I figure it would only take one or two to hold her down while they take turns. Then again, she's so thin now from the addiction, they probably wouldn't have to work at it. Maybe she'd beg them to do it as long as they promised her a hit."

In all this time, I knew Grace was a monster. I've seen what she's capable of. But this cuts me, dragging a dull knife across the deepest parts of me.

"You can't do this," I repeat dumbly.

"I can. And what's more, I would make you watch what they do to her. I'd watch, too, and love every minute of it. Because it's justice. Because she has it coming to her just like you do. The Lord rejoices when sluts like you and your bitch of a mother get what they deserve."

The desire to fly at her, to try and strangle her with my bare hands almost overwhelms me. But that image of my mother going through the same hell I went through keeps me in my seat.

"I've seen your file." She sits down in her chair but leaves the video of the men playing on the monitor behind her. "Your mother gave up on you. She cared more about getting high than you. If I had a mother like that, this—" she waves her hand at the screen "—wouldn't burn me too badly. Which is what I told the Prophet when he suggested we take her and bring her here. 'There's no way this will work,' I told him. Respectfully, of course. But he disagreed." She points at me. "He knew you were weak and sentimental. And he was right. Look at you. Blubbering over poor addicted, whoring mommy who doesn't give two shits about you."

"Shut your mouth." I dig my nails into the arms of the chair.

"I won't. And I'd watch my tone if I were you." She opens her drawer and pulls out a black binder, then slides it across to me. "We need to get started on our lessons for the day. You wouldn't want to disappoint the Prophet, not when your mom's on the line."

I stare at the black binder as Grace watches me with hawkish eyes. What little choice I thought I had has vanished into the ether. I reach out a shaking hand and take the notebook, settling it into my lap.

"Good." She folds her hands on the desk. "Let's talk about your future husband."

I open the binder. But I do something else, too. I make a decision. Killing my sister's murderer isn't enough anymore. Torching Heavenly isn't enough. If I want to destroy the evil, I have to start with the base of the tree and cut it down, then dig out the roots one by one, and salt the earth when I'm done. Each piece of it must wither and die, and I have to be sure that nothing will ever grow in this place again.

"He enjoys watching other men fuck his toys." Her grin spreads wide across her face. "Did you know that? You're going to be ripped apart by strangers while he films it." She points to the binder. "Flip to the third tab. We have stills from a few videos. Research material for you."

I hold her gaze for one more moment, a silent message on the air between us—her, transmitting smug power; me, transmitting the truth.

You'll be the first to die.

CHAPTER 12

NOAH

"*I*f you know where he is and you aren't telling me." My father's eyes dart around his office, his dark irises huge. "You know. You're probably the one who took him. You must know!"

I wish I did. But I've gotten nowhere on trying to figure it out. "Dad, if I knew, I'd tell you." *Pants decidedly on fire.*

He swipes his hand across his desk, knocking off a paperweight and some documents, though he's careful not to scatter his precious coke container. "Castro! Bring Rachel!"

"Dad. I swear I don't know." I scrub a hand down my face, my several days' worth of beard scratching my palm. "I was with you when he was taken, remember?"

"You were?" He sits down, his shoulders slumping. "That's right." He waves a hand at Castro who'd headed for the door. "Forget it."

The iron band around my heart relaxes as Castro re-takes his seat.

My father stares at me, and I wonder if he's slept at all. When he found out Adam was gone, he sent every one of his minions out onto the compound. Every building has been searched, and the grounds have been combed by men with dogs. A trail led away from the cross, into the woods, and onto the road, but then it vanished. Whoever took Adam had access to a vehicle.

"You could still know." Dad's words come out in a mumble.

"I don't." I shrug and hold his gaze.

"I want the grounds searched again. He has to be out there somewhere. Maybe—I don't know—maybe he's hiding out on the land you're about to clear for farming. Maybe he hopes that you'll find him."

I could point out that there's no way Adam would survive out in the cold—no food, no water, no shelter—but I don't. "I'll have some men go through the area again."

"I want him found today!" He fumbles for his cross-shaped box of white powder. "This is a disgrace. An affront to me, to the Lord, to the Father of Fire. Whoever took him will be up on the cross next to him." He points at me. "Do you understand? I want that traitor found and nailed up like the thief he is. No mercy for him. No mercy for anyone who seeks to undermine my will. I am the Prophet of the Lord!"

It's amazing to me that I believed in him for as long as I did. Watching him now—an old man, unhinged and addicted—I can't link him to the all-powerful Prophet that I thought he was. Instead, he's a decrepit monster, one who preys on young, hopeful women, with big dreams and bright eyes. What's worse, I've been a part of it all along. I may not have killed Georgia, but I didn't stop all the bad things from happening to her. I could have saved her a million times over, but I never did. Because I was a fool. Because I believed that this broken down man in front of me, snorting cocaine with a practiced sniff, was holy. Now I know that, if anything, he's evil incarnate.

Maybe my hatred shows on my face, because he narrows his eyes at me. "Why are you looking at me like that?"

"I'm not looking at you like anything. Just thinking about all the discipline my new Maiden requires."

His face sours even more. "That bitch is a fucking pestilence. Nothing but trouble from the moment she got here. Ruined my son. Tried to ruin this deal with the senator. What was she on about last night? I saw her hit you. But you got her in line eventually." He points at me. "A firm hand Noah. No leash for that one. She has to be ready for her post. The senator is too important."

"I can't believe he still wants her."

"He does, but he's a fool for it. She'll poison him the same way she did Adam if we don't get her under control." He finishes his coke communion, then leans back, his mood growing lighter. "But I've got her under my thumb now. She'll fall in line."

"How'd you manage that?"

"I found her pressure point."

I swallow hard—anything he does to her is going to complicate things for me. I promised Adam I'd look out for her. Do I see a way to do that? No. Not right now, but a promise is a promise.

"I have her mother over at the Rectory." An easy smile takes over as the coke hits his bloodstream. "Leverage."

Complication? Check.

I stand and stretch. "Well, it's time for my visit. I'll see if she's more inclined to be a good girl."

"No marks," he warns. "Now that she's damaged, we need to keep her as clean as we can for Senator Roberts. He's not too happy with the delay, so we need to mitigate that with other things. No marks ..." He taps his fingers on the desk. "And don't fuck her in the ass. I don't want any evidence that she's been touched more than she has been already."

I feign outrage. "But Dad, if I can't—"

"I said no." His voice remains gentle, as if he knows what a crushing blow this is to me. "But you can still have her suck your cock. That doesn't leave a mark."

I sigh. "I guess I'll have to live with that."

"That's a good boy." He nods. "You always were my favorite, you know?"

His favorite because I'm dumb and gullible. Yeah, I know. "Thanks, Dad. I'll get to it, if that's all right with you?"

"A firm hand, don't forget." He waves me away.

"Yes, sir." I stride out and head down to the basement, my body loosening with each step. Just being near him bunches my muscles, twists them until it almost feels like a cramp.

"Hey." Castro follows me down the steps.

Shit. I don't know what he wants, but it can't be anything good. Then again, maybe he knows where Adam is?

"Outside." He pushes through the back door near the bar, and we step out into the cold night.

"What?" I keep my voice down and lean against the brick wall.

"Your mother has a message for you." He pulls a pack of cigs from his pocket and offers me one.

I shake my head. I love my nicotine, but I have standards about who I'll share a smoke with. "What's the message?"

He takes a long drag. "She knows where Adam is."

"She took him?"

"No." He blows the smoke up until it forms a plume above his head, a comic bubble over an idiot character. "But we know who did. He's on the compound."

"Where?"

"That's not important. What you need to know is that the plan is still on. Everything will be in place for a smooth transition. Now that Adam is safe—*pendejo*." He spits, then continues, "Rachel still wants him to lead. But, if he can't, she'll make you the new Prophet. Either way, the old Prophet will be gone, and *she* will be in charge. Understand?"

"I'm not Prophet material."

"Neither is your *puta* brother, but it is what it is." He shrugs. "That's what she wants, and I'm going to give it to her."

"When is all this supposed to go down?"

His gaze shifts away. "Soon."

"Like tomorrow soon or next week soon?"

"Soon. Your mother has it all well in hand, and I'll be there beside her taking care of business."

"Why? I mean, why are you backing her?" I stare at him. Castro is maybe forty, dark hair, fit build. I can't say he's attractive—mainly because I'm almost certain I hate his guts—but he could find a woman, settle down, maybe have some kids that take after him and turn into total assholes. Mom isn't ugly or anything, but the two of them together doesn't make sense to me.

He takes another long drag, though he keeps his eyes on me. "For years, I've served your father. For years, he doesn't make me a Protector. When he promoted Zion, that should have been my time. When that fucker Newell got popped, that was definitely the time. He should have done it then. Instead, he promotes that piece of shit Trey. Not me. Not the one who's been there day in and day out for years."

"So, you're jealous of Zion and Trey."

He flicks the cigarette. "Sometimes I think you're just as dumb as your brother."

"Douche." It's a reflex.

He shakes his head. "Jealous? No. I'm *righteous*. Your mother knows I'm worthy. She treats me with the respect I deserve. She doesn't hold this against me." He gestures to his face. "Doesn't care where I come from or who my parents were."

It clicks when he says that. For years, my father has been privately teaching what Adam calls "white supremacy for dummies." It's not the in-your-face pointy hats and cross-burning, but there's a reason why all the Maidens are white. Even when we opened a Heavenly branch in the poorer section of Birmingham, it was just for appearances. Nothing more. My father wanted to stop the influx of all people of color to the main Heavenly campus.

"*Build them their own church, collect their tithes, and that's it,*" he'd said. "*Problem solved.*"

"You aren't better than me. Your *pendejo* brother is certainly not better than me. Your mother knows that. She sees that I can lead." He straightens, his chest puffing a bit. "That's what this is about."

I scratch my jaw. "Okay, then. I get it now. So you're jealous and mad that Dad discriminates."

He throws his hands up and launches into a litany of curses in Spanish, then opens the back door, walks in, and slams it behind him.

For the first time in a while, a genuine smile pulls at my lips. No wonder Adam likes fucking with that guy. It's easy and way too fun.

CHAPTER 13

DELILAH

I look up when the door opens and Noah walks in. So different from Adam. He doesn't seem inclined to make me kneel, to dominate me in all the animal ways that Adam thrives on. I wonder for the millionth time where Adam is and if he's okay.

"Hey." Noah walks over to the bed and sits down beside me. "How was your, um, day?"

I would laugh at the banality of his question, but I can't. I can't laugh or smile or seem to do anything other than endure. "I've had better."

"You and me both." He leans back and spreads out on my bed, tucking his hands behind his head and closing his eyes. "Lie next to me."

I clutch my dress, my body unwilling to move. Not for him.

"Come on, Maiden. I'm here to work on your obedience." He drops his voice to a whisper. "Do it or we'll both be fucked in the ass."

Point made. I scoot next to him, lying on my back. My ass still stings, but Abigail came by earlier to check on me. "*Healing*," she'd said. "*Seems like you're always healing these days.*"

Noah is a big man like his brother, but he keeps to his side of the bed, the only encroachment from his elbow on my side of the pillow.

"What did you and Grace get up to today?"

Small talk. Is this small talk?

"She showed me—" A bunch of depraved photos taken by my fiancé. I try again. "She showed me some information on the senator. Things I'll need to know to be a good wife to him."

"Is that what you're going to do?"

"What?"

The smirk in his voice is biting. "Be a good wife?"

"Yes."

"How will you please him?"

"I'll be in perfect obedience."

He turns to look at me, his blue eyes searing despite his nonchalant tone. "I mean how will you fuck him? How

114

will you use your mouth, your hands, your pussy?"

His words are like physical blows, and I cringe away from him.

"Not so fast." He reaches out and grabs me, wrestling me until I'm astride him, my dress tight and twisted around my right hip, the marks on my backside stinging.

My heart slams against my ribs, and fear momentarily dazes me.

"Show me." He tucks his hands behind his head again, his eyes on me. "Show me how you'll ride his cock."

"Noah, please—"

"A firm hand, Delilah." He glances toward the camera. "That's what I need to have with you. A firm hand that guides you back down the proper path."

This is all a show. He's in on it. I tell myself these things over and over again, but it doesn't change the shame that creeps into my cheeks. It doesn't stop tears from pricking behind my eyes. He has to degrade me for the camera. For show. But my humiliation is as real as it ever was.

Reaching up, he grabs my dress, freeing it from my hip and bunching it in his fist. "Ride me, Maiden."

I close my eyes and move my hips. My skin scrapes against the seam of his jeans, but I keep undulating. With my eyes closed, I can pretend Adam is beneath me. Even though everything tells me it's another man. Noah doesn't smell the same, doesn't speak in the same gravelly voice. *No, it's Adam.* I force my mind into compliance, and imagine Adam staring up at me with his unfathomable dark eyes. *"Ride me, little lamb."*

My hips loosen, and I let myself go more, let myself feel Adam beneath me. His cock hardening, his thighs tensing, his breathing speeding up. His hands digging into my hips as I rub myself against him again and again. My nipples harden, tingling with need as I lick my lips and think about him, his hands, his belt, his tongue.

"Fuck." A voice. Not Adam's.

I slow and stop. Opening my eyes, I find Noah beneath me, his jaw tight, his eyes heavy-lidded and intense. More shame, more embarrassment—everything piles onto my heart. I cover my face.

"Delilah." His voice is gruff. "That's enough for now. You're learning. The senator will be more than pleased with your fucking skills."

I climb off him and lay back down.

He turns toward me, his back to the camera. "I'm sorry," he whispers.

"It's okay." Is it?

"We have to. Understand? We have to do this."

I nod and meet his gaze. "I know."

His brow furrows. "Don't cry." He swipes my tears with his thumb. He's gentle. His nature is far softer than Adam's, but I can sense something steely underneath.

"I want to be strong. I'm trying."

"You are. You're just like your sister." His throat closes on the last word, and he's silent for a long while.

How could I have thought he was the one to hurt Georgia? God, I'm so blind. It wasn't Noah. Then again, Noah knows who it was.

"Tell me who hurt her. Please."

"I can't."

"Why?" My whisper gets a little too loud, and he presses his finger to his lips.

I try again. "Why won't you tell me?"

"I just can't. Please don't ask me."

"Was it Adam?" I blurt.

"No. But that's all I'm saying. Maybe a time will come when you'll find out, but I can promise you it won't be from me."

I have the urge to reach out and pinch him. I don't. "Who are you protecting? It has to be someone close to you."

He flinches but doesn't answer. Instead, he changes the subject. "Something's coming. A change. I don't know when, but it's on the way."

"What kind of change?"

"There's going to be a fight. You just need to keep yourself safe. If anything happens to you, Adam will kill me."

"Is he okay?"

"I think so. He's somewhere on the compound."

"Where?"

"I have a guess or two, but I can't follow up on them right now. Dad is too suspicious. Paranoid since Adam disappeared. I have to watch my back."

"Can you do something for me?"

He lets out a breath through pursed lips. "Doubt it. But what?"

"My mom, they have her in the Rectory. Could—"

"I can't get her out."

This time I do pinch him.

"Ow." He glowers.

"I wasn't finished. They have her. Could you visit her at least? Tell her that everything's going to be all right?"

"What good will that do?"

"I've been where she is. I know what it feels like. If you can just get to her somehow. Tell her—" I swallow hard. "Tell her that I'm going to get her out. It won't be long."

His eyes soften. "So you want me to lie to her?"

I fist my hands. "It's not a lie."

"Sounds like one to me."

"I'm getting out of here. I'm going to—"

"What? You're going to what? Look, I don't want to burst your rescue bubble, but you're trapped in here. No escape for you or your mom or any of us. Unless you have an arsenal I'm not aware of, you aren't blasting your way out."

"I agree." Everything he's said is true. But I have one option, one way to bring this place down. It's not with guns and war. At least, not yet.

Though I try not to think about it, I have one card left to play. One checkmate that will cost me dearly.

His brow furrows. "If you agree with what I'm saying here, then what are we even talking about?"

"Just tell her, okay? Tell her I'm coming for her. Can you do that for me?"

"I'll try." He sits up. "Till tomorrow, Maiden." He rises and strides to the door, opening it roughly. "Work on your cock-handling skills for next time. And I hope your gag reflex is non-existent." He slams the door.

I curl into a ball and stare at the wall, my mind clicking with plans and strategy. Adam is safe for the time being.

Mom is not. These are the parameters I have to work within. I can do it. I can save them both.

Even if the cost is higher than I can admit, even to myself.

CHAPTER 14

ADAM

"*H*oly shit, where'd you get this?"

I keep my eyes closed. Lying on Jez's couch, I've heard plenty of interesting conversations over the past three days. This one is the most interesting of all.

"You know how Noah has crews clearing all those acres for farming?"

"Yeah," Jez replies.

"They're stockpiling dynamite to take care of the stony areas that they can't dig out with regular equipment. Going to break the rock into smaller pieces they can get with their bulldozers."

"Are you shitting me?" Jez cackles. "We won't need the gasoline at all if we've got more of this."

"This is just a sample. There's more. A ton more in a storage shed on that side of the compound."

"How much can you nick?"

"Enough."

"When?"

"It'll take me a few days. I'm only supposed to be out there to take lunches and refreshments to the workers, and that's once a day. If I'm lucky, they don't pay me any attention, and I can sneak by the shed on my way back. I can hide what I take under the seat of my golf cart, then stash it somewhere safer. But if anyone's looking, I'll have to skip it and try again the next day."

I open my eyes and watch the back and forth between Jez and Chastity. They don't pay me any attention, either believing I'm asleep or knowing I'm awake and not caring.

Jez holds a stick of dynamite that looks just like what you'd see in the movies—a narrow tube in a khaki wrapper with warnings all over it and a black fuse hanging out one end.

"We'll need to bring the sanctuary down. This Sunday, got it? Can you get that many sticks?"

"How many of these will that take?" Chastity retrieves the stick, holding it gingerly as she whispers to Jez.

Mass murder. That's what's being planned right in front of me. My father has driven these women to this, pushed them over the brink and into the dark abyss below. I've done things that will haunt me until the day I die, but all of it pales in comparison to what Jez and Chastity are planning in urgent whispers. But that's what my father does. Poisons everything and everyone he touches. This is his evil—their entire plan is just another rung on his ladder of hatred, murder, and power.

"So, I'm thinking twenty. We place them around those wide, round columns in the atrium area and around to the sides and back." Chastity glances at me and frowns.

"Nice to see you again. So you're in on the mass murder plan, too?" I stretch, my phantom toes stinging.

Chastity turns to me, her eyes shrewd. "It was my idea, so I'd say so."

"I see."

She glares. "No, you don't."

"Let me rephrase. I see that you and Jez here have lost your fucking minds and intend to slaughter thousands of people. Judge, jury, and executioner. A death sentence all because they were desperate enough to fall for the Prophet's lies. And not just them." I sit up and wince as blood rushes to my foot. "Their children, too. You'll kill them all."

Chastity steps toward me, her shoulders back, her eyes alight. "You think we came to this decision lightly?"

"I don't care how much hand-wringing it took, what you're talking about is the worst sort of evil."

"No. Your father. He's the worst sort of evil."

"So kill him. Just him." I hold up my bandaged hands. "I hope you can see that I'd be happy to help with that plan. He needs to go, and I'm more than willing to help out. But that doesn't mean you have to kill all the—"

"I do." Chastity shakes her head. "I have to destroy Heavenly. Cutting off the head of the snake isn't enough. Another head will pop right up." She jerks her chin at me. "You, your brother, one of the Protectors, some asshole in the crowd who thinks he's touched by God. And then it will never stop."

"So kill the Protectors. That's been my plan."

Her eyes widen. "You planned to—"

"Kill every last one of them right along with my father. Yes."

"What about the guy in the crowd?" Jez plops down on her golden tufted chair and slings one leg over the dingy arm. "How are we going to stop him?"

"Deal with that when it comes up." I lean forward and pluck a piece of cheese from a tray they've left out for me. "Surely, you can see that killing so many is wrong."

"Wrong." Chastity laughs. "Adam Monroe is lecturing me about right and wrong." She giggles. "Ah, God, that's rich." Still laughing, she doubles over, her hand over her mouth as she tries to control her mirth.

"It's wrong, and you know it."

She jerks upright, the laughter dying on a sour note. "No." Her fingers fly to the buttons at her throat and make quick work of them down her front.

I take a too-ripe strawberry, chewing it as Chastity turns and strips her dress down. "This is wrong. What he did to me and to Jez, to the girls in the Chapel and in the Cathedral." A vicious criss-cross of scars mars the pale skin of her back. Circles of pink, raised skin are dotted here and there. Cigar burns, courtesy of the Prophet. "I'm not even the worst one. Two of the girls at the Cathedral are missing fingers. You know why?"

I nod.

"Say it," Chastity hisses and buttons her top back into place.

The words don't want to come out, the truth just as disgusting and diseased as my father. But I say it all the same. "They miscarried."

"Goddamn." Jez rubs her eyes. "I'd forgotten about that. Maybe blocked it out. Fuck if I know."

"A finger for a miscarriage. There's plenty more that goes on there. Ruth probably just gives us the highlights."

"Ruth is in on this mess?" That's more of a surprise than even Chastity. Ruth is from the first crop of Maidens. Quiet, level-headed, and unfailingly calm, she's been like a mother hen to all the girls that wind up in the Cathedral.

"Yes. Her and more. And we all know the plan. And we *all* agree that to stop the rot, we have to destroy every bit of Heavenly."

"You heard from Ruth?" Jez asks Chastity.

"Yeah. Earlier today. Said she got busted for having contraband at the Cathedral. Had to spend a day in the Rectory, but is out now."

"Damn. I thought she was too smooth to get caught."

Chastity shrugs. "Me too, but all's well now. She's ready to get back to work."

"Good." Jez nods. "Sunday can't come soon enough."

"You're wrong." I realize I'm treating them the same way I treat my father when he's ranting or plotting. I stay as placid as possible, letting him rage and answering with even tones, reasonable words. Of course, it doesn't work on him, and, from the expressions on Jez and Chastity's faces, it's not working on them either. "Why am I even here? What's my place in all this? I'm not going along with your murder mission. You may as well throw me back to the Prophet."

"You're insurance." Chastity grabs her black coat and pulls it on. "If things go south, we'll offer you to the Prophet for our freedom."

"I don't think that'll work. He crucified me, remember? Not sure he's interested in having me back."

Chastity smirks, and I see the darkness in her that wasn't there a few years ago. She was right about one thing; the Prophet corrupts everything he touches. "He's still tearing the compound apart looking for you. He's desperate to have you returned. Probably so he can put you back up on that cross where you belong."

I can't argue that point. Sarah's blood on my hands is plenty to condemn me to death, not to mention my other sins. "Let's pretend trading me goes according to plan. You hand me over, he gives you freedom, you walk out of here. His men will have you hunted down and dragged back in a matter of hours. You know that right?"

Chastity shrugs. "We'll tackle that when it comes."

"*If* it comes," interjects Jez.

"So I take it I'm a prisoner?"

"For the time being, yes." Jez rises. "If you make any trouble, we'll tie you, gag you, and stick you back in the box."

"Good to know." I lean back, pretending to make myself comfortable while my insides twist and bubble like lava. It's not smart, but I have to ask. "I realize I'm in no position for favors, but I was hoping you could add Delilah to your little venture on the off chance it actually works."

"I will keep her away from the church on Sunday. I owe her that much."

"You owe her?" I'm lost.

"This is for her sister." She snatches her gloves off the small table by the door. "I'm not doing this for you."

"Her sister?" What the hell? Nothing in Emily's records ever mentioned a sister. "What are you talking about?"

Chastity shakes her head and steps toward the door, her lips pressed together in a hard line.

"Chastity, please. Who's her sister?"

"I've done enough for the Monroes." She turns her back on me.

Fuck. A sister? A memory ghosts across my mind, some fact that I missed, some bit of information that I should have followed further. But it's gone. It doesn't matter. I don't care the why of it. I just want Emily safe and away from this place if it's at all possible. My past days have been spent with thoughts of her. Jez wouldn't answer any questions about her, wouldn't even tell me if she'd been sold to that bastard senator. But I've refused to believe it, refused to give in to despair. There has to be a way to save her. Since Jez and Chastity are hellbent on a suicide mission, I'll have to search outside of the Chapel for help. But that won't be easy, not when everyone on the compound is looking for me.

Jez rubs a hand down Chastity's back. "Calm down. You need to look saintly when you walk out of here."

Chastity takes a deep breath and lets it out in a shaky burst. Then she and Jez embrace and share a decidedly non-chaste kiss.

"Be safe." Jez reaches for the door that leads to the rest of the Chapel.

"One more question, Chastity." I peer up at her. "When you're done with your explosive endgame, what do you plan to do with me?"

She pulls her hood up and walks out, giving me nothing more than the hint of a smirk, the promise of my death.

CHAPTER 15

DELILAH

*W*e file out of the Cloister and get onto the white bus. We're headed to the Temple for the LSD ritual, but it's on a Thursday night this time. It seems Adam's disappearance threw everything into disarray, and even now, I can see a few flashlights off in the woods—the Prophet's goons still searching for his lost son.

Chastity eases down next to me. I look up, but Grace's back is to us, her eyes focused on the road ahead.

"Sunday. Stay in the Cloister for service. Pretend you're sick. Do whatever it takes to stay behind."

"Why, what—"

She rises quickly and moves down the aisle toward the back.

Damn.

I need to know more, especially since I intend to make a move tonight—one that will likely land me in an even more dire situation.

"What was that?" Eve huddles beside me.

"Don't know." I turn to her. It's been days since I've had a chance to speak with anyone besides Grace or Noah. They keep me separate, making sure I eat at a separate table, alone, and not allowing me to go to training with the rest of the Maidens. Maybe that last part is a blessing, but the isolation chafes.

I lean closer to Eve. "How are you holding up?"

She stares at her hands. "Not so great. I had to meet my suitor two days ago." Her shoulders slump even more. "He's from South Carolina. Runs some sort of guns and ammunition manufacturing thing out there. Old. Fat." She shivers. "Handsy."

"I'm sorry." I want to say that I'll get her out of here, that she won't have to go to the old fat man in South Carolina, but I can't be sure it's true. Not yet.

"At least he doesn't want me yet. But he's told the Prophet what sort of training I need." She crosses her arms over her stomach and squeezes her elbows. "He's got a thing for blood. For cutting. Leaving scars in weird patterns."

My mouth goes dry. Eve will leave the torture of the Cloister only to be sent into an even deeper hell. I can't tell if I'm raging or sorrowful. A mix of both, I suppose.

All I can see is her profile, her skin wan, her eyes clenched shut. If I could paint a picture of her at this moment, I could easily title it 'Despair.' That's all the Maidens have left—except the ones who are true believers. For them, they think a heaven awaits them after their trials here on earth.

The bus rumbles through the compound. There are men along the road at intervals, guns slung across their backs. No wonder the Prophet is aiming to get a gun manufacturer on his hook.

We pull to a stop in front of the Temple and file out of the bus into the shivering evening. The overdone walls of the Temple meet us, paintings of the Prophet following our every step down the hallway. We strip outside the golden doors leading to the round room, the Spinners taking our dresses. No shame amongst us anymore, we stand in a line, obedient and still.

When we're led in, my eyes automatically go to the spot where Adam used to be, his gaze locked with mine as he knelt on the floor. He's not there, his absence an open wound. Noah is on his knees in his usual spot, and this time he watches me instead of his previous Maiden.

The Spinners guide us to sit on the floor in front of the throne, all of the Maidens herded inside the large pentagram that transverses the floor in veins of gold. I try to keep myself grounded, to control the fear that eats away at my insides. The path I'm on—it doesn't lead to a happy end. Not for me. But maybe my actions tonight will clear a way for me to start the systematic dismantling of everything Heavenly stands for.

"My children." The Prophet smiles, though he seems aged somehow, worn thin. His forehead more wrinkled, the lines next to his eyes darker. Maybe I'm not the only one losing sleep over Adam.

The Spinners bring in the trays of poisoned food and set them amongst us before walking out and closing the doors behind them.

"I'm so pleased to have each of you. Eat, drink, enjoy yourselves. Be as children. 'Truly I tell you, unless you change and become like little children, you will never enter the kingdom of heaven.'" He gestures toward the food. "Eat, my loves. Tonight we shall delight in the love of the Lord."

I grab a grape, pretend to eat it, then reach for another, all the while keeping the same one in my palm. The other Maidens take the wine, drinking and eating with abandon. I understand why. The drugs give a reprieve from this place. Even if it leaves you open and empty in the end, it's still better than the cutting touch of reality.

"We've had our trials, difficult times, and disappointments. But, tonight, I feel that we are on the correct path.

Here with you lovely angels, I don't know of anything that can stop Heavenly from spreading God's word to all those who need to hear it." He smiles, his beady eyes devouring all the Maidens before him.

I saw a movie once where a mummy would suck the souls of the people he killed until they dried up and blew away. The Prophet reminds me of that, the way he hungrily surveys the women before him, as if he wants to steal every bit of youth and heart and soul from each of us.

"Come, little one." He motions to Hannah. "Sit with me and share your perfect innocence for just a moment."

She stands, her posture bent, the drugs not in full effect yet, and sits next to him. He pulls her close to his side and whispers in her ear. She doesn't react, her eyes downcast. It's hard to square her with the girl who almost escaped with Sarah, Eve, Chastity, and me. What we did took guts, and perhaps it was a stupid attempt, but Hannah saw her chance and took it. Now, she's empty. Whatever light she had in her has been extinguished, and I wonder if it will ever shine again.

The price for our freedom was too dear. We paid, and Sarah most of all. A hot needle pierces my heart when I think of her, how strong she'd been to even dream of finding a way out. I hope I can make her proud some-how, even if I don't possess but a fraction of her courage.

The Maidens next to me giggle and paw at each other as Hannah leaves the throne and settles onto her royal-blue pillow. She grabs a handful of grapes and eats them.

"Delilah." The Prophet's gaze finds me, and he motions me up to his dais.

I thought I'd have more time. I don't. I stand and walk to him, sitting on the crimson cushion as he wraps his arm around me.

His hand is dry and leathery as he squeezes my upper arm. "And how is my fallen angel enjoying her feast?"

My stomach churns and the desperate urge to run whispers up and down my spine.

"Doesn't matter." He grins. "The drugs will make you have a good time whether you want to or not." His hand moves up and over my shoulder, his fingertips reaching for my nipple. "There's one thing I regret, you know?"

I swallow, trying to keep my bile in check. "What's that?"

"I wished I'd asked Adam—before I had him nailed to the cross—what your pussy felt like."

My shoulders tense, but his hand clamps down on me, and he brings his other around to my stomach. I clench my legs together.

"Don't be like that." He draws his fingers over my skin, moving lower as I scream inside my head. "You gave it to Adam. Why not share it with me?" His fingers stop.

"Though I hate to say that your senator has insisted that you not be spoiled any more than you already are." He strokes lower, his fingers invading the sensitive skin between my thighs.

My eyes water. I want to tell him to stop, but I know that will only make it worse. He doesn't violate me completely, his fingers skirting along the bare skin, but it's enough. It's enough that I want to vomit, to run, to scream.

"So soft and pale." He removes his hand and grabs my breast with it, squeezing hard. "How did something so fragile ruin my firstborn son?" The edge in his voice grows jagged. "How did you, a worthless piece of ass, cause his downfall?" Pinching my nipple, he twists it then lets go.

I draw in a shaking breath as his hold on my shoulder loosens.

"I suppose it doesn't matter now." He adopts a more congenial tone. "What's done is done, and the senator still wants you."

"I was hoping to talk to you about that." Just saying those words is like pulling a dagger from my body.

His eyes widen, then an indulgent smile crosses his lips. "What does my lily-white whore have to say?"

I can take his insults. They mean nothing to me. Just as he means nothing to me. But I'm here for more than words. "I spoke with Grace earlier today, but she refused my request to speak to you."

"Go on." He puts his hand on my thigh, resting it there as if I'm a piece of furniture.

"I'm ready for my assignment." I hold his eyes, though their serpent-like nature sends a chill through my heart. "I'm ready to be what you need me to be for the senator."

He arches a brow. "You're ready to be in perfect obedience?"

"Yes, Prophet." I drop my gaze. "I want to do your will."

"Oh, my darling." He pinches my leg. "I wish I could believe that."

"It's true." I wring my hands. "If you send me to the senator, I promise I will be obedient to him and serve your will. You'll see."

"Why this sudden change of heart?" His hand inches up my leg. "What's made the difference?"

"I see now that I have sinned against you. Grace and Noah taught me that. I was so wrapped up in myself that I didn't open my heart to your words. But now I know better. And I'm sorry. And one day, I hope to be worthy of all the love you've shown me."

He tilts my chin up. "How am I supposed to believe you? After all you've done? You tried to escape, led my son to ruin, then threatened to kill your one true mate."

"I know." I think of Sarah, of her blood, and of Adam, his screams on the cross. My eyes water, just as I intend. "And I will spend a lifetime trying to be the good girl you want me to be." I slide to the floor and kneel at his feet. "I will make you proud. Please give me this chance to atone for all I've done." Though I run the risk of retching, I take his hand and kiss the back of it. "Please, Prophet. Let me show you."

"Show me?" He runs his other hand through my hair.

"Yes, please."

He grins, and a shudder courses through me.

"You can show me what a good girl you are." He opens his crimson robe and reaches for his pants. "With your mouth."

My gorge rises, but I force it back down. I will do what I have to do. I blink, and a tear rolls down my cheek.

"Perfect." He unzips his pants, and I close my eyes.

CHAPTER 16

NOAH

I hurtle out of the Temple and into the night. A light drizzle floats down and coats everything in misery as I hurry to my car. The white bus has barely pulled away when I tear off after it, then take a left as it turns toward the Cloister to the right.

Blinking, I see Delilah on her knees, her teary eyes locking with mine for only a second before my father takes her attention again.

Fuck. I screech to a halt next to the small white church, gravel flying from under my tires. Jumping out of my car, I rush up the stairs. The usual guard is on duty and pays me no attention as I barrel through the double doors into the bedrooms. A few girls give me tired looks, then return to chatting. Only a couple of them are working, their fake moans floating around me like cheap perfume.

I hurry past to the door at the end of the center aisle, giving zero fucks when one of them screeches at me, "You can't go in there!"

Jez's door handle doesn't yield when I turn it, so I bang on the hollow wood, demanding she open up.

"The fuck?" she squawks, and I hear movement.

"I'll kick it in if you don't open it by the time I get to five." I don't have time for her bullshit. He's here. He has to be. I've searched everywhere on the compound that he could be. I even questioned Castro more this afternoon, though that fucker didn't give me anything other than an assurance he wasn't in the main house. Useless. But if Mom didn't have him squirreled away somewhere, the Chapel is the only spot.

I count down. When I get to five, I take a step back and kick. Right when my foot should bust the door, Jez swings it open.

Topless, and with a bored look, she asks, "Where's the fire?"

I storm in and slam the door behind me. "He's here. I know he is." Despite my rash entrance, I keep my voice down.

"Who?"

I step toward her and glower down into her face. "I don't want to hurt you, but I will."

She snorts a laugh and turns her back to me, showing the cigarette burns that run down her spine in a neat line. "More than Daddy did?" The look she throws over her shoulder is a mix of mocking and sultry, and I want to strangle her.

"Hand him over. Now."

"Nothing but girls here, baby." She twirls her index finger in a circular motion. "This is a cathouse. No boys allowed unless they're paying."

I push past her and peer inside her bedroom. Nothing there. Nowhere to hide a grown man, anyway. When I turn, I see another one of the Chapel girls lounging on one of the gold chairs. Babylon, I think is her name.

"She wasn't there before." I point at her. "You. Where'd you come from?"

"I've been here the whole time." She spreads her legs, the tiny scrap of lace meant to cover her pussy revealing everything except the spot where the baby comes out. "Want to see more of me?"

"No, I want to know where my brother is." I look up at the leaves, two colorful birds staring back down at me, silent as always.

"We don't know." Jez grabs a short robe from the rack of clothes just inside her bedroom and throws it on. "Haven't seen him. Guards have already searched us twice."

I hear a quiet thump, and sharply turn my head toward the wide stained glass window at the back of the church.

Babylon kicks one of her feet down to the floor, making a similar sound. "Let's go out to my room. Get a few other girls." She stands and struts to me, her hands grasping the front of my shirt. "We can have a good time."

Another thump, this one definitely coming from the baptistry.

"Lay off." I push past her and walk around the edge of the wide planter, the dark dirt covered with trailing vines and lush greenery. "You have him here. Somewhere." Peering down, I see a smaller concrete planter that is slightly off-kilter.

"I told you. We've been searched already." Jez approaches, tension rolling off her.

"No." I hold up a hand. "Stay back." Grabbing the planter, I yank it away. Dirt spills over the side, and some of it cascades down the blue-green stairs that lead down into a narrow well—what's left of the old baptistry.

"Noah, come on." Jez's voice has risen an octave. "There's nothing back there but fertilizer for the plants. Let us show you—"

"Fuck off." I drop down the stairs and feel along the back of the wooden structure that supports the garden above. A pile of goodies lies to the side, all sorts of contraband that would result in a one-way ticket to the punishment circle. "Naughty girls." I cluck my tongue and pull on one of the wooden cross slats. It comes away with ease and reveals a pine box hidden behind it.

"Noah, I'm warning you." Jez has disappeared, her voice coming from the main sitting area.

"If you're going for a gun, I hope you've got a silencer for it. Otherwise, if you fire a shot, the guard will be on you faster than a chigger on a nut-sack."

"Faster than a what?" Babylon mutters.

I grab one end of the box and yank.

"Fuck!" Definitely Adam's voice, though it's muffled.

A wound-up coil of tension lets go inside me, and I feel like I can finally take a deep breath for the first time in days. My brother is alive. I can't stop the grin that spreads over my face and seems to reach all the way down to my toes. With another yank, I have the box far enough out that I can open the lid.

I pull it up and slide it back. "Morning, sunshine."

"It's about fucking time." He blinks up at me, looking beat up, worn out, a little pissed off and a lot relieved.

"Nice to see you, too."

He sits up with a grimace. His hands are wrapped with clean, white bandages. But there's something wrong with his foot.

"What's that about?" I jerk my chin at the bandaged foot.

"Lost some toes. Frostbite."

"Seriously?"

"I don't joke about losing appendages."

The sheer ridiculousness of his words hits me right in the funny bone, and I snort. He smiles, too, and I pull him to me in a hard hug.

I'm not crying. That's not what I'd do. Ever. Happy tears aren't a thing for me. But my eyes are tingling, and I can't seem to stop squeezing the shit out of him.

"It's all right." He pats me on the back awkwardly with his injured hands. "I'm okay, Noah."

I take a deep breath, though it hitches a few times, and let him go. After a quick swipe at my (super dry) eyes, I give him another once-over. "You able to walk?"

"Yeah. It's weird, but I can still feel my toes."

"All of them are gone? I can't believe that." I stare at the bandages.

"Just two. Pinky and the one next to it. I'll be able to walk fine."

"That's not so bad, then. I guess." I shrug. It's still super bad, but there's no point freaking out about it.

"Get me out of here." He dusts off his too-big white t-shirt—must be whatever the Chapel had on hand.

I help him down. "Jesus, you still weigh a goddamn ton."

"It's all in the cock."

I snort again.

"So glad this has been a heartwarming reunion." Jez stands at the head of the stairs, a long hunting knife in her hand. "But Noah, you need to be going."

"I'm not going anywhere without him." I throw Adam's arm over my shoulders and help him toward the stairs. "So you might as well back the fuck off."

"He's ours." She moves away so I can get by and sit Adam on the sofa.

He rubs the wood dust from his hair. "I can't stay here forever, Jez. Someone will find me eventually."

She waves the knife, coming closer. "You leave when I say. And I *don't* say."

"I don't want to hurt you." I hold up my hands.

"That's novel, coming from a Monroe." She smirks and points at me. "Just leave."

"Nope."

Adam sighs. "Jez, you have to let me go. If I'm found here, they'll kill you and maybe all the girls up there. That's how my father is. Scorched earth. You know this."

"I'm willing to take that chance. I took you. You're mine. Chastity has plans."

CELIA AARON

"Chastity?" I picture the nice Spinner, the one with the scar. "She's a part of this?"

"She's the head of this." Jez says it with pride. "I know you two think you've got some way to overthrow the Prophet, but we've got this on lock. You just need to sit back and let us handle it. In any case, Adam stays here."

Adam turns to me. "They plan to blow the church up during Sunday service."

My jaw literally drops, and I look at Jez like she's a stranger. "Have you lost your fucking mind?"

"No. As I explained to your brother, this is the only way."

"It's the crazy way, sure." I stare at her, looking for some crack in her resolve. There is none. She believes in what she's saying. *Fuuuuuck.*

There's no reasoning with her, but there's no way I'm leaving my brother behind. Not again. "Look, if you want to come at me with that pig sticker, go ahead, but I'm taking Adam."

"And how do you expect to get out without them seeing you, genius?" She points the tip of the knife toward the camera in the ceiling.

I lunge at her. Caught off guard, she tries to swing the blade down at me, but I have her wrist.

"Get off!" She shoves me with her other hand, but I keep my grip on her and increase the pressure.

"Drop it." I haven't used all my strength on her, but I will if I have to. "This was never going to work, okay? Just drop it."

"Fuck you." Her knee to my crotch makes an agonizing impression, and I feel my lunch creeping up my throat at the peculiar pain that must be what dying feels like.

Letting go of her wrist, I fall back, both hands reaching for the damage between my legs. She springs toward me, but Adam throws himself off the couch and topples over onto her. Shit, with a knife between them, nothing good is about to happen.

I can't breathe. Not yet. The goods hurt too bad. But I push forward onto my knees. Adam has her wrist pinned with both of his bandaged hands, but she's trying to gouge his eye.

Scooting forward, I pry the knife from her, then yank Adam back.

He groans and presses his fingers next to his eye. "Goddammit!"

She scrabbles back until she bumps into one of her ridiculous chairs. "Shit."

I finally gasp in a breath, though I suspect my balls may be lodged in my throat for the foreseeable future.

"Jez, you know that wasn't a fair play." He points at my crotch.

149

"Fuck your fair." She eyes the knife in my hand.

"Come and get it." My voice has a wobble to it, but I finally get to my feet.

"This doesn't change anything." She rubs her reddening forehead. Adam must have gotten in a headbutt.

"I'm taking him. That's final. If you rat me out, I'll rat you out, and around and around we go." I pull Adam to his feet. He's winded, and his color seems more off than it did only minutes ago. I worry he'll pass out before we even get out the door.

Turning to Jez, I ask, "You have a back way out of here?"

She crosses her arms over her stomach and mean mugs at me. No help there.

"You know, if we get caught leaving here, you'll be in trouble, too."

"That's a chance I'm willing to take. Chastity has my back." She hasn't lost her swagger. "Who has yours?"

"Fuck." I walk past her and into her room. There's no "exit" sign pointing to a door, just more stained glass and wood paneling. Maybe I haven't thought this through all the way. Actually, I'm sure I haven't. Thinking things through isn't, strictly speaking, my strong suit. Turning again, I stop and stare at the rack of clothes that serves as Jez's closet.

An idea—not a good one, of course—forms in my mind, and I pull a dress off its hanger and head back out to Adam. "Strip."

His eyes widen and he drops onto the couch. "No way."

"It's our only chance."

"It's dumb." He shakes his head at the black dress with its long skirt and severe black habit.

"Why do you even have a Spinner costume?" he asks Jez.

She shrugs. "Some of the guys that come here are into it. The kink of the unavailable."

"You going to change your mind about helping us get out of here?" Adam pulls his shirt over his head.

"I was supposed to keep you here. I'm not going to help you get out. Not when I'm letting my girl down." She doesn't move from the floor.

I hold the dress out to Adam, unable to hide my amusement despite the dire circumstances. "Act girly, okay?"

He snatches it from me. "Just get me out of here, and I'll kick your ass for that later." He pulls the dress over his head. It's too tight, but it'll have to do.

"Follow my lead. You're a drunk whore. I'm a drunk john. We'll stumble out into the night together. I'll hold you up so you don't give away the fucked up foot."

"This is never going to work." He pulls the wings of the habit tight around his face.

"Might want to up your enthusiasm a bit." I pat him on the back. "After all, you'll be the one blowing the guard if anything goes wrong."

CHAPTER 17

DELILAH

Grace fetches me from my room earlier than usual, her face an unmoving mask of ire. "Get dressed." She throws me a white robe—the kind Maidens only wear when we're leaving the Cloister.

I don't ask questions, just slip the robe on over my white dress and step into my flats. Besides, I can guess why she's angry. I went over her head last night, asked the Prophet face-to-face if I could go to the senator. I'd asked Grace earlier in the day. She'd scoffed at the idea and assured me I was nowhere near ready.

"Move." She shoves me out the door and into the main dormitory area. With brisk steps she overtakes me and leads down the hallway and out into the cloudy morning. "This was a mistake on your part." She starts the golf cart, no driver today. "You'll see that." We take off, heading up the hill toward the main house. "I hope he does every horrible thing he can think of to you."

CELIA AARON

"I know." I pull the robe closer around my neck to ward off the cold. "You've been over this."

She turns her icy gaze on me. "Maybe he'll kill you. A man like him, he'd never get in trouble for it. Killing a disposable slut like you wouldn't matter."

"Maybe." I've thought about the grim possibility. These people were able to get rid of Georgia. It probably would be even easier for Evan, especially now that my mother won't even have the chance to look for me. I'd like to think that if I disappeared and she were free, she would come searching, demanding answers. Thinking that is easier than facing the truth.

We lurch to a stop near the back door.

Grace grabs a fistful of my robe and yanks me toward her. "I'm not getting through to you. If you leave here with that senator, you aren't coming back. Ever." She shakes her head, confused. "Why are you running toward him?"

"Why are you trying to convince me to stay?" I return her icy glare. "You've been trying scare tactics for days, doing everything you can to keep me here and away from Evan. Why?"

She flinches. Because I see her, because I can easily spy the outline of her web and avoid its silky strands.

She shakes me a little, her frustration boiling into the heightened tone of her voice. "Self-preservation isn't working on you, probably because your freak DNA is

154

broken. Since you don't seem to be following along with the rest of the class, let me make it clear for you. If you leave here with him, I will walk out of this house, ride this golf cart over to the Rectory, and start cutting pieces off your mother."

My ears ring, my body going cold. "No."

"Yes." She releases her hold on me. "I'll do it. Start with her fingers, move to her face, then to other parts. But I'll make sure she'll live. I won't kill her. I'll tell her the reason why this is happening to her—because her bitch of a daughter didn't care enough about her to save her."

I clasp my shaking hands together. "Why are you like this?" The question is as honest as it is futile. In my experience, monsters don't self-reflect, they just act. Again and again, destroying whatever they need to in order to get their way.

"I'm strong, Delilah." Her blue eyes are stone, her back straight. "Something you'll never be. Now, unless you want me to send the pieces to you in boxes, you'll stop this stupidity right now. Go." She turns and stands, then smooths her already-smooth black dress.

I stand numbly, my body in some sort of shock from the painfully vivid image Grace painted. *What am I going to do?*

"Come on." She grabs my elbow and pulls me into the house.

The Prophet's bodyguard is standing just inside, his dark eyes locking on Grace when we walk in.

"Stay." She shoves me against the bar and walks a few feet away to have a whispered conversation with the man. When it's over, she returns to my side, some color in her cheeks. It must have been good news.

We walk up the staircase to the main level, and she leads me to the familiar room with the piano and the couches. My stomach churns, and for once I'm glad the Cloister doesn't offer breakfast. Just being in here, remembering what Evan did to me on this very couch, would likely have me vomiting in the corner if I had anything in my stomach.

"Don't move." She deposits me and walks to the door, then pauses. "And don't forget about sweet little Mommy over in the Rectory."

When she's gone, I switch to the other couch. The one I haven't been assaulted on... yet. My fingers tangle together just like my thoughts. I had a plan—not a great one—but it was a plan. Now, Grace's threats have turned it all upside down. I can't leave here. My mom hasn't been there for me, but that doesn't mean I can turn my back on her now. Not when I know Grace is absolutely serious in her threats and dedicated in her follow-through.

I rest my head in my hands and hold in the scream that echoes through my mind. I can't let it out. And worse, I can't *get* out.

"Darling." Evan strides in.

I jump. And I hate that I jump.

He smiles and sits next to me, stretching his long legs out in front of him. "I hear you're desperate to be mine. That true?"

My strategy is shot. For now. But maybe I can turn this around somehow.

"I've changed."

"You have?" He slings his arm around my shoulders and pulls me close, his expensive cologne spicy and masculine. "What made you come around?" Taking my chin, he pulls my face around to his. Then he squints. "What's this?" He strokes his finger along the bruise next to my eye.

"I had an accident." I shrug. "It doesn't matter."

"Don't lie." His expression sours.

I scoot closer to him, even though I hate every bit of contact between us. "Okay, someone hit me. But it doesn't matter now. You're here." I can't feel the bruise, but I remember perfectly how I got it. Last night, when the Prophet wanted me to suck him, he couldn't get it up.

Somehow, I was to blame, and the bare knuckle hit to the side of my face was my punishment.

He laughs lightly. "What are you up to, darling? I know you don't want anything to do with me. It's one of the reasons I'm crazy about you." Nuzzling into my hair, he says, "Tell me how you want to kill me again."

I push away from him. It's instinct. And not what I'm supposed to be doing. Damn.

"See?" He smirks. "You haven't changed."

"I have!" I climb into his lap and straddle him. My heart clenches and shudders, but my mind is right where it needs to be.

His eyes light with surprise, and he rests his hands on my hips. "This should be good."

"Look, I admit I don't want any of this. I want to be free."

His fingers dig into my skin. "Never."

"I know." I shift forward until my core rests over his erection, even though I'm dry as dust. "I know I can't be free. So I'd rather be with you than here." I run my fingertips along the bruise. "They hurt me at the Cloister."

He grins. "I'll hurt you, too, darling."

My palms go clammy, and I rest them on his shoulders. "I know. But you'll give me pleasure, too, won't you?"

"Yes." He says the word as if it's obvious.

"I don't get that here." I move my hips slowly, stroking him through his pants. "All I get is pain."

He moves his hands around to my sore ass. "I'll give you plenty of that, but I'll throw in some pleasure. Though I'm not sure if you'll be a good girl for me. Only good girls get to come."

"I'll fight." I run my hands up my stomach and cup my breasts. "But I can't win, can I?"

"No." His voice lowers, his eyes locked with mine. "You'll never win." Kneading my ass, he leans forward and bites my nipple through the fabric of my dress and robe.

It hurts. He bites too hard. I whimper just the way he wants.

"But I can't go yet." I move back, but he yanks me back to his erection again.

"Not yet?" He glares, his eyes somehow darker. "Why not?"

Have I played him too hard? I want him on my side, want him desperate for me. But I can't leave yet. I need to back this up some. "There are a few more lessons on how to please you. I want to make sure I understand your needs."

"I don't think so." He pushes my dress up, then rubs his palms along the bare skin of my thighs. "You need to come with me now."

"No." I shake my head.

He slaps my ass. "There she is. Buttering me up one second, defying me the next."

The sting almost draws tears to my eyes, my skin still recovering from the Prophet's belt. "I can't leave yet. I'm not ready." God, I've botched this.

"You're ready when I say you are." He pulls me against him until we're nose to nose. "And I say you're ready right now."

"Now, Evan." The Prophet walks in, his hands behind his back and slight chiding expression on his face. "You can't go too far with her."

Evan grabs my chin and wrenches my face around to the Prophet. "I told you I didn't want any marks on her. Look at this. Care to explain?"

He sits on the sofa across from us. "Accidents happen. Especially when a Maiden is clumsy or rude." His withering stare doesn't affect me. Not anymore.

"I want her now." Evan pulls my dress down, making sure my ass is covered.

I suppose he doesn't want his property on display just yet.

"Now?" The Prophet shakes his head. "She isn't ready."

"I say she is. She wants to come with me."

"Is that true, Delilah?" The Prophet asks.

"Yes, but I—"

"Well, then we can make a deal. But I'm afraid given her damaged nature, I'll need you to wed her before you bed her. A little insurance policy. I'm sure you understand. I can't have you using her up and then dumping her out of spite."

"I'll keep my word." Evan sits me beside him, his icy eyes locked on the Prophet. "I hope you aren't suggesting otherwise."

"Of course not." The Prophet adopts a placid expression. "I think I have a solution that should make us all happy. How about we have a brief ceremony at this Sunday's service, make it official, and then you can take her and be on your way. Plan a big to-do later, once you've gotten her broken in."

Evan's fingers wrap around my upper arm, pressing hard enough to leave bruises. "I'd rather have her today."

"I'm afraid you can't." Though he wraps his tone in silk, there's metal underneath. "But Sunday would be the perfect time."

Evan turns to me. "Can you wait that long, darling?"

I nod, hiding my relief in an obedient, downward gaze. "Yes."

"Well, I guess that'll have to do." He sighs. "Though I fucking hate to wait."

"It's for the best. You'll see." The Prophet stands. "I've got the paperwork in my office. Shall we?"

"Give me a minute with her."

The Prophet's eyes narrow, clearly not liking the command in Evan's voice, but he walks away all the same. "Of course."

Evan slides his arm behind my back and pushes me down onto the couch. Fear coats every thought in my mind with an oily haze, but I have to keep it together. He presses his body onto mine, his unforgiving muscles and hard cock promising me that he'll always be bigger, stronger, faster.

"God, the things I'm going to do to you, darling." He runs his teeth along the line of my jaw. "You'll hate me so much." He clenches his arm behind me, squeezing the air from my lungs before letting up and kissing my neck.

"Are you—" The question gets stuck in my throat.

"What?" He pulls back and stares down into my eyes, the monster barely restrained.

"Are you really going to share me?"

He smiles, as if he thrives on my fear. And maybe he does. "Does that upset you?"

"I saw the video. I saw what you like to... do."

"I like to watch, to film, to savor it frame by frame. And then I like to fuck." He presses his lips to my ear. "Worried?"

Yes. I fold in on myself, making myself small on the inside, trying to hide my soul from him. But I know I can't. There's no escape from him.

"I'll share you, darling. With friends. Haven't decided if I'll let them fuck you proper or not. But you'll have to suck them, let them in your ass, rub their come all over your tits. Then I'll fuck you while they watch. How's that sound?"

He must feel me shaking, because he laughs low in his throat. Pressing his lips to my ear, he whispers, "I like you angry, darling. But I *love* you scared."

CHAPTER 18

ADAM

"*J*esus Christ, this is fucking insane." Noah kneels at the foot of the bed, his gaze on my unwrapped foot. "They're just gone."

"I know."

"What do you think they did with them?"

"What?"

"What did they do with the two toes they cut off?" He scratches his ear and stares.

"I don't know. I guess they threw them away." I sigh. "Are you going to check the sites for infection or just gawk?"

Gregory stands stoic in his tank behind Noah's back, and Felix slinks around near the door. I'm in the spare room Noah uses as his pet sanctuary. No cameras in here. Noah keeps the room locked ever since the "roasted

Gregory" ruse we pulled on Dad. My brother's become adept at navigating around the surveillance.

"I mean, they sewed you up. Everything looks clean. I don't think I can take the stitches out yet. The skin is still sort of ... raw where they cut them off." He presses the back of his hand to his mouth and gags a little.

"Pussy."

"Yeah." He nods and stands, his hands on his hips. "In this case, I concur. Cannot handle that shit. Do you still feel them?"

"Yep. As far as my brain knows, those two toes are still alive and well." He sits next to me and grabs my right hand, then starts unwrapping the gauze.

"I really thought we were going to get busted at the Chapel. Fuck, that was close."

"I was doing fine. You were the one who was acting suspicious. All we had to do was stagger past, but you had to go and start talking. 'I sure did drink a lot. I'm really trashed. Wow, I don't know if I can drive. Man, I had too—'"

Color rises in his cheeks. "Yeah, yeah. We got out though."

"You're a nervous talker."

"Whatever." He finishes unwrapping my hand and stares at it. "This is..."

"I know." I can't close my fist on either hand. I've tried several times, but the pain is too intense. "Some of the damage is permanent."

"Fuck, Adam." He turns my hand over and stares at the stitches in my palm. "Fuck."

Honestly, it's the only thing to say. I just nod and relax as he unbandages the other hand and inspects it.

He clears his throat. "Nothing's infected. Those hookers know how to close a wound and keep it that way. God bless the Chapel."

"Don't get ahead of yourself." I wince as he feels around the back of my right hand. The first day I woke up—really woke up—I vomited from the pain. But Noah doesn't need to know that. This is bearable. I can take it, even when he smooths some antibiotic ointment onto the wounds.

"Good point. But surely Jez will reconsider this whole dynamite plan." He pulls some fresh gauze from a box and gets to work.

"I don't think so. Dad has pushed her too far for too long."

He stops mid-wrap and peers at me with blue eyes that I don't think will ever look anything but boyish to me. "Maybe I'm a fool, but I can't believe Jez would actually go through with this."

"It's not just her, though. Chastity, Ruth, and several of the other women are in on it. And it's not new—they've been planning for a while. They'd originally thought they could burn the place down, but thanks to Dad's farm plans, now they've gotten their hands on the dynamite."

Realization breaks across his face. "Oh, fuck. The stuff we're using to clear the stone outcrops."

"Exactly. They've already stockpiled enough to bring the church down, and they intend to do it during service. They think it's justice."

"All those children. How the fuck could that ever be justice?" He slaps the gauze onto my hand.

I tense from the shock of pain rushing through my arm.

"Sorry, man." He eases up and goes slowly. "Sorry."

"It's fine. I know it's a lot." We have to stop them. That part goes unsaid between us. No matter what the Heavenly church members' sins may be, they don't deserve to die.

After a while, he says, "So we have to deal with whatever Mom's cooking up, the dynamite bandits, and what else? I feel like I'm missing something." He scrunches his nose. "Oh yeah, that's it—our insane father. Got all the bases covered. Wait, one more thing. Deli—I mean Emily's mother is in the Rectory."

My eyebrows hit my hairline. "What?"

"Yeah. Apparently, Emily wasn't playing along like Dad wanted, so he whipped her at the Cathedral and kidnapped her mom for insurance."

I swallow everything he's said, but it'll take a while to digest. I'll have to circle back around. But for now, I need to ask about the one topic that he's avoided. "So, she's your Maiden now?"

He hesitates, then resumes wrapping my other hand. "Yeah."

"What have you done with her?" The words fucking burn on the way out, but I have to know.

He shrugs. "I threaten her super loud so Dad can hear. Then I lay next to her on her bed—"

My fingers close, but the pain forces me to open my palms again. "What else?"

"Hey, I haven't fucked her in any form or fashion. I would never get my dick wet in your girl, okay?" He still doesn't meet my eyes.

"Tell me all of it. Come on, Noah."

"Why?" He finishes the bandages then moves back to my foot. "Why does it matter?"

"Please." I clench my eyes shut as he dabs the ointment onto my ghost toes.

"I made her..." He takes a deep breath and spits out the rest of the words in a tumble. "Dry hump me a little for the camera."

My heart wrenches in my chest, and a blinding rage threatens. I want to throttle him, to fucking beat him into a puddle for touching her. *Not his fault*, I tell myself. Even though I know he's blameless, the feeling remains, the need to protect what's mine at all costs.

"She doesn't like me, if that makes you feel any better."

It does. I hitch up a shoulder noncommittally.

He hurries on, "She asks about you constantly. And when I touch her, she doesn't—like, I don't know—she doesn't respond like chicks usually do to me. There's nothing there. Not really. She doesn't want me."

"Do you want her?"

His split-second pause is a knife to my gut, but then he says, "I like her. I used to think she was weird-looking, but now I see her better. She's beautiful. Strong. I can see why you're into her."

"That doesn't answer my question."

He wraps my toes, his head down so I can't see his eyes. "I don't want her, not the way you do."

I let my breath out slowly, trying to put his last words on repeat and burying the earlier ones. If I don't push the thoughts of them together down, down, down, it'll tear me apart. And I can't let anything come between any of us ever again. We have to stick together to make it through this.

"There's more," he says quietly.

"More?" I brace myself. "Tell me."

"She isn't who you think she is. Well—" He shrugs. "I mean she is, but not all the way."

"I don't follow."

"Remember the Maiden that Mom—" He audibly swallows. "The one she killed?"

"Yeah, Georgia." Something starts to fire in my mind, a memory that I can't quite put my finger on. "What about her?"

He wraps gauze around my foot, and I can tell he's wrestling with the rest. He thinks I don't know how Georgia's death affected him. But I do. I can't say if he loved her, but he cared for her deeply. When she was found, he changed. Grew darker. And I suspect that's when the drinking started.

"Noah, go on."

He clears his throat. "Emily is her sister. Well, half-sister. Different moms. Georgia would talk about her sometimes. Her Firefly—that was the nickname Georgia gave her. I didn't put it together when I should have. But Emily told me. That day she tried to kill me? She thought

I was the one who hurt Georgia." He shakes his head. "I never would have hurt her. I was even thinking about... Well, it doesn't matter now."

My memory comes back full force. A gut punch would have been less of a blindside. I blink when I see the clue that should have led me to the real Emily. When I spoke to her mother, paid her off to stop asking questions about her daughter, she'd said, *"Please don't kill her. Like you did Georgia."* At the time, I'd just assumed she'd read about the murder when it happened. But now I think about it, that doesn't make sense. She was an addict in Louisiana at that time, and Heavenly did its best to keep the story off the front pages. There's no way she would have known about it. Not unless she had a connection. Emily was it.

I dig the heels of my palms into my eyelids. "Fuck."

"I take it you didn't know."

"No." I can't fathom the dedication it took for Emily to follow her sister down the twisted path to Heavenly. She's been here trying to find Georgia's killer all this time. "She never told me." Why didn't she tell me? I try to switch places, put myself in her shoes. She's in a strange place and doesn't know who to trust. Not even me. The thought stings, but I understand. And once she believed it was Noah? *Fuck.* I run my fingers through my hair and pull. Of *course* she couldn't tell me if she thought my brother did it. And the truth is somehow worse. Not Noah, but my mother. My mother took her sister's life. There's nothing to solve this, no way out of it.

"It's kind of a mess." Noah seems to read my thoughts.

"You didn't tell her it was Mom, right?"

"No fucking way." He finishes bandaging my foot and finally looks at me. "I couldn't do it."

I don't blame him. I've come to learn that Emily is a force. She doesn't have a lot of power in the Cloister, but what she has, she uses to devastating effect. "You're supposed to see her tomorrow night?"

"Yeah." His answer is wary.

"I'm going."

"No way."

Felix jumps on the bed and stands on my chest, then turns around three times before settling with his tail in my face.

I try to push his fluff away from me, but his claws dig into my shirt. "Fuck." I speak around him. "I'll wear a hoodie. Hurry in, keep my head down, and be you."

"You can't even walk, dipshit."

I point to the joint on the bedside table. "I'll smoke up enough to dull the pain."

"Too risky. If someone sees you, you're fucked. And someone *will* see you. Especially if you're lit. You'll probably ask Zion if he has any Cheetos." He stands. "I'm not letting you out of here just so you can get nailed to the cross again. Forget it."

He's right. I know he's right, but I can't deny my need for her. I have to see her, have to do something to soothe her broken heart. Her *sister*. I can't believe I didn't see it before. I knew she was holding something back from me, but a righteous vendetta was not something I could have guessed—not until I got the clue from her mother. But I was too thickheaded to put it together then. This revelation changes everything and nothing. I still have to see her. A dangerous idea forms. "Wait, how about you bring her here?"

He arches a brow. "I can't just borrow her from the Cloister. She's not a library book."

"Why not?" I pick Felix up and place him beside me on the bed. He gives me a surly look, his orange eyes half open.

"He's just going to crawl right back on you in a minute," Noah deflects.

"Bring her here, okay? Think of something, but get her here. Please?"

Felix, true to Noah's prediction, climbs onto my chest again, this time opting for settling with his face up against my chin.

"Come on, Noah. I'm whoring myself out for your cat. It's the least you could do."

He smiles at the orange furball that's trying to suffocate me, then sobers when he looks me in the eye. "Look, I can't promise anything. But I can try."

"That's all I'm asking."

"No, you're asking for more trouble on top of the shit heap full of trouble we already have."

"Maybe." I give in and pet Felix. "But I have to see her. I can't do what needs to be done until I know she's safe, okay?"

"Fine." He lifts the lid on Gregory's terrarium and uses his index finger to stroke the old lizard's head. "But once that's done, we have to get serious. About Dad, about the Chapel, about everything."

"I'm serious." I settle back and close my eyes. "We're going to deal with it all, including Mom."

"Man, I wouldn't tell her about Mom and her sister. I hope that's not part of your reason for seeing her."

"I don't know." I'm not sure if I can tell her, let alone if I should. But she deserves to know... at some point.

Felix digs his claws in again, making himself at home, perfectly at ease with the swirling shit storm all around us.

Everything is coming to a head, like a slow-moving wave on the ocean that grows higher and higher the closer it gets to land. When it hits, some of us will be able to weather it, and some of us will be swept away. I can only hope Noah, Emily, and I are sturdy enough to keep our feet on land.

CHAPTER 19

DELILAH

I pace the short length of my room. Grace didn't come get me today. Instead, I went to the TV room—this time with a Spinner stationed just inside the door—and watched videos on "The Journey of the Prophet," consisting of multiple propaganda pieces focusing on his life.

Though boring, there were some bright spots. Adam featured in a few of them, always in the background, his dark eyes surveying everything going on as if he was taking names. The younger version of him didn't smirk as much, but he was still in there, the calculating mind and the forceful character that leaps out of the screen even now.

After a lunch of steamed vegetables, I was escorted back to my room and dumped for the afternoon. I've been pacing ever since. The sun has long since gone down, and

I haven't bothered to turn my light on. I continue my walk in darkness.

Sunday looms large in my mind, the black tornado from my dreams waiting to swallow me up. Grace didn't say a word to me as we left the Prophet's house yesterday, but I could feel her seething. I'm still here like she wanted, but Sunday is just two days away. If I marry the senator and leave, I know what Grace will do to my mother.

I turn sharply when I'm almost to the far wall and pace back to the door. Getting on Evan's good side worked a little too well. I underestimated him and assumed the Prophet would still opt to keep me around for at least a month or two. I would have used that time to get under Evan's skin during his visits, to try and convince him that Heavenly is a threat. But all that's shot to pieces now. I can still work on him, try and turn him against the Prophet, but I'll be utterly under his control. And Evan isn't the sort to bend easily.

My foot hits the wall next to the door, and I turn again, my dress whirling out from my body dramatically as I tread the same path over and over. Noah didn't come yesterday, so I couldn't explain anything. Had something happened to him? It feels odd to worry about Noah, especially when I was convinced that he'd murdered Georgia. But now, I care for him, even though I wish I didn't. It seems like anyone I care for gets crushed by the Heavenly machine.

My door swings open, halting my progress.

Grace's sneer greets me. "Get your shoes on. We're going out."

I hurry around my bed and slip on my flats. "Where are we going?"

"Shut up." She turns and walks away.

I follow, keeping up with her clipped pace. No point in asking any more questions. She didn't bring me a robe this time, so I guess we aren't heading to the Prophet's house. That's a relief, but it also begs the question of where we're going.

The cold night greets us, and we pile onto a golf cart. She heads up the pavement, the cold wind biting through my thin dress. When we come to the main compound road, for a moment I think she's going to turn right toward the Rectory—either to give me a cruel visit to my mother or to have me join her—but she turns left toward the main entrance.

I hunch forward against the wind as she speeds up the hill, the golf cart's engine only a quiet hum. She passes the rear of the Prophet's house and stops in front of one of the smaller ones that flank it.

"I'll return in one hour. Be outside waiting. If you set foot outside this house otherwise, you will be found and taken to the Rectory. I'll be sure to accommodate you next to your mother so you can hear her screams. Understand?"

I nod.

CELIA AARON

"Go." She points to the black front door.

I want to ask who lives here, what I'm doing here, and about a dozen other things, but I don't. I simply step off the golf cart and walk to the door. It swings open as I approach, and Noah stands just inside wearing a hoodie, a hand-rolled cigarette or a joint hanging from his mouth. He motions me inside.

"You know the rules," Grace calls.

"I got this, and you got what you wanted." He points down the road leading to the Cloister. "Now hop on down the bunny trail, and I'll see you in an hour."

I step inside, and Noah slams the door behind me, his hood pulled up.

"I hate that bitch. Like, I used to think 'oh, I feel bad for her because x, y, z, but a few years ago, I realized she's just rotten all the way through." He says it all with what is—from the smell—definitely a joint dangling from his lips.

"I could have told you that." I peer around at his house. It's nice—dark wood floors, conservative but contemporary décor, and large—a great home for a family.

"You probably know her better than I do." He shrugs. "Which is shit luck for you."

I'm suddenly keenly aware that I'm alone with him in his house. "What am I doing here?"

He pulls the joint from his lips and offers it to me. "You want?"

"I'm good." I shake my head. The forced LSD trips have changed my mind on indulging ever again.

"Okay, cool." He walks ahead of me, his bare feet silent on the floor. "Come on upstairs. Where I am *most definitely not going to fuck her!*" He points the joint at the ceiling fan in the living room as he passes, as if he can see whoever's watching him and communicate directly.

I'm no less confused than I was when Grace came to get me, but I follow him up the stairs. "What did you give Grace to get me here?" I ask quietly.

His jeans hang low on his hips, the elastic of his boxers visible. I drop my gaze and watch the stairs as I climb.

"Information."

"Oh."

He turns left at the top of the stairs and walks to the end of the hall. "In here. Strip and get on the bed."

My insides clench. A large bed sits in the center of the dim room, the white sheets and duvet mussed. "What are you—"

"Just do as you're told, Maiden." His tone turns gruff and he steps into the en suite bathroom, then closes the door.

I swallow hard, my hands shaking as I reach for the hem of my dress. Maybe I'm wrong about Noah. Why else would he have me brought here? He's going to hurt me, use me. Trusting him was a mistake.

I pull my dress off and lay it across the foot of the bed. My heartbeat pulses in my temples as I crawl between the cool sheets and pull them up to my chin. They smell like him, but also like some sort of detergent. I itch to flip on the lamp beside me so I can see what's coming. But that might be a bad idea. Maybe it's better if I don't know. I remember the lamb at the Winter Solstice, the way it looked around with guileless eyes, completely unaware of its fate. Would it be better to be ignorant?

The bathroom door opens, and I clench the sheet. I'm shaking, my body in open revolt as Noah crawls into bed beside me.

"Noah, please don't do—"

"Shh." A cool hand rests on my shoulder, and I turn to look at him.

I blink. He slaps a hand over my mouth. "Not a word." His voice is quiet, a low rumble, the hoodie keeping his face in shadow.

Tears obscure my view, and I kiss the bandaged palm. *Adam.*

He pulls his hand away and moves closer, wrapping his arms around me as I turn to him and bury my face in his neck. I hold him, squeezing so hard that I don't know if he can breathe. My soul stitches back together, enmeshed with his as he strokes down my back.

"Shh, little lamb. My Emily."

I try not to sob, but I can't hold it back. Relief unlocks a pool of emotion inside of me, and I entwine my legs with his, melding our bodies together to convince myself that it's him, that he's really here.

He continues to soothe me, his voice in my ear, his hands moving along my bare skin.

When I'm finally able to speak, I whisper, "Your hands."

"They'll be fine." He kisses my forehead, then drops kisses all down my cheeks. His hoodie covers most of his hair, hiding him from the camera.

"I was so scared."

"I know." His lips move to my neck, tracing a trail of fire.

Cold worry skitters across my mind. "Is this safe? Can you be here?"

"I don't care." He moves back to my face and claims me in a kiss that obliterates every thought from my head. His taste, his hands, his everything. I've been starving for it. And though I knew I needed him on some level, I didn't realize how badly.

His tongue sweeps across mine, and he moves on top of me, his hips between my legs as I open for him. He kisses me like he'd die without it, and I return it with just as much passion. Messy and seeking, we share pieces of our souls, and I want to give him everything. There's so much I need to say. I have to confess about Georgia, tell him who she was, tell him who I am. I have to tell him what seeing him on the cross did to me, the deep scar it left on my heart. But all I can do is kiss him.

I whimper when he thrusts, his hard cock pressing against me in the most delicious way, only his jeans separating us. "I want you," I breathe when he breaks the kiss and moves to my neck, kissing and biting.

"We can't." He moves lower and captures a nipple in his mouth, lashing the tip with his tongue as he kneads my other breast.

Each touch sends a jolt of heat spiraling between my thighs, and desire, thicker than honey, pours over me. "Please." I dig my hands in his hair, squeezing the strands as he kisses lower. "I want to taste you."

He groans against my stomach, then rolls over onto his back, pulling me with him. "Sit on my face." With rough hands, he positions me until I'm straddling him, my knees on either side of his shoulders, my face even with his waist. When he licks, I jolt. I want to say his name, but nothing passes my lips except a hard exhale. His tongue comes again, and I burn with need. Scrabbling at his jeans, I free his cock and lick the tip, the wetness salty on my tongue.

I take him as far into my mouth as I can, eager to please and be pleased. When he presses his mouth to me and pulls me down onto his face, I moan around his thick cock, then suck his head. He doesn't let up, his fingertips pressing into my hips, forcing me to sit right on top of him as his mouth takes over.

My arousal twists tighter and tighter as I try to focus on him. Bobbing up and down, sucking and licking, I use one hand at his base, working it in tandem with my mouth. His hips rock up to meet me, and he matches my rhythm. When he presses his tongue inside me, my thighs shudder and I stop sucking. I want more. I want all of him inside me. Maybe it will make us whole again, hold us together despite the ground fracturing beneath our feet.

"Please." I kiss down the side of his cock then drag my tongue back up. "Please," I whimper again.

"Fuck," he grates out, then pushes me off him.

In a quick blur of movement, he's behind me, his hands on my ass. "Spread for me."

On my knees, I scoot them out, and he rubs his wet cock head up and down my slick skin.

He drags his fingers along one of the belt lines. "I hate his marks on you."

"I hate them, too."

Bending over, he bites my ear. "We have to make it look like I'm reaming your sweet little ass."

I know he's taking an even bigger risk, but I can't go another second without him inside me—that bond that I only share with him.

He positions his cock and pushes forward. I grip the sheets and let my head drop, hanging between my shoulders. Sliding farther, my wetness urging him onward, he seats himself inside me. I curl my toes and let out a hard breath. So full but needing more, I move forward and then press back into him.

"Fuck." He groans and bites my upper back. When he pulls out again, he slams home. He doesn't hold back, fucking me hard, destroying and rebuilding me with each impact. I bury my face in the pillow, crying out my pleasure as he reaches around me, his fingers playing my clit.

My breaths come in short bursts, everything inside me tightening around the single point that his fingers stroke. He's relentless, his cock filling me perfectly, his sweat-slicked skin slapping against mine. I press my forehead into the pillow and use my hands on the headboard to push back.

He groans and slams me harder, my resistance spurring him faster. I love every hit, the sounds, the sweat, being full of Adam.

"I can't—" I don't know what words I was going to say next, but my orgasm rushes at me in a blinding haze. It hits me from nowhere and everywhere, my body folding in and expanding outward on a streaking blaze of pleasure. Waves roll over me, and I can barely breathe. My hips lock, my breath stops, and all I can feel is him—us. Nothing exists outside of us.

He slams hard a few more times, then pulls out. His come coats my ass, the warm spurts strong, his grunts tortured and erotic. My legs slide apart farther, and I lie all the way on the bed. He lets up on my hip, his palm massaging the spot where he'd been squeezing.

I want to tell him I love him. I can't. Not here. Not now. It isn't safe. Down from the high, I realize this was a mistake. What if he gets caught? Fear filters through, and I turn to look at him.

He gives me a crisp nod and steps off the bed. With a hobbling gait that raises plenty of questions in my mind, he goes into the en suite and returns with a washcloth. He silently cleans me off, then lies next to me.

I throw the sheet over us and snuggle up to him. After several long beats of silence, my breathing returns to normal, and I feel the danger in the air. It coats everything like soot. We shouldn't have done this.

"Are you all right?" He tucks my hair behind my ear.

"Me? What's wrong with your feet?"

His gaze flickers to my lips. "Does it matter? We only have a little time left."

"Yes, it matters." I lean in and bite his ear. "Tell me."

He slides one hand down to my hip, squeezing. "It's not a big thing. I just ... I just lost a couple of toes to frostbite."

I wince. He suffered to save me, to keep me out of Evan's clutches, and he's paid so dearly. I close my eyes and nuzzle against his neck. "I'm sorry."

"I didn't really need them. They were sort of extra anyway, right? You just won't be able to do 'This Little Piggy' on me like you've dreamed about." He kisses my crown, and I smile at his ridiculous words. His sense of humor hides behind a scornful exterior, but it's there— warm and rich. I wish there was more time for us so I could explore all his nooks and crannies, the facets that make up his personality.

His kiss lingers. "You have to go soon, but I need you to know some things. Stay away from the church service on Sunday. Shit will be going down. Can you do that?"

My heart sinks into an acid vat, bubbling and blistering as he tries to warn me away from a destiny that's already written in stone. "I have to be there."

"Why?"

I clutch him closer to me, afraid of losing him, afraid of so much. But I can't lie. Not now. "Because I'm supposed to marry the senator at the service that day."

He pulls me away from him, his dark eyes burning into me. "You can't marry him."

I shake my head, my eyes watering again. "I have to."

"No." He grips my arms. "No way."

"I don't have any other choice. The Prophet has my mom. I can't fight this place from within. I have to do it from outside. Maybe if I can convince Evan—"

"Convince him of what?" His voice is tight, and he's straining to keep it down. "He's not someone that can be reasoned with."

"I have to try. It's my only chance to stop the Prophet. I'm going to use Evan, to turn him against Heavenly."

"How do you intend to sway him, Emily?" Fire rages in his eyes, his body tense. "What are you going to use to do that?"

Shame flames in my cheeks, but I tell him the truth. "I'll have to give him what he wants."

He presses his forehead to mine, his hands clutching me close. "He wants *you*, Emily. He wants to break you in half and suck out your fucking marrow. That's the kind of man he is."

"I know." My voice shakes. "But it's the only way."

"No."

"It's already decided. It's over, Adam." I press my palm to his cheek. "I'm marrying him on Sunday. And I'll do what I have to do to turn him to our side."

"I'll die before I let you go to him." He grits his teeth.

"I want you alive." Tears slide across the bridge of my nose. "Away from here. You deserve so much more than this life. You deserve love, a family, a place to call your own."

"I only want those things with you." He puts his hand over mine. "I love you."

Everything inside me tears apart at his solemn words. I want him so badly, and I want the life I described. The two of us, free from the Prophet's web. But it can't happen. We were doomed from the moment we saw each other. Nothing can flourish under the Prophet's harsh sun.

"I love you, too." I let the words spill out. Freeing, yet somehow a prison.

Those words tie us to each other, even when we're about to be ripped apart. He pulls me into his arms, crushing me to him. I feel his brand on my heart, scorching my soul. Letting him go is the hardest thing I've ever done. But I have to. It's the only chance I have to save him.

"I won't let this happen," he whispers in my ear. "I love you too much. It won't happen."

It's already done. I hold onto him, wishing our love could stop the inevitable.

A faint knock at the bathroom door shatters the quiet.

"Fuck." He kisses my forehead, down my nose, and to my lips. "It's time."

I kiss him with all the heart I have left, and I hope he feels my seal on his heart, my promise that I will always love him, no matter what happens. It's all I can give. And I offer myself to him freely. His little lamb. I will gladly sacrifice myself to save him, to give him a future, and to watch Heavenly burn.

CHAPTER 20

GRACE

*N*ight cloaks me as I creep into the main house and hurry to the metal door in the basement. Castro waits inside, the tip of his cigarette glowing orange in the dark.

"What?" He leans against the wall, nonchalant even though his greatest enemy is just above us. If we were caught down here, the Prophet would kill us both.

I stand next to him, so close I can smell the stale cigar smoke in his dark hair. "Noah took Adam. He's no longer at the Chapel."

He glances at me. "How do you know?"

"Noah told me."

"Why?"

"He needed a favor." My blood boils at what I had to give up just to get this information. That whore Delilah spending time at Noah's house. I have no doubt she warmed Adam's bed, spread her legs and gave him whatever he wanted. That's all she has to offer anyone—her freak pussy.

"Anything else?"

I nod. "The Chapel traitors are planning something for Sunday. I don't know what, but it could interfere with our plans."

"We're moving forward no matter what. The time has come. The Father of Fire has told her—" he glances at the ceiling, as if he can see Rachel through the timbers. "The time is now, and it must happen on a holy day. This Sunday. What have you heard about the Chapel whores?"

"Nothing specific, but Chastity has been visiting more frequently." I shake my head. "She thinks I don't know. What a twit. Of *course* I know. She even chanced a visit to the Cathedral two days ago to speak with Ruth. It's something big. I can feel it."

"Should I pop them now and bring them to the Prophet?"

"I don't think so. Ask *her*, of course. She knows best." I feign deference to Rachel. I'm on her team, sure. But I could never bow to a woman. It goes against God's law. Once Adam is firmly on the throne, I'll convince him to get rid of her and this jumped-up wetback. "But it could play in our favor."

He shrugs. "I'm fine with letting them stage their little rebellion. It'll be more fun to shoot them down than get rid of them quietly."

I don't know. Seeing them swing from ropes or hang on crosses sounds like justice to me, but it's six one way, half a dozen the other. They're a problem that must be dealt with once Adam is Prophet. We'll use them—either as a distraction or a scapegoat—until the time is right.

"Anything else?" He tosses his cigarette onto the concrete floor and crushes it with the sole of his boot.

My gaze wanders deeper into the room to the spot where Adam cradled his dying Faith. A chill creeps through my bones. Is she here, watching me? Judging me? I wish she were still alive. Then Adam wouldn't hate me. If it weren't for Faith, Adam and I would still be together, maybe already ruling over Heavenly. But that child ruined it all. I should have gotten rid of her at the first sign, but I didn't. I foolishly thought a child would bring us closer together. Stupid.

"Grace?" Castro has been speaking to me.

"Apologies. I missed it. What?"

"Do you have anything else?" His impatience riles me. Though he's a man, he doesn't hold any sway over me. Not with his dark skin and questionable heritage.

"Just one thing. Sunday. I want Delilah dead. She has to be a casualty. Otherwise, she threatens Rachel's plan.

That freak is able to turn Adam's head, and she'll lead him away from Heavenly's future glory. She has to go."

He shrugs. "Not a problem. I'll handle it." Launching off the wall, he strides past me.

The same chill creeps down my spine, and my gaze returns to the spot where Faith died. I straighten my back. She can haunt me all she wants. It doesn't matter. I'm still alive, and I intend to stay that way. She's just dust, and I won't let her separate me from Adam any longer.

CHAPTER 21

ADAM

*E*mily sits on her bed. Head down, eyes closed, as if she's praying. Does she pray? I assume she doesn't believe in God, not after what she's seen here. The small screen flickers. I pop the side of it with the heel of my palm, and it evens out again. Noah ran the cords for it down the hall from his bedroom, under my door, and to a small monitor he set up on the dresser next to Gregory's terrarium.

Saturday morning means she should be in class with the rest of the Maidens. But she's alone, her fingers twining with each other, her mind troubled. But there's no way to soothe her from here. Besides, what would I say? She's set on her path, even though I'm going to block it, saving her in the process.

"He's here." Noah speaks through the door. I didn't hear him come down the hall.

"Bring him up." I flick off the television and sit up in bed. Looking weak isn't an option.

Noah retreats, and I whip the blanket over my feet, hiding the bandages around my missing toes. I can't do anything about my hands, but he'll already know those are fucked.

Footsteps on the stairs, and then Noah opens my door. Castro enters first, his head on a swivel as he surveys the room. When he's satisfied no one's going to jump out from a corner, he rests his gaze on me.

"Sad to see you're still alive, *pendejo*." He doesn't need to spit for me to feel the disdain rolling off him.

Like I give a shit. If this motherfucker makes it past Sunday service, it'll only be because I'm dead. "Say what you came to say and then get the fuck out."

He glowers. "I should turn you in to your father."

"Go right ahead." I let out a bored sigh. "See how Mom feels about that."

His eyebrows pinch, but he doesn't continue down that road. No point. Mom may be far more ruthless than I'd ever imagined, but she doesn't want me crucified. I'm part of her grand scheme, after all. Besides, she's known that I'm here ever since Noah made the deal with Grace to get Emily to his house for my visit. A costly quid pro quo, but worth it. And if Mom hasn't spilled by now, she isn't going to.

"Your mother has been told that this Sunday is the day. The Father of Fire will crown you Prophet once the old one is destroyed. You need to be ready to do what needs to be done."

"And what's that?" As if there wasn't enough already riding on Sunday. Fuck.

"Take your father's place—that you don't deserve." He's quick to add that last part. "And follow your mother's direction for the future of Heavenly. After the transition is complete, you have to deal with the whores. All of them."

Noah leans against the doorframe, his head cocked to the side. "Which whores are we talking about? Dad seems to refer to all the women here like that without any distinction."

"All of them," Castro says. "No more Cloister. No more Chapel. And we'll have to raze the Cathedral and all within it. It shouldn't be difficult. A fire would take care of it. Bar the doors and burn it down."

Noah looks past him to me. "Why do I get the feeling he means 'bar the doors' to keep the women and children inside?"

"Because that's exactly what he means." The cold bastard has bought into my mother's vengeful scheme and intends to see it through to its bloody end. I didn't think I could hate him more. But I do.

Castro nods. "None of the people there are on the grid anymore. They'll just disappear. Some of the Maidens we'll have to keep—make them Spinners to serve Rachel and yourself. Some will have to burn for the Father of Fire in gratitude."

"And the Chapel girls?" Noah's eyes are wide to an almost comical degree. But nothing about any of this is funny.

Castro shrugs. "They can't leave the compound. We can either lock them in the Cathedral or do it some other way. Waste a few bullets on them for target practice, I guess."

Noah stuffs his hands in his pockets. "So, let me see if I'm following here—you want to murder most of the women and all the children on the compound?"

"It's God's will." Castro stares at me. "And it will be done at the order of the new Prophet. Understand?"

"What?" I smirk. "Mom is too shy to order the genocide?"

"You are the new head. You will follow her lead, but she will remain invisible. Much the way she is now." He almost smiles, his lips twitching. "And I'll be your second, though I answer only to Rachel."

"Sounds like a shitty second." I lean my head back, doing my best to remain nonchalant while Castro calmly explains all the terrors my mother has planned. "So, how's Sunday going to go down?"

"All you have to do is be there. Get into the crowd somehow without a Protector seeing you. I'll handle the rest."

"No offense, Castro." Noah pauses, then reconsiders. "Actually, all the offense. You're a low life foot soldier with no clue what you've gotten yourself into. So why should we trust that you're able to do anything to stop the Prophet?"

Castro whips his head around. "The more you sound like your brother, the more expendable you become. We only need one Monroe asshole for all this to work. Not two."

I lean forward. "Keep speaking to Noah like that and you won't live to see this glorious Sunday you've outlined."

Castro turns his attention back to me. "All you have to do is be there. I've been by your father's side long enough that I can stick the knife in and twist it before he even realizes I have a blade."

"You going to execute him in front of the congregation?" I raise an eyebrow. "Seems like bad form. That would definitely start a panic."

"You don't need to know the particulars. Just be there. The Father of Fire has promised Rachel that this will work out perfectly." He glances at his watch. "Fuck, I'm late." Turning, he brushes past Noah. "Be there and be ready. The Father of Fire will make sure everything falls into place." His steps thump away down the stairs and the front door slams.

"I fucking hate that guy." Noah closes the bedroom door and sits at the foot of the bed.

"He's an idiot to believe Mom." I rub my eyes and second-guess myself. Should I have told Castro about the dynamite plot? Then again, maybe I just need to let things play out. Confusion and chaos are both to my advantage. "Any word on where Jez and the gals hid the dynamite?"

"No." He pulls the blanket away from my foot and peers at the bandage. "I can't go to the Chapel now. Jez has the girls on high alert. But I've searched all along the road in between the storage shed and the main compound. If they've hidden it out there, they've done a damn good job. I didn't see anything out of place."

"They wouldn't be dumb enough to store it in the Chapel. At least I don't think they would." I wince as he unwraps my toes. Even though I expect the pain, it's still a shock to my system, just like seeing my mangled foot. "We may not find it in time."

He reaches across the bed for the gauze, and when his sleeve rides up, I see an ugly red circle of burned flesh on his inner wrist.

"Hey." I point. "What the fuck?"

He pulls his hand back quickly. "Nothing."

"Noah." I lean forward and stare him down. "Tell me."

He gives a half-hearted shrug. "Dad called me in first thing this morning. Saw the video from last night."

My hands dampen. "And?"

"I wasn't supposed to fuck her in the ass. Senator's rules. So, I got a little reminder. That's all." He grabs the gauze. "It'll heal."

Fuck, I'm a dick. "I didn't even think—"

"God, if he knew what really happened in that room." He snorts. "Don't worry. It's just a little burn. You've had a lot worse." He kneels and gets to work on my toes.

"You should put something on it." I inspect my stitches. They're holding up, the raw skin melding together without any care for the fact that pieces of me are missing.

"Sure." He sighs. "Dad was off this morning."

I give him a wry look.

"More than usual, I mean. He kept talking about the fire. He said the fire was talking to him and telling him his downfall. And he was worried. Like to the point that he couldn't sit down. He just paced and mumbled until he yelled at me to get out. I don't think he's slept for days."

"Batshit." I still don't believe my father has any divine intuition, but maybe his regular human warning signals are twitching at the shit storm forming around him.

"He was coming unglued. I just left. Castro was there, but he stayed out of the way. It's all a clusterfuck. Speaking of that, what are we going to do about tomorrow?"

"We'll do what Mom wants. I'll show up, melt into the crowd, and wait for my moment. We'll both have to keep an eye out for Jez. If she, or Chastity, or Ruth shows up with a backpack full of dynamite, things are going to get dicey real quick. We just need to get them the fuck out of there before they do anything stupid."

"I'll see if I can meet with Chastity today. Talk some sense into her. She's the ringleader, seems like."

"She's harder than I thought. Smarter, too. But she's got a soft spot for Emily. Use that, if you can. Tell her that Emily will be at the service this Sunday. She has no choice but to show up." My jaw clenches at the thought of *why* she has to be there. It's her goddamn wedding day. My guts clench. I'll kill that piece of shit senator with my bare hands if I get the chance. I'll gladly reopen the wounds in my palms if I do it while I'm snapping his neck.

"Adam." Noah peers up at me. "Evan won't get her. Relax."

"I'm relaxed," I reply, a little too loudly. Felix jumps on me, as if my raised voice is an invitation. "Great," I groan.

He settles on my chest, his head tucked beneath my chin.

Noah smiles at him indulgently. "Let Felix work his kitty magic. You'll feel better."

"Better?" I pet him against my better judgment. "He makes my eyes itchy as hell, that's about all."

"He'll keep you sane. He does that for me." Noah shrugs.

I keep stroking the purring fur ball. "There are too many moving pieces, and I can't see the whole board." The lack of control eats at me. I want to know what happens next. More than that, I want it to happen because I *make* it happen. But that luxury is long gone. There are too many factions, and far too many variables. I have to concentrate on what's important—keeping Emily and Noah safe and thwarting the dynamite attempt.

Noah stands. "I'm going to see if I can accidentally bump into Chastity and get her in a choke hold."

"Good plan." I loathe lying in this bed instead of doing something. But I can't move around without suspicion, especially not during the day.

He opens the terrarium and drops a couple of live crickets inside. "Just relax here. Keep that brain firing to find us a way out of this. I'll go do the footwork." Closing the lid, he bends down and watches as Gregory ignores his lunch. "Asshole." He points at Felix and says, "Be good," then does the same to me. I flip him off as best I can.

When the front door shuts, I turn the TV back on and watch Emily. She's lying down now, her face resting on her folded hands. An angel. No, a firefly. I smile at the reference, because her sister was right. Emily *does* shine in the darkness, bringing light into the grimmest parts of my soul.

She jumps and sits up. I push Felix off and lean forward. "What the—"

My father walks into view and offers her his hand. What is he doing there? After a moment of hesitation, she looks up, her eyes wide, and takes it.

He yanks her from the bed. Rage pools inside me like molten steel, and I squeeze the remote in my aching palm.

When he drags her from the room, I can't hear her scream, but I can feel it in my bones.

CHAPTER 22

DELILAH

The Prophet drags me from my room, his grip painful and his gait fast yet unsteady. Chastity plasters her back to the wall as we pass, her eyes questioning but her mouth silent. I keep up, my bare feet slapping the wood floor.

"The Father of Fire tried to speak to me this morning." His words are half-mumbled, and I can barely make them out. "He told me that you are my downfall. *You.*" He stops so quickly I almost bump into him. Turning his dark eyes on me, he glares. "But if I kill you, my downfall will be even swifter. Why is that? Why you?" He shoves me against the wall, his usual calm façade gone and the astounded face of a madman in its place. "Why? Who are you?"

I shake my head. How can I respond? There's nothing to say.

"You." He jabs a finger into my chest. "You are nothing." Spittle flies from his lips. "No one. Just another whore. That's all."

Did he talk this way to Georgia before he had her killed? The thought erupts and burns. He can threaten and blame me all he wants, but his downfall—whatever that means—is all of his own making. His sins will come back to him tenfold, and I will be the one watching him as he's crushed under their weight.

"Come with me." He yanks my arm again.

Grace stands at the back door, holding it open as we barrel past and into the sunny, cold morning. I can't read anything other than her usual smugness as we pass.

He shoves me into a waiting car. I scramble away as he sits next to me and slams the door.

"Go!" He slaps the headrest of his driver, and the car rockets up the hill from the Cloister, then turns right. Away from the Prophet's house and deeper into the compound.

The Prophet grabs my throat. I press my back to the door, but there's no escape from him. A thin coating of white powder outlines his nostrils, and there's whiskey on his breath.

"You know where he is, don't you?" He squeezes, but not hard enough to stop my breath.

"I don't know—"

"Adam!" he yells in my face. "You took him. It had to be you. You spirited him away somewhere. Witch!"

I shake my head. "No."

"'I will destroy your witchcraft, and you will no longer cast spells.'" He shakes me, the back of my head beating against the glass. "'Thou shalt not suffer a witch to live.'"

My heart spasms in my chest, and I can't catch my breath. He's lost what little bit of self-control he had. If it weren't for his pronouncements about his swifter downfall, I have no doubt he would kill me.

"I'm not." I can barely get the words out. "Not a witch."

He grimaces. "You are what I say you are, what the Father of Fire tells me you are. You disobey your Prophet with your heathen ways. I will make you suffer." His voice lowers, all the softness from his usual tone gone. "Tell me what you've done with my son."

"I didn't—"

"Tell me, you whore of Babylon!" My ears ring as he screams in my face.

I close my eyes, trying to hide from him, to disappear into myself where he can't follow.

"Sir." Another voice invades my self-imposed darkness. "We're here."

The Prophet's hand disappears, and a waft of cold air enters the car as the driver steps out.

I open my eyes and scrabble at my door handle. It doesn't catch. My need to escape is primal, beating in my soul like a drum. *Out, out, out.* When my door opens, I heave myself from the car and stumble on the gravel path leading into the short, dark building—squat and silent like a tomb. The place where I broke. The place where my mother suffers.

The Prophet is on me, his rough grip on my arm dragging me forward.

A scream rips from me, my cowardice given sound. But he doesn't stop, even as my feet skitter along the rocks and I try to yank free of his grip. There is no 'free'. Not from him. Not from this place.

The guard at the door abandons his post and grabs my other arm, the two of them dragging me into the gloom and turning down the long, narrow hallway. I know this place too well, and a single phantom drop of water trickles onto my forehead.

"Which one?" The Prophet asks.

"Here." The guard stops at a door in the middle of the hall and swings it open.

Inside is nothing. The black hole at the center of the galaxy, the inky water of a fetid well that has no bottom.

A click, and then harsh light from a bare bulb overhead blooms across the cinderblock walls and the woman tied to the table. Her bleach blonde hair matted, her eyes closed against the light's assault. Stripped, her body is marred with bruises and cuts, and she shivers as the drop of water falls from above and taps her in the same spot where I can feel it even now.

I can't stop the sob in my lungs, the despair that spreads across my body like a million spiders, their tiny legs invading every nook, caressing every nerve until I'm tormented. "Let her go," I choke out.

"She's staying here." The Prophet shoves me into the guard's steely arms and stands next to her.

She opens her eyes slowly. When she sees him, she tries to pull back, but there's nowhere to go. Strapped to a cross, flat on her back, she's at the Prophet's mercy. I can feel the wood pressing into the back of my skull, taste the rubber and leather of the gag.

"Mom." I try to reach for her, but the guard gives me no room.

Her gaze flickers to me, her eyes wide.

"Your mother belongs to me, witch. She will never leave this compound. As long as you are alive, I will keep her here." He turns to me, his eyes black pools of hate. "Not in the Rectory the entire time. I'm not a monster." He grins, as if he's fully aware he's the worst sort of monster and revels in it. "She'll serve as a Spinner. Make herself

211

useful instead of continuing down her path of ruination." He jabs at the needle tracks on her inner arm. "We found her in an abandoned house. High, barely conscious. They told me that from the look of her, she'd just whored herself out for a hit. Come still crusting on her worn-out cunt."

I can't stop the tears coursing down my cheeks. Like so much else, I have no control. There's nothing I can do for her. The guard's grip and the Prophet's insanity will keep running wild, and I have no power to stop it. Not yet.

"The reason I brought you here." He turns to me. "Is so you know that if you disobey me, if you do anything to jeopardize your placement with the senator—" He walks farther into the room and pulls a scalpel from a table in the corner.

"Don't." I strain against the guard's grip. "Please."

"You need to learn, witch." The Prophet returns to Mom's side, knife in hand.

She makes a high-pitched sound in her throat.

"Please!" I yell, but the guard slaps a palm over my mouth.

He cuts her. Slow, shallow, tracing the knife down her chest.

"Stop!" I scream against the guard's hand. Mom closes her eyes, the high-pitched noise dying in her throat as he finishes his stroke. Blood pools along the line, spilling down her sides in thin rivulets. A tremor passes through her, and she can't seem to get enough air in through her nose.

My knees go weak, and I can barely stand. I have to help her, to comfort her, to do something to stop this.

The guard releases his hold on my mouth and wraps his arm around my waist, keeping me upright.

"Please, I'll do anything. Please don't hurt her anymore."

He drops the bloody scalpel onto the table and returns to me, his demeanor smoother now, as if drawing blood soothed him like a lullaby. "You will do everything I ask, and you will do as the senator says. If you comply, your mother won't be harmed. If you don't, I'll cut her life away bit by bit."

He motions toward the door. The guard drags me out. I reach for my mother, but don't get close enough to touch her, to tell her I'm going to fix it, to tell her this is all a temporary nightmare and that I'll save her from it. The Prophet slams her door as he leaves, throwing her into darkness so complete that it eats you alive.

"Please," I whisper, though I don't know who I'm talking to. My entreaties have never moved the Prophet or anyone in this godforsaken place. There is no compassion here, no help.

The guard walks me out into the chilly morning, the sun playing across my face but offering no warmth. He shoves me into the back of the car, and the Prophet sits next to me. He hums a little, the torture pick-me-up lifting his spirit as mine mires in despair.

I shrink against the door as he turns to me, his lips almost in a smile.

"I must have misread the signs. The flames can do that. It's more of an art than a science, you know?" He grabs my chin and wrenches my face to his. "But it makes more sense now. You will *not* be my downfall, witch. I will be yours."

Noah slinks into my room and gently closes the door behind him. He's early. I don't move from the bed as he slides in next to me and turns to face me.

"Hi." He rests his hand on my hip.

"How is he?" I don't say Adam's name, but he knows who I mean.

"Fine. Well... Worried. He saw Dad come to get you." His light blue eyes, so unlike Adam's, peer deeply into mine. "I found out he took you to see your mom. Are you okay?"

"No," I whisper.

He pulls me closer but keeps his hips back. "I went to see her afterwards, fixed up the cut. Assured her that she wouldn't be here long."

"I hope you're right." I let him stroke my hair, even though it's wrong and he isn't the one I want. A little bit of comfort from a friend—my thoughts halt. It's odd that I think of Noah as a friend now, when only a little while ago I wanted him dead. But Heavenly creates strange bedfellows.

"I have to get her out of here." I haven't changed my plan. Swaying Evan to my side is my only chance of saving her. And I'll give up everything to get her and Adam to safety.

"We will."

"What's going to happen tomorrow?" I press my forehead to his shoulder.

"A lot. Too much. But you're my priority. I've sworn to Adam that when shit goes down, I'll keep you safe."

I don't like the hardness in his voice, the promise of blood, possibly his and Adam's. "Tell me everything."

"The short and sweet version goes like this: Chastity, Jez, and some others are planning to blow up the entire church at service."

I move back and gawk at him. Chastity would do that? Kill thousands of innocents. "No."

He pulls me to him again, holding me tight. "Just listen. That's their plan. I'm going to stop them. In the meantime, Adam will be in the crowd. Mom, Castro, and Grace are planning a big coup, probably just before the service or after. She won't kill Dad in front of everyone. But—" he shrugs, "She's a little bit crazy so I don't know. Castro is on her team and won't tell me anything other than some vague bullshit. I guess they don't want me cocking up their big reveal."

I can't fathom it all. Rachel? I always thought she was cowed, a hostage in the Prophet's game of control. But I was wrong. If she's come up with a way to destroy him, then she has a lot more guts than I ever dreamed. A glimmer of hope ignites in me, and I swear I could kiss Rachel. So many people coming together against the Prophet. Is this the way out for all of us?

"I've been trying to get to Chastity to talk her out of her plan, but she's slippery these days. I'm going to try again when I leave your room. If she could just hold off, maybe Mom will take out Dad, and then we can sort of work it out from there."

"What does your mom want to do with Heavenly once your dad is gone?"

"That's more complicated." He sighs. "She wants to keep it going. Different, but really the same."

"Keep it going?" I clutch his shirt. "Why?"

"She has her reasons. But I'm hoping Adam and I can talk her out of it."

"It has to burn, Noah." Acid rises in my throat. "All of it. We can't let it go on."

"I know." He squeezes my shoulder. "I know, okay? But we have to get through tomorrow first. Once we do that, maybe we'll see the right way to shut it down."

This news changes the entire game. Maybe I don't have to marry Evan to get what I want. But it all rests on the edge of a blade, and if I don't marry him, I run the risk of getting cut. "What about the senator? And my mom?"

"Depends on timing."

"We're supposed to get married at the start of the service," I hiss.

"I don't know." He shakes his head. "It all depends on what Mom does."

"I'll have to go through with it, then." I take a deep steadying breath, and remind myself that this was my goal all along—getting out and swaying Evan. All these other webs could fall apart. So I need to stay strong and follow through.

"Maybe." He hugs me again. "But we'll sort it all out afterwards. You won't have to... you know, stay with him or anything."

"We'll see." I bite back my bitterness. Noah's dangled a way out in front of me, but I can't take it. Not yet. Not until I know for sure that Heavenly will be destroyed.

He rests his chin on the top of my head. "You're kind of crazy."

"What?"

"This whole thing you've got cooking to take the place down. I mean, it's brilliant but also insane."

I shrug. "Evan's a powerful man. If I can use him, I will."

He swallows. "Because of Georgia?"

I push him away and meet his gaze. "Yes. All this is because of her. And because I don't want any other girls to fall into the trap of the Cloister. I know this is what she'd want."

His blue eyes are glossy. "I know."

Something inside me melts, and I can feel my connection to Noah. "You loved her, too, didn't you?"

He blinks, his lashes wet. "I don't think I was capable of it then. I was too blinded by my father. Stupid, you know? But now…" When he blinks again, a single tear escapes. "Now, yeah. I think I loved her."

I wrap my arm around his neck and pull him close. He holds onto me, and he shudders just once, his tears falling on my pillow where no one can see. We stay that way for a while, lost in thoughts of her and what could have been.

"Please tell Adam I love him," I whisper. "In case I don't get the chance."

"He knows." His voice is clipped, thick. "He loves you, too."

When he clears his throat and gently pushes me back, he says, "I need you to know I'm not on the fence anymore. Not about Georgia or anything else. Whatever happens tomorrow, I will get justice for her and for us."

I nod, and a vow is created between us. A bond forged in pain and loss. A bond that cannot be broken.

CHAPTER 23

DELILAH

*G*race floats into my room at the crack of dawn on Sunday. "Wake up. Today is your day." She stands at the foot of my bed, a smile on her face. A real one that shows what she could have been. Beautiful in another life, but in this one, there is only spitefulness. I wonder who died to make her so happy, but I don't ask.

"Your wedding gown." She drapes a white dress over my comforter and holds a flowy white veil. "Get up. Get ready. It's going to be a big day." Her tone is chipper, which sends a shiver down my spine as I stand and walk to the bathroom.

Looking in the mirror, I see the lack of sleep has taken its toll, not to mention what the horrors of the Prophet have wrought on my face and body. Aged ten years, too thin, and dull—I am a ghost of myself. No longer the glowing Firefly, I'm an apparition, one that can pass unnoticed.

When I'm done in the bathroom, I find Abigail walking through my door, her makeup case under one arm.

"I'll take it from here." Grace grabs the case and shoos Abigail out.

I sit on the bed, unsure of this new, happy Grace.

"Perk up." She opens the case and pulls out a hair brush. "It's your wedding day, after all." Pushing the case back, she sits next to me and turns my shoulders so she can brush my hair. She hums a little as she runs the bristles through the tangles, the knots created from tossing and turning during my sleepless night. Her touch is firm, but she doesn't hurt me any more than she has to. I have to wonder why. But I don't ask.

"White hair." She giggles and focuses on the ends. "Some heathen women would pay for this sort of color. Platinum blonde they call it." She makes a pfft noise at the silliness of anyone wanting hair like mine.

This Grace makes more sense to me. Ridicule has always been one of her favorite weapons.

"There, that's better." She drops the brush into the case. "Turn around. I'm going to add some color to you."

I obey, watching as she digs through Abigail's limited color palettes. She chooses a compact with a variety of pinks and another with light browns. The colors are jarring, reminding me of another time, another place.

"You can pull off just about any color, you know?" Georgia leans down and looks at me in her vanity mirror. "Like a blank slate."

"Is that supposed to be a compliment?" I try to hide my nerves. Mom doesn't want me wearing makeup. She says it gives the wrong idea and always looks garish on me. Then again, when I'm with Georgia, I'm away from Mom's prying eyes. Playing a little couldn't hurt, not when I can wipe it right off.

"It really is." She digs through the stacks and stacks of pallets in her top drawer, some of the colors worn down to nothing and others not even touched. "My coloring means I have to stay away from blues and reds. Blues just look terrible no matter what, because they clash with my eyes. And reds highlight the pink undertint to my skin. It's a mess."

"Mmhmm." I've never noticed any 'undertint', but there's no point mentioning that. I'm well acquainted with Georgia's ability to lay out each of her perceived flaws and lament over them for hours on end.

"But you, everything's even and perfect." She peers at my nose. "I don't even see any pores."

"Is that bad?"

"It's amazing, and I'm jelly!" She returns to her drawer of colors and draws out a pallet of browns and another of pinks. "Let's start conservative, okay? Maybe once we've *done the subtle look, we can start over and go for a mermaid look or—" her eyes widen. "A peacock look!"*

"Subtle sounds better." I lean back.

"Don't be a ninny." She tilts my chin up. "Now close your eyes."

"Close your eyes." Grace stands above me, a hint of impatience showing through her too-bright countenance.

I do as she says and wait as the tickling brush does its work on my eyelids. Like this, I can pretend it's Georgia again, delightedly highlighting and contouring and doing God knows what else. But I didn't mind it. Because it made her happy. I mind now, because it makes Grace happy.

"Better." She dabs some pink on my cheeks. "Too much." Grabbing the hem of my dress, she wipes some off. "A little bit goes a long way on your corpse-white skin, doesn't it?" She scrubs a little with my dress then drops the fabric. "You look alive now, at least. Let's do something to your lips. They're like two starved worms. And that eye—" she frowns at the bruise the Prophet left when he couldn't get hard. "I think there's some concealer in here."

She works for a few more minutes, adding mascara and some other touches to make me look "like something other than a dead body." When she's done, she stands back. "You'll never be beautiful, but this is as close as I can get."

"You're so beautiful, Firefly. With or without makeup."
Georgia's voice tiptoes across my heart.

"Now, your dress." She snaps her fingers. "Up. I want to see it on you."

I stand, tired to my soul. "I thought you wanted me to stay? Now you're happy I'm going?"

She cuts her gaze to me. "I did want you to stay. But things are different now. It's a new day. You can go. I'm happy for you to disappear."

"Why the sudden change?" I know why. She believes today is the day when the Prophet falls.

"Can't I just be happy for you?" She holds the dress up to my shoulders. "You're getting married. That's something to celebrate, right? Now, take that dress off and let's see how this one looks."

I grab my hem and lift my dress over my head. Her apprizing gaze takes in every inch of my emaciated body.

"At least you lost some weight while you were here. Not enough, though." She steps closer. "Arms up."

Once the dress is on, she stands back. "Perfect."

I look down. I'm wearing what could be considered a boxy white sack that flows down to my ankles. Not that I care what my "wedding gown" looks like. Even if I wind up marrying Evan today, in my heart, I'm already wed to Adam.

"I picked out a veil for you, too, but we can put that on at the church." She smiles again, her teeth reminiscent of a crocodile even though they're straight and smooth. "Get your shoes on."

"We're leaving now?"

"Yes. The senator wants a little time with you before the service begins."

I slip on my flats. "I thought it was bad luck for the groom to see the bride before the wedding."

She laughs, the sound explosive and loud.

I stare at her, trying to parse through whatever is going through her mind. Reading her is impossible, but I know something wrong is simmering just underneath the surface of what I can see. Everything is off-kilter. A queasy feeling slithers through my stomach.

She tapers off her giggles. "Oh, I think you're right about that tradition. It will *definitely* be bad luck."

CHAPTER 24

NOAH

I shove Chastity against the wall, her choked cry just what I was aiming for. "Call it off."

She recovers, her eyes shuttering, her face going stoic. "Not a chance."

"Why?" I glance down the hallway. The Cloister's walls have ears, but we're alone for the moment.

"*Why?*" she asks, incredulous. "I can give you a million reasons. All of them good."

"To murder innocent people?"

"They aren't innocent." She shoves me back.

I let her. "The children are. The people who are fooled by the Prophet—"

"You mean the ones who are fine with oppressing everyone who isn't like them? The ones who agree with the Prophet that homosexuals should be imprisoned, women who've had abortions killed, and mixed race marriages annulled?" Her voice shakes with fury. "Those people? The ones who are raising their children in this cesspool, who are teaching them the same *values* as the Prophet?"

"They still have a chance. To learn. To choose differently. To get out!" I force myself to keep my voice down. "If you sit in judgment of them and wipe them out because of it, you're no better than him." I shake my head. "No better."

"Wrong." She steps to me, her face red, the scar at her temple an angry slash. "They've killed themselves with their own sins. What I'm doing will free all the women on this compound. Every sex slave—and that's what we are—will finally be able to choose for themselves. And no more will be brought here to be abused, sold, tortured, *murdered*." Her eyes soften the slightest bit. "Don't you care about what they did to her? To Georgia?"

"My mother will pay for that."

She nods. "You know, for the longest time I'd thought you'd killed her."

"I never would have—"

"I know. This conversation alone tells me you don't have what's required to commit to taking life." Her earlier softness disappears. "But I do. For all the lives the Prophet has stolen, there must be an answer. This is it."

"No, it doesn't have to be. This isn't you. You're kind. I've seen it. The way you treat the Maidens, the way you keep your head up no matter what happens."

She shakes her head. "You don't know me. You don't know what they've *done* to me." Her eyes water, but she bites back her tears. "The time I've spent at the Rectory. The things they did to me, to change me. They did them to Jez, too." Her voice trembles at the mention of Jez's name. "Over and over. Man after man. We were raped and beaten and raped again. The Prophet said that it would change us, make us women who the Lord would love. Women who would cling to men as our only salvation. And so for days after our first attempt to escape, the men would come. And we were gagged, strapped down, forced to endure their touches, their degradations." She points her finger in my face. "So don't you *ever* think you know me. You don't know a goddamn thing."

I take her words in. Sickeningly, they don't surprise me. "I'm sorry for all of it, for everything that was done to you. But you can't—"

She barks out a laugh. "Sorry?" Tapping the scar on her forehead, she says, "And this, not done by a man at all. This was Grace, showing me that I was worth less than nothing when I disobeyed her." She straightens her back. "No one here is holy. No one here deserves to live one more day. The people who go to that church support every act of cruelty that happens here. They turn a blind eye, close their hearts to the truth. I can't save them when they've made no efforts to save themselves."

She's too far gone. I see that now. This place has wrecked her. The same way it's done to Grace, to me, to countless others. I can't get through, even though I have to give it one last try.

"What about Emily? She'll be there. She has to be. The other Maidens? They'll be in the front row like always. How do you plan to save them?"

Her lips compress into a thin line, everything about her stony and harsh.

I pinch the bridge of my nose. "You don't intend to save them at all, do you? You've condemned them right along with everyone else. You say you want to free them, but if you do this, you've signed their death warrants."

"I don't want to hurt them, but this is war. And this has to end bloody." She takes a step back. "Killing them is a mercy, really. Better to be dead than enslaved by the Prophet. It all has to go. It's the only way to be sure."

"No matter who gets hurt?"

"It's war," she repeats, as if it's something she tells herself often.

I've lost her. I probably never had her. "I can't let you do this."

She backs down the hall, her head high. "Do what you have to do, Noah. But I won't stop. Not until there's justice." With a whirl of her skirts, she turns and jogs down the corridor. Her footsteps dissipate and eventually go silent.

I pull a flask from my pocket and take a long drink, the cool liquor doing nothing to calm me. "Well, fuck. That went well."

CHAPTER 25

DELILAH

*G*race is blessedly silent on our short trip to the Prophet's house. Maybe she spent all her venom earlier, though I doubt it. We enter through the basement, the house quiet as we walk up the stairs and into the grand foyer.

My stomach lurches as we pass my least favorite room in the house, the piano silent in the corner. But she doesn't guide me there. Instead, we cross the marbled foyer, the wide staircase to our right. The scents of bacon and biscuits waft through the air, and the light clink of silverware on china greets us as we enter an ornate dining room.

Evan sits near the head of the table, smiling and talking to the Prophet as the men eat breakfast. The Prophet's bodyguard—Castro, Noah calls him—sits in a chair in the corner of the room, his watchful eye on me as I follow Grace.

"Here's the blushing bride!" The Prophet doesn't stand as he beams up at me. All the disarray from the previous day is buried, hidden beneath his thin veneer of civility and kindness. "Have a seat. Let's enjoy a good breakfast together before service."

Grace takes the seat closest to the Prophet, and points to the chair beside her. I take it, my eyes down as a servant places a plate of food in front of me. Not the stuff we get at the Cloister, but real food—a biscuit covered in sausage gravy, fluffy scrambled eggs, and three slices of thin, crispy bacon. My stomach growls loudly, and Evan laughs.

I catch his eye. He's looking especially handsome today, his face closely shaved and his hair neatly clipped. Wearing a crisp dark gray suit, he is the picture of masculine beauty, his blue eyes shining like ice as he surveys me. "Eat up, Delilah. You'll need your energy for today."

Encouraging words when delivered by anyone else—from him, they're a threat.

Grace hands me a napkin, and I smooth it in my lap. "Do as your husband commands."

He's not my husband. I bite my tongue to keep the words from coming out. But Evan smirks, as if he knows I thought them.

I pick up my silverware and slice off a piece of biscuit. When I put it in my mouth and chew, the room seems to relax, as if the walls had been holding their breath.

"Now, Evan. Tell me more about Washington. I've never had much of a hankering for politics, but DC sure seems like the fast lane, you know? All that power swirling around."

Evan finally turns his hawk-like stare back to the Prophet. "It's definitely different than being here at home. There's always something going on, some sort of deals being made, and tons of trouble to get into if you're up to it."

"I bet you're always up to it." The Prophet laughs. "A young buck like you. What I wouldn't give to turn back the clock."

Grace eats with prim precision, her faint smile brimming with viciously positive energy. I try to eat, but my stomach rebels, aching as the too-rich food hits it.

The Prophet and Evan continue to make small-talk. I'm relieved that they don't expect anything from me. Not right now, anyway. After all, Grace has always taught us that Maidens are better seen and not heard.

I take small bites and sip the orange juice by my plate. It's too sweet, the shock of sugar like a revelation on my tongue.

"We have big plans. So much can be accomplished here at Heavenly, and we can do even more with a little help from our friends in Congress." The Prophet finishes his meal.

Evan places his napkin next to his plate. "You know Heavenly always has my support."

The Prophet pauses, as if expecting more of a pledge, but Evan doesn't offer it. A sour note seems to grow for a moment, then the Prophet stands, his jovial mask in place. "Service will be starting soon, but I have some business to attend to first." He glances at Grace and me. "And I think it'll be a treat for all of you to see it. You, too, Evan."

"Sure thing, though I'd like to have some private time with Delilah first, if that's all right?"

"Of course." The Prophet motions for Grace to join him. "We'll just be in my office. Come on over when you're ready."

"Thank you." Evan doesn't take his eyes off me as the Prophet, Grace, and Castro leave us. Once the room is cleared, he stands and walks to my side of the table.

When his hands come down on my shoulders, I jump.

He squeezes. "Almost mine, darling."

I don't move, barely breathe, but he takes my arm and pulls me to my feet, then embraces me. I force myself to return his hug, wrapping my arms around him even though it feels wrong, every bit of it off and dirty and tarnished.

"Don't worry about this dress." He kisses the top of my head. "We'll have another ceremony in a few months. A real one. You can have any dress you like. A big cake, huge reception, dancing, flowers—all of it. This hillbilly ceremony is just a little formality." Pulling back, he stares down at me. "I'm not like them."

I'm too unsure to respond. What does he want me to say? That I believe him? I don't.

"You'll see." He grips my upper arms. "I have some quirks; I can admit that."

"Quirks?" I can't hold back the incredulity.

"My dark side, yes." He peers at me, and I swear for a moment that he's actually trying to speak to me on a level as equals. "I can't deny it, and I want you to revel in it like I do. You have it inside you—the fight, the fire. You'll come to want our sessions, you'll see. But that's just one part of our lives together. I want this marriage to work. I want you to shine on my arm wherever we go. You are my future." He strokes my cheek, his palm warm, his words treacly sweet like concealed poison.

I will never be your anything.

He glances out into the foyer. "These rednecks are just a stepping stone for us."

I nod. He's saying exactly what I want—that he doesn't care about Heavenly, has no stake in what happens to this place. It will make it so much easier for me to convince him to destroy the Prophet. But I still hold onto hope that I won't have to do any convincing, that I'll be with Adam, safely away from Evan's grasp by the end of the day.

"Come on." He sighs. "Let's go get this over with so I can take you home."

"Home?" I ask.

"I have a house in Birmingham, remember?" His smile sends a shiver down my spine. "It's all set up for us. Everything we need for our little honeymoon." Pulling me along with him, he leads me across the hall into the Prophet's office. Noah and Castro are already there— Noah drinking and Castro scowling. Grace is perched on one of the leather chairs like an attentive bird, and in the far corner sits Ruth, the kind wife from the Cathedral. Both of her eyes are swollen, her lip split, and silent tears spill down her cheeks.

"What's this business?" Evan walks to the chair next to Grace, sits down, then pulls me into his lap.

Looking around at the miserable faces, I sit there, Evan's hand on the small of my back, his thumb rubbing a circle on the stiff fabric of the dress. I'm a prized possession, a pampered dog. Ruth doesn't make a sound, but her tears are fresh and the bruises are just now forming around her swollen eyes. What is happening?

"Just a little something to show you how serious I am about Heavenly's future." The Prophet smiles, his blue seersucker suit doing its best to convince everyone he's a southern gentleman instead of a sadistic devil worshipper.

I don't look at Noah. I can't. I feel certain our secret would be out, our alliance obvious if we were to make eye contact. So I stare at the arm of the chair and wait for whatever the Prophet has in store for me, for Ruth, for whatever victim in his web he's chosen to devour.

"Bring her." He points at Castro.

The man rises and leaves, but his footsteps don't go far.

The Prophet opens his top desk drawer and draws out a blade.

I swallow hard, and black spots fill my vision. It's the same blade that cut Sarah's throat. Her face flashes through my mind—the empty, dead look in her eyes as her blood spilled. I unwillingly cringe away, back into Evan's arms.

"Shh," he whispers in my ear. "It doesn't matter. Nothing here does. He won't touch you, darling. You're mine."

The Prophet runs his thumb lightly along the blade, then nods. "Sharp enough."

Castro returns dragging a woman in a Spinner's dress. Her light hair is too familiar, and I lean over to see her better. I grip the arm of the chair and shake my head. *No.*

"You see, even for a man like me, there are problems that I have to solve before they become too big, too over-

239

whelming." The Prophet walks around his desk and leans against the front as Castro yanks Chastity's hair, exposing her badly beaten face.

Noah shifts on the couch, but doesn't intervene.

"Just a few days ago, I learned from Ruth that some of my sweet, devoted girls were planning to kill me." The Prophet tsks and looks at Evan with comically raised brows. "Can you believe that?"

Evan pulls me tighter against him. "That's a surprise."

That day Ruth didn't come back to the Cathedral—was that why? Had the Prophet gotten wind of her plan?

"It is." The Prophet nods. "It was quite a shock, I can tell you that. But Ruth was truthful, eventually. I had to get my son involved, poor boy. Ezekiel is tough like his mother, though." He points at Ruth. "She raised him well. He didn't cry... at first."

Ruth gasps in a breath and covers her mouth with her hand.

"She's a good mother. That's why I'm going to let her live." He turns his attention to Chastity. "But you, my dear, have no value anymore. Too many mistakes. Too many attempts to disobey me. 'God's wrath comes on those who are disobedient.' You, Chastity, have flouted my law for far too long. I've been forgiving. But now that time has passed. You and your friends planned to destroy the church." He steps to the sofa where Noah sits, stone-faced, and reaches behind it. Grabbing a satchel, the Prophet stands and pulls a stick of dynamite from it. "Foolish woman. What good would that do? Even if you killed us all, more warriors of the Lord would rise to take our places." He shakes his head and gently drops the bag on his desk, more khaki tubes rolling around inside.

"Fuck you." She spits on the polished wood floor.

"Dad, you don't have to do this." Noah stands and runs a hand through his hair. "Send her to the Rectory. Or maybe you could—"

"Noah, I didn't ask for your input." The Prophet's voice goes chilly in an instant.

"I know, but you can't do this." He steps toward his father.

The Prophet whirls on him. "I can't? Have you forgotten I have been chosen by God to lead the faithful?"

"I haven't forgotten anything, but Chastity doesn't deserve to die." He puts so much faith into his words, as if they aren't falling on the deaf ears of a madman, as if he thinks his plea for mercy might work.

Some of me hopes right along with him, but most of me despairs.

"I decide what people deserve, son. Not you." The Prophet turns his head toward the hallway and yells, "Zion!"

"Dad, don't." Noah shakes his head. "Don't do this."

One of the Protectors walks in, his assault rifle in his hands.

"Zion, please escort my son to the church for morning service."

The Protector's eyes pinball from Chastity to me to the Prophet, but he does as he's told. "Come on." He points the gun at Noah.

"Dad—"

"Go!" The Prophet bellows.

"Move." Zion walks around to Noah's back and presses the barrel into him. "You heard him. Get going. Now."

"No." Noah's voice is strong. "I won't let you do it." He brings his fists up, his only weapons.

"I thought you might betray me like this." The Prophet scowls and jerks his chin at Zion, who turns his gun and brings the butt down hard on the back of Noah's head. Noah groans and crumples into a heap at his father's feet, unconscious.

"No!" I yell, helpless in my captor's arms. Hot, angry tears form, and my hate roars inside me. For the Prophet. For Castro. For the man who holds me captive and allows this horror show to continue.

"Drag Noah to the sitting room." The Prophet waves a dismissive hand. "I'll get him in line later."

"Yes, sir." Zion shoulders his gun and grabs Noah's feet, pulling him out of the room.

"Now." The Prophet turns back to Chastity. "Where were we?"

"I was telling you to go fuck yourself," she grits out.

I freeze, Evan's arms holding me tighter as the scene plays out to its inevitable end. *Stop, please stop.*

The Prophet grabs her face, squeezing viciously. "Still defiant. Even after everything I let Castro do to you."

She laughs, the sound hard. "I couldn't even tell when he was inside. That's how big of a man Castro is."

"*Puta!*" Castro shakes her, her arms flying like a rag doll. One of them moves too much, as if it's broken in several places.

No. I can't sit here and let this happen. I won't. Noah took a stand, and now I have to do the same.

The Prophet approaches her, the blade in his right hand. "And don't worry about your other conspirators. I have men out looking for them. It's only a matter of time. They'll be rounded up and taken care of. Jez especially. I'll give her a little extra lesson in pleasing men before stringing her up like the witch she is. She and her handful of whores will hang in the punishment circle, a meal for the crows and whatever other beasts will lower themselves to partake."

"Let go." I struggle against Evan's hold, kicking his legs and trying to push out of his lap. "Let me go."

The Prophet shoots me an amused look. "You sure you can handle that one, Senator?"

"I'll do just fine, thank you." Evan yanks me against his chest, one arm around my waist as his hand claps over my mouth. "You have to get through it, darling," he whispers in my ear. "The rules are different here on the Prophet's turf."

I scratch at his hand, and scream, desperate to get to Chastity.

She turns to me, her light eyes clear. "Light it up, Firefly. Don't let them get away with it any longer. For Georgia. For me. For Sarah. For all of us. Light. It. Up."

"That's enough silly talk. The Father of Fire is waiting. You aren't pure, but he'll take you. Use you. Burn you from the inside out." The Prophet directs Castro, "Hold her good. I don't want to get any on my suit."

I fight against Evan's arms, but I get nowhere. And when the Prophet's blade opens Chastity's neck, a crimson river flowing to the floor, I scream and scream and scream.

CHAPTER 26

ADAM

Keeping my hoodie up, I dissolve into the crowd that hovers in the entry to the sanctuary. The Prophet smiles down from enlarged photos posted along the walls, his gaze always on the congregation, counting his minions.

I ease past a couple talking about their daughter's grades in school—they find them too high in math. The murmuring jumble of souls has molded themselves to fit my father's edicts. The women's dresses almost brush the floor, and several of them have thick makeup to cover bruises. The children are still jubilant, running and giggling with each other, but they'll be broken soon enough. Once their parents move them into Monroeville, there will be no escape. Their childhoods will end as abruptly as mine did, and with just as much grief.

My hands shoved in my pockets, I limp toward the double doors that lead to the classroom section of the church. Some people are inside, most of them bustling about and getting ready for the service. Keeping my head down, I push into the nearest room. It's dark, and I don't touch the light switch as I survey the nearest support column. Wide and painted white, three men could barely hold hands around it. There are a dozen of these in the structure, each one supporting an essential piece of the church. Circling this one, I don't find anything—no tampering, no dynamite. One down, eleven to go.

I open the door, then quickly let it close. The women from the Cathedral file in, their antiquated dress and hair styles covering over the fact that they are sex slaves. Their children aren't with them. Odd. My father doesn't like for my brothers and sisters to ever miss a service. I peer through the sliver of a window in the door, seeing but unseen. Noah should be here by now. We'd agreed to meet up and search for the Chapel saboteurs. But he isn't here. I'll have to go it alone. Worry creeps into my thoughts—for Noah and Emily. But if I dwell too much, I won't be able to get this done, or maybe I'll make a mistake. No good options.

Once the hall clears of the Cathedral wives, I open the door and ease to the next room. This pillar is half-buried in the wall, but the accessible sides are clear. I double check it, but hear the door opening behind me.

Fuck. I press myself to the wall in the small crevice created by the pillar.

"Where is she?" Jez's voice reaches my ears.

"She was supposed to be here thirty minutes ago."

"Do you have any?" Jez's voice rises.

"Dynamite? No. She kept a close eye on it. Was supposed to bring it."

"We're screwed without it. Where is she?"

The door opens again, light from the hallway creating a rectangle on the floor before going dark again.

"Ruth and Chastity are missing." It's the old Spinner, Abigail. "Someone says they were both taken to the Prophet's house over an hour ago. Haven't come out."

Stunned silence. Their plan has gone to shit. Somehow, the Prophet found out about it.

"What are we going to do?" The woman's voice I don't recognize is a mouse's whisper. "If he has Chas—"

"She'll be okay." Jez is vehement. "She's tough. But we need to do this without her for now. We still have the gasoline stockpiled under the Chapel. I'll take some of the girls, head over, collect it all, and bring it here. We'll just go back to plan A. No problem."

"But there *is* a problem." I walk out, my foot aching with each step.

"Shit!" Jez backs away, then stops. "The fuck are you doing in here?" She wears a modest blouse and skirt, and, with her hair up in a severe bun and not a scrap of makeup on her face, she's become someone else. Not Jez,

247

the madam, but another one of the Prophet's followers, devotion in her bones.

"I was checking for explosives. You're never going to believe this, but I heard some psycho assholes were going to try and blow up the church. Crazy, right?"

She pulls a knife from the pocket of her denim skirt. "You and your smart mouth. I should gut you on principle."

"I'm not the one you need to worry about. If he took Ruth and Chastity, he knows what you're planning. You're lucky the Protectors haven't swept you up yet. Once they do ..." I let out a low whistle.

"Fuck." She shakes her head. "This is a cluster."

"If you want to survive, you need to get what girls from the Chapel you can and make a break for it. They'll capture some of you, but not all. Most of the Protectors and some of the guards are here in the church for the big service."

"We aren't running." Jez puts the knife back in her pocket.

"Then you're dying." I'm not a fan of their murder plot, but I'm not a fool either. They're victims of this place, tainted by the purest form of cruelty. To them, their plan is warranted—justice, even.

"What about you? I don't see you limping away from here despite all your advice to turn tail and run."

"I still have a part to play." *I still have my love to save.* "Doesn't mean you can't save yourself and some of your girls."

The girl I don't recognize shifts from one foot to the other. "Maybe he's right. Maybe we should—"

"No." Jez turns to the door. "Get into the crowd. Keep your eyes peeled. I'm going to the Prophet's house to find Chastity."

Abigail sighs, her wrinkled forehead even more furrowed than usual. "That place is a death trap for you, girl."

"I have to go. For Chastity." Jez leaves, the door clicking shut behind her as Abigail wrings her hands.

"All falling apart," the old Spinner mutters to herself, then leaves, the other girl on her heels.

I peek into the hall, watching as they disappear into the sanctuary proper. The people are thinning, most of them taking their seats for the big show. Where the fuck is Noah? I press my forehead to the door and try to think of where he could be. Maybe on the other side checking the supports for the dynamite that will never come? I refuse to think of the grimmer alternatives.

I stare at the stage door at the very end of the hall. That's where my father will make his entrance just before it's time to start. I balance on my good foot, waiting. After about ten minutes, the door opens and my mother walks in, her limp slowing her down. Castro holds onto her elbow and leads her up the stairs and through the door. They're going to make their move. My mother usually comes to service, but she has an assigned seat in the crowd, surrounded by members of the Heavenly Police Force and Protectors. She's breaking protocol. Expectation hums through me like a funeral dirge. It's all about to go down.

Running my fingers over the pistol in my pocket, I reassure myself that if she doesn't get it done, I will. My father has to die today. Heavenly has to *end*. Before more people are lost, before Emily is sold to a monster, before anyone else falls into my father's trap.

The door opens again, and my breath freezes in my lungs. Emily walks in, Evan at her back. Her face is drawn and pale, and her shoulders are curved forward, as if she's in a protective stance, seeking to shield her softest parts from attackers. Evan whispers something in her ear, then leads her to the stairs. When she gets to the top, she turns, her gaze resting on the door where I stand as if she can see me in the dark. The sadness in her pulls at me, yanking me toward her no matter the consequences. I rest my hand on the door handle, my heart pumping as if I've been sprinting through the trees again, racing after her. She stares for a moment longer, her gray eyes seeking. I turn the handle and start to open it.

She turns, Evan leading her through the door to the stage and closing it behind them. My hand relaxes, the door clicking shut. She's gone, but I feel her. In my soul, in every part of me that's still alive. I won't fail her. Not anymore.

I wait, biding my time until everyone is in place. When the door opens once more, my father strides in with half a dozen Protectors. He hands a black satchel to Zion and gives instructions that I can't hear. When he's finished, Zion nods and motions for the Protectors to follow him. My father climbs the stairs to the stage in what I hope is his last performance.

After a few minutes, I leave the dark room and push through one of the side doors to the sanctuary. The seats are already filled, an ensemble onstage singing a hymn as the crowd murmurs quietly. I ascend the stadium stairs and choose the only empty seat on the right side aisle.

"What a blessed morning." The man in the seat next to me is already too chipper for my tastes.

"Morning." I keep my voice low, my hoodie up.

He doesn't take the hint. "You a regular?"

"Something like that."

"Well, I'm Gene. Pleased to meet you." He holds his hand out.

Mine are still bandaged and in my pocket. "I'm sorry, but I'm getting over a cold, so it wouldn't be—"

"No need to say more." He chuckles. "I don't need to bring any sickness into my house. Got a newborn at home with my wife. I've brought my daughter and son to service, though. Don't like to miss, not when the Prophet's on fire like he has been the past few Sundays."

I could laugh, but I don't. Instead, I nod along as he continues waxing warm and fuzzy about my father. I still haven't looked the guy in the face, but I can picture him. Good ol' boy. Maybe a beard. Laugh wrinkles next to his eyes. Seems harmless. But if he's enjoying the Prophet's teachings, there's a part of him that hates. Hates so deeply that he comes here to indulge it once a week, to let it free under the guise of religion. Jez wants to destroy him for that hate. I hold onto hope that he can change, that his children can choose a different path. Perhaps I'm naïve. The more he talks, the more I'm sure of it.

"—and what he said about the women needing to cover up? Amen. He's right on, don't you think?"

"Mmhhm." I tune him out even further as the singers near the end of their song.

It's almost showtime.

CHAPTER 27

DELILAH

*T*he choir's voices drone quietly over the backstage speakers, their version of "Great is Thy Faithfulness" steady and smooth.

"We're up first." Evan holds my hand, his confidence suffocating.

All I can see is blood. Chastity's life flowing all over the perfectly polished floor, the Prophet stepping back so his shoes wouldn't get splattered, Castro lowering her to the floor. Nothing will ever make it right. My body is numb, my heart sedated. I have a purpose, but it's lost behind a veil of crimson—the thick, syrupy liquid coating everything I see.

"You get through this, and we're home free." Evan squeezes my fingers lightly. "Then things will be fine. You'll forget about this place, these people. I promise."

His promise rings hollow like his soul. There is no forgetting what happened here. Not to me, or Georgia, or Adam, or Sarah, or Chastity. Even if Heavenly is reduced to rubble, the scars it has inflicted will remain inside me forever. Indelible, raised marks that I can't explain and don't want to touch for fear of opening the old wounds.

A young man fusses over the Prophet as he sits in front of a mirror with large, bare bulbs, just like you see in any decent showbiz film. Powder on the face, product in the hair, and then the final touch—a microphone looped behind his ear and poised near his mouth.

The Prophet rises, but something catches his eye. He turns toward the darker depths of backstage, and I follow his gaze. Something is moving back there.

Someone touches my hair. I turn my head to find Grace behind me, bobby pins sticking out of her mouth.

She scrunches her forehead. "Dt moooooo."

I take it she means "don't move," so turn back toward the stage. Utterly unaffected by Chastity's murder, she pins the white veil to my hair and tosses the fabric over my face. It hangs to my chest, a white blur on everything.

"Beautiful," Evan says as the choir crescendos toward the end of the song.

Noise behind me catches my attention, and I cast a glance toward the commotion.

The Prophet, red-faced and irate, points his finger at Rachel, his voice rising. She must have been the one moving in the wing. Castro stands beside her, his face placid, his hand in his pocket.

"—lying whore. This will not go unpunished. Castro, take her down to the congregation and keep an eye on her."

"Can't do that." Castro pulls a pistol from his pocket and aims it at the Prophet. "It's best you do what Rachel says. Make the announcement. Step down."

I move toward them to try and hear better.

Evan grabs my elbow. "Don't."

I shake him off and take another step before he grabs me again. "Delilah, this is clearly a family matter that we need to stay the hell out of."

"You, Castro?" The Prophet shakes his head. "Bastard of an ingrate. After all I've done for you. 'He who shared my bread has turned against me.'"

"Don't try to use the Bible on me, old man." Castro's dark eyes rage, his voice shaking. "After all I've put up with from you. All the times you passed me over. You're the betrayer, not me."

"Leon, there's no point arguing." Rachel holds up a hand. "All you have to do is announce that you are stepping down and that Adam will be taking your place as Prophet. If you don't, Castro will shoot you dead, and I'll make the announcement myself."

The Prophet seems to ignore the threat as he looms over his wife, every bit of him tense. "You're the one who took Adam? *You*?"

It's as if I'm watching a movie through a frosted window, trying to follow the characters and guess what's going to happen next.

"That's neither here nor there." Unafraid, she glares up at him. Her weakness is gone. Was it always a charade? In its place, iron seems to run through her spine, and the malevolence in her gaze is only tempered by the veil that dims my vision. In the hazy light, I can see that Adam has her fire, the same indomitable will to survive, to carry on, and to win. Maybe she can pull this off. My heart leaps at the thought of it, how easy it could be if she cuts the Prophet down to nothing in one smooth stroke.

"You're a witch!" the Prophet yells, his voice likely carrying to the Maidens along the front row. "An evil thing sent here to torment me!" He turns to Grace who's been silently watching near the stage door. "Go get Zion or any Protector. I want Rachel and Castro detained until after service."

Grace reaches for the door and flips over the sliding lock. Her smug smile resurfaces, and for the first time, the Prophet seems to lose some of his steam. "Grace, do it now!" His voice quavers.

She leans against the door and crosses her arms with a curt shake of her head.

"You!" He points to the young man standing frozen next to the makeup chair. "Get out there and get me some help!"

Unsure, he drops his makeup brush. "I, okay—"

"Now!" The Prophet yells, and the man glances at the bright stage and starts to move.

Grace tracks him like a cougar on a deer.

"Don't!" I lunge toward him, but Evan drags me back.

"Leave it, Delilah," he growls against my veil.

The poor man takes half a dozen steps toward the stage before Grace is on him. I don't see the blade, but I can tell by the jerking motion of her arm that she's stabbing him in the back again and again. His yell is covered by the final notes of the choir, and I feel his body thump to the floor. Grace wipes her knife on his white shirt, then stands.

"Witches, all of you!" the Prophet cries.

The choir quiets, the song over.

"Maybe I am." Rachel smiles, drawing his attention back to her. "But it doesn't matter. Either you do what I say or you die now, choking on your own blood. It's up to you, dear husband."

"The Father of Fire will punish you." He smooths the front of his jacket, his tone returning to even and reasonable. "You will not win this, Rachel. And once it's over, you'll be hung with the other whores in the punishment circle."

"Your threats don't scare me. Not anymore." She clasps her hands in front of her, her simple white shirt and black skirt hiding the complicated woman within. "Are you going to oblige?"

Castro raises his pistol to the Prophet's forehead as a green light blinks on the front wall of the stage just behind the shimmering gold curtain. It's time for the Prophet to address his congregation.

"Or shall I have Castro shoot you?" She shrugs. "Either way, your time is up. This is Adam's world now. His to rule."

"You mean *yours*," the Prophet sneers. "But I have news for you, sweet wife, Adam can't be controlled. Not by me. And certainly not by a weak-willed female like you."

She shrugs. "I doubt that's the case, but even if it is, I have another son."

Evan wraps his arm around me and slowly pulls me back. "We need to go. Now."

Grace catches his movements and scurries around us, cutting off our exit. A few more steps and we'd be bathed in the stage lights, the coup attempt on full display. But those mere feet are like a football field with Grace blocking our path.

"We're leaving." Evan puts a note of command in his voice that is wasted on Grace.

She holds the blade out toward my face. "Senator, you're free to go. But Delilah is staying here. Sadly, her usefulness is at an end."

"She's mine."

Her eyes flick up to his, and I see the fullness of how unhinged she is. How far gone. She'll kill both of us. I know it, and so it seems, does Evan.

His grip loosens. "We had a deal."

"Heavenly is under new management." She waves the blade back and forth, a snake charming herself. "And no former deals will be honored. You leave now, or I gut you. She's dead either way. But you have a choice."

Evan lets me go and scoots me to the side, then brings up his fists. "You don't have a chance. I'm stronger, faster."

Grace laughs and points her knife at the bloodied man a few paces away. "I bet he thought the same thing."

I look for any escape. Only the darkness at the back of the stage is an option, but I don't know where or how far it goes.

Evan grunts in frustration, his gaze bouncing from me to Grace.

"She'll kill you." Rachel calls, her motherly voice at odds with her dark words. "She doesn't care who you are. I don't either."

"Evan, you need to help me here." The Prophet tries to flip the southern gentleman switch, but he just winds up sounding scared. "We can't let these women—"

Grace darts toward Evan. He jumps back right when she swings, and the knife barely misses his stomach. "Fuck!" he yells and scurries away toward the stage door.

I take the opening and run toward the darkness in the rear of the stage, past the fabric backdrops that hang from the ceiling and the scenery from the Christmas pageant. My heart pounds, and I rip the veil from my face but keep it clutched in my hand.

A tall, wide open door beckons to my left, but it's the first place I'd guess. *"You need to stop picking the first good place you see to hide. Be a little more sneaky."* Georgia's voice whispers across my mind.

Dashing to the right, I find a white tent set up against the back wall. Inside, dozens of life-sized angel wings are perched on metal stands, their white feathers gloomy in the dim light. It's the best chance I have, so I hurry inside and pick my way toward the wall, then hunker down amidst the sea of white. My breathing is labored, fear and exertion seeking to give me away. I press my mouth to the back of my arm, using it to dull the sound. Is Grace on my heels?

I don't have a good view of the tent entrance, but I know she's out there, her knife at the ready. Evan is long gone. I have no delusions that he'll try to save me. The fear on his face when she swung told me that he had no problems abandoning me to save his own skin. Something hits the concrete floor—a loud *click* in the gloom. I shrink down a little more, my back pressed to the cinderblock wall.

"Delilah," Grace's voice tickles through the gloom, coming from the dark room I passed up. I wipe sweat from my brow. I have to hold on, stay hidden, and when I see an opportunity, take it.

My thoughts skitter into my memory again—Georgia hunting me in the backyard as I tried to stay as still as I could despite the mosquitoes and the stuffy summer heat. The need to pee is the same now as it was then. Hiding was never my strong suit.

"I'd be able to find you in the dark. You shine no matter where you are, Firefly." For once, I hope Georgia was wrong.

CHAPTER 28

ADAM

*T*he choir has been done for too long, and the sounds from backstage have the audience tittering. Shouts and thumps and whispered voices—a deeply odd start to what is usually a flawless service. My mind itches, like bugs crawling all over the gray matter, as I wrestle with my need to keep Emily safe. She's back there. I'm out here. If I move too soon—I glance at the Heavenly police officers scattered along the aisles—I won't be able to help anyone, especially not her. Fuck. Where is Noah? I scan the crowd again, looking for him in the throng of faithful. He still isn't there.

The static whine of a microphone going hot pulses through the speakers, and my father appears onstage. He strides out slowly, his steps measured, as if he's planning what to say. I lean forward as the crowd hushes, their attention on the mythical Prophet who looms on large screens all around the sanctuary.

He stops in the middle of the stage, his head down, his hands clasped in front of him. Like this, he looks like just a man. Nothing more. His graying hair a little mussed, his shoulders down, his stance a little wider than a young man's because he needs more help to balance. Even in the bright spotlight, he's faded, frail, mortal. Can anyone else see it?

Slowly, he lifts his head until his eyes search the silent crowd. Someone sneezes on the other side of the sanctuary, and a baby lets out a short wail that's quickly cut off. The Prophet lifts one hand up, palm open, and says nothing.

The worshippers turn to each other, some of them shrugging, a few of them whispering. Even the Maidens perched along the front row seem unsure as they lean and speak amongst themselves despite the fact it's forbidden.

After a few more long beats of silence, a child down front stands and raises her hand, keeping it in the air just like the Prophet. Another child near her does the same, then another. Soon, the gesture spreads until the entire congregation is rising, hands shooting up. Beside me, Gene gets to his feet. I follow and raise my hand, hoping no one notices the bandaging.

The entire sanctuary is silent, reflecting the Prophet back to himself. This is his perfect world. What he's strived after for so long—conformity with him, his ideals, his goals. What the congregants likely view as an act of support is truly an act of sublimation. They are shoved under in a hellish baptism, their individuality denied as they take on the shape and desires of the Prophet.

We stand long enough for me to wonder how badly my hand is going to hurt when the blood returns to it. Gradually, the Prophet lowers his palm and gestures for everyone to sit. A cacophony of seat cushions compressing, old folks groaning, and people getting settled fills the wide space and then dies away.

"My beloveds." He opens his hands and motions toward the entire congregation. "You are blessed, and you have blessed me. Without your love, Heavenly would not be what it is today. Strong, Godly, and devout. Your generosity has allowed us to flourish, our influence to grow. We have spread the Gospel to every corner of the planet, and we did it together in the light of the Lord."

The "amens" come from all angles. Gene beside me adds a hearty one once the others have died down a bit.

The Prophet pauses, building the anticipation like water adding to a droplet, growing larger and larger until its weight drags it down. His whisper is barely a hiss. "But in every garden, there is a *snake*."

Some members gasp, others stare straight ahead, their attention demanding that the Prophet point out the traitor.

"Our little church is no different. Here, we have made a new Eden, each of us working toward our heavenly reward. But just as Adam and Eve prospered in the garden and were set upon by the serpent, we too are under attack. I've told you many times of the forces of evil that live outside our walls that seek to harm us. They are still there, my friends." He shakes his head. "They will always be there. But the true downfall of man always comes from within. And it always comes from a *woman*."

Gene shifts in his seat, and the restlessness flows through the audience, each of them glancing at their neighbor or their neighbor's wife, wondering who the culprit is.

"While we've been working to build, a rot has set in at the core of our church. At the very base of our tree, if you will. Sometimes, a rot is so strong, that you can't save the tree, no matter what you do. In cases like that, it's a mercy to cut it down, burn the stump, start anew."

Movement around the periphery catches my eye. The Protectors are flipping the latches on the double doors that lead out of the sanctuary. Silently, they engage the locking mechanisms, then close the doors. The hackles on my neck rise, and I grip the back of the seat in front of me.

The Prophet shakes his head dramatically. "I should have known when my firstborn turned on me."

Another gasp rocks the crowd. Gene spits out a "the fuck?" then turns to his two girls next to him. "Don't listen to Daddy."

The smallest one nods. "Didn't hear nothing."

I grab his arm. "You need to get out of here."

"What?" His bushy brows rise as he looks me in the eye for the first time. "Hey, you're—"

"You need to leave, understand? If you stay here, you and your girls will die." I point to the nearest door that hasn't yet been locked. "Go now or stay and die."

"—redemption doesn't apply here. I thought it might, when Adam first started going wrong. But that was a false hope. He never returned to the fold. Too far gone, mired in his love for yet another serpent, and turned his back on his Prophet. But she is not the one who caused the rot. No. She could have been dealt with. The decay goes much, much deeper. And it's the sort that must be burned out."

Gene sits frozen, his eyes wide.

"Listen to him." I point at the Prophet and grip Gene by the front of his weathered t-shirt. "Listen to what he's saying."

"Only holy, cleansing fire can save our immortal souls. And it has to happen today. Right now." He drones on, but I turn my focus to Gene. I can't save them all, but I can do this.

Gene swallows hard and stands. "Girls, come on." He takes the smallest one's hand and the other follows as they edge past me and push out the door. Another family follows, and then another lines up to go, but a Protector blocks their way and pushes them back as he locks the door and shuts it.

Panic spreads slowly, a grass fire after a wet summer. But the alarm grows as the Prophet continues to preach fire and brimstone. Polite at first, they try the doors that won't budge. I stand and make my way down the stairs. No one pays attention to me now, their concentration on the rising fear.

"And my son," my father laments, "his disobedience hurt the most. But I know why. Now I know the cause." He takes a deep breath and shoots both hands heavenward. "Why, Father, have you cursed me with a wife such as Rachel? She is the serpent. *She* took him from me. She turned my children, my Maidens, my wives against me. Her. But the Father of Fire came to me, warned me in a dream last night. So I can save us all right now. I will not let the snake eat us alive. Your Prophet will always protect you, and the Lord has given me the ability to do so."

I make steady progress toward the stage as the panic grows, jumping from one person to the next like hot cinders or a disease.

"The snake will not win. I'll never see my son again because of her. He won't make it to my Heavenly home. He is lost. But all of you will be there with me. In glory. We will not wait for the terrors of the world to come here and rob our lives away. And we will *not* give in to the serpent who stalks us even now. You see, my Protectors have placed dynamite throughout this holy place. Dying as martyrs is a far better end than falling prey to the lure of the snake."

Now, men throw themselves against the doors, the timbers shaking but not giving. Children cry and somewhere someone is wailing. Even the Heavenly police officers are shouting—some trying to calm the throng, others kicking at the doors.

I cut through the crowd and rush down the center aisle. "Here! I'm here!"

Dad looks my way, his eyes widening when he sees me. "The Prodigal has returned."

CHAPTER 29

DELILAH

*T*he sanctuary is oddly silent, the stillness a promise of terrible things to come. I pick at the wings in front of me, pulling away a piece of the wire that forms their shape. The white metal doesn't give easily, and the tips of the wings scoot across the floor as I pull. I yank some, then stop, listening for Grace.

"Delilah," Grace's voice, dripping with menace, moves closer. I peer at the side of the white tent nearest to me, then freeze when I see a shadow ease by. She's close, too close. I give the wire slight pressure, a light touch that doesn't make a sound, but also doesn't do much in the way of pulling it free.

The Prophet starts his sermon, but I can't pay attention to the words.

The shadow moves on, disappearing beyond my view. The entrance to the tent is on the other side, so I angle

271

myself to watch the white flaps. I take a breath and use a little more force on the wire. It's almost loose when a ripping sound makes me jump.

I turn toward the noise. A silver blade slices down the side of the tent only a few feet away. Everything comes into sharp focus, and I can't seem to move. My heart beats in my throat, and my dress sticks to my sweaty body. The knife slides lower, clinks against the ground, and disappears.

Move, Emily. Fucking move! Abandoning my wire, I step back and edge around the next set of wings, then duck down as Grace pushes into the opening, a black phantasm invading the feathery white space.

"I know you're in here," she sing-songs.

I want to close my eyes, to pretend I'm somewhere else, to *be* somewhere else. But I can't. I can only watch as she moves through the angel wings, her black dress swishing against the floor and stirring up tiny bits of white feathers that float through the air. Pressing my back to the wall, I reach forward and try to feel for any loose bit of metal in this set of wings. My fingers graze sturdy construction, and nothing gives until I reach the very top where the wings join in the center. A piece of the wire there is undone on one side. I pull as Grace creeps closer. It gives a little, but not enough.

"Just come out. No need to dirty up all these pretty wings with your filthy blood."

I stop moving, stop breathing as she walks just to my right, her back to me, her head turning this way and that. She steps away, aiming for the tent flaps. She pushes out of the tent, the flap slapping back closed. I give the wire one more soft tug, and the piece pulls free. It's only about four inches long, but when I touch the tip, the metal is sharp. I wrap my veil around the end in my hand and scan the tent.

Speakers pump the Prophet's voice through the backstage area, his tone growing more and more dire.

I ease toward the back corner, only scraping one set of feathers across the floor as I go. Stopping, I listen for Grace, but the noise from the sanctuary is too loud now. I don't know what's going on, but I can't think about it. My attention has to be on survival and escape. Creeping along the cinderblocks, my dress catching on some of the rough edges, I stop when I get to the corner where the tent meets the wall.

Taking a deep breath, I re-check the wire in my hand, making sure the veil is wrapped enough for me to use it without cutting myself open. I try to calm my breathing, to ready myself to sneak out of the feathers and try to circumvent Grace.

When the knife plunges through the tent next to my face, I scream.

"Bitch!" She slices down the tent as I push over the row of wings in front of me and run.

Stumbling out of the tent flaps, I see her barreling toward me, the knife out in front of her.

I gain my feet and run. I'm almost to the fabric backdrops when fire swipes across my back. A scream rips from me as I fall, then roll to the side as Grace comes down next to me, her knife sticking in the wood floor of the mainstage.

She yanks at it as I scramble back. "You should have kept your veil on. I wanted you to look like a perfect bride when Adam found you covered in blood."

My back hits the wall and I force myself up despite the ripping pain across my shoulder blades. "You don't have to be like this." I keep the wire at my side.

"Shut up." She wrenches the blade free and stands. "You think you're the first bitch to come between Adam and me?"

"What?" I try to steady myself, to get ready for her.

"I had a daughter. Did you know that? Faith was her name." She rolls her eyes. "A little brat. I thought if I gave him a child he would marry me and we'd eventually dethrone the Prophet and rule together. But no." She swipes the blade in a dangerous, angry arc. "He doted on her, fawned over that little shit. Ignored me. Only cared about her."

"He said she died." I swallow hard, my eyes on the steel she's waving around.

"She died." She nods and stills. "After months of poisoning, she died. It was only supposed to take a few weeks. I looked it up. Arsenic. A little in her food every day." She makes a motion with her free hand as if she's sprinkling seasoning onto food. "Simple, right?"

I can't stop the horror that sets my hair on end, my teeth on edge. My bowels loosen, and utter disgust constricts my throat.

"No, of course it wasn't," she growls. "It took months. *Months* of her calling for Daddy every night, sleeping in his bed, wanting cuddles, taking all the attention that should have been mine. Instead of bringing us closer together, she drove us apart. I thought killing her would fix it. But then, he just got further away!" She steps closer, almost in range to strike.

The Prophet's still speaking, the word "serpent" twisting around us, punctuating Grace's confession.

Her face turns to a pout, her lips in a petulant frown. "She ruined us. Adam never wanted me after that. But at least he didn't want anyone else either." Her eyes focus on mine. "Until *you*."

I grip the wire harder, the gauzy veil compressing around the metal. "I wish I could say I pity you, that you're a victim of the Prophet just like everyone else here." I let her gaze go, kicking it to the dirt as I focus on the knife in her hand. "But you aren't. You're a monster of your own making."

275

Her pout dissolves, hard hate in her eyes. "At least I'm still alive." She lunges forward, the blade aimed at my heart.

I dart to the left, my injured back scraping against the wall. She comes at me again, holding the knife low and stabbing upward. I jump again, and her blade scrapes against the wall behind me.

With a cry of rage, she rushes me. I stumble backwards, my feet tripping over some piece of scenery, and I fall backward into the fabric sheets hanging from the ceiling. They cushion me, but also keep me upright and within range of her blade. She stabs toward me again. I roll sideways, then shove my right hand out hard. The metal makes contact, and I twist, grunting from the effort to push it even deeper. The end cuts through the veil and pushes into my palm, but I don't let up. Not until she drops the knife, the blade slapping against the wood slats beneath.

I shove her back and let go of the metal, the veil still caught around the end. Blood stains the white fabric, some of it mine but more of it hers.

She stumbles away and grabs the wire, then looks up at me, surprise in her wide eyes. "You cut me." Disbelief colors her tone as she stares down at the blood spilling from the wound. Staggering farther, her heel catches and she falls. "I'm bleeding." She holds up a red hand, then gives me a look more vicious than any before. "I'll kill you." Her foot comes out from beneath her and she tries to push herself up.

I step back.

But she falls, gasping for breath as she leans over on her side. She can't get up, and I uncurl my shaking hands. My right one bleeds, the droplets coloring the floor beneath me. But I don't care. Jubilation races through my blood. *I beat her*. I'm still alive. I take in a gulping breath and wrap my arms around me to try and keep myself together, keep myself from blowing apart with the enormity of what I've just done. I beat her, but I've taken a life. I should be sorry... I'm not.

"I beat you," I whisper.

She lays her head down, her eyes closing. "You bitch."

The world rushes back—sounds of panic and the Prophet's voice cooing about his "Prodigal son."

I turn and walk away, the floor reeling beneath me as I try to center myself. The Prophet's voice is gone, only a deep static tone emanating from the speakers. The area begins to brighten the closer I get to the side of the stage.

"—have to do it now." Rachel's voice is just up ahead.

"I can't get a shot."

"Don't shoot Adam!"

"I know!" Castro bites back.

I lean on a support beam. Blood trickles down my back, and my hand burns, the sting like a thousand bees going at my bones.

"Take it when you can. Then we need to go before he brings the whole place down. It's such a mess."

"—crucified you, and then you were gone. I thought maybe the angels—" The Prophet's voice wafts in and out. He's nearby on the stage. Thumps, yells, and screams emanate from the sanctuary. A riot, but contained. Why can't they get out?

I keep moving until I see Rachel, her face ghostly because of the garish makeup lights aimed at her.

"It's over, Dad. All of it."

"Adam," I breathe and take a few more steps forward.

"Just take me. You don't need to kill all these people." Adam sounds so reasonable, so *close*. "I'm the one—"

"This should have gone to plan." Rachel crosses her arms over her stomach. "I don't understand. The Father of Fire promised me. He promised! I carved and sacrificed that virgin. She was stupid and pretty, *perfect*! I did everything he asked of me. It wasn't supposed to be like this. Something was wrong with her. Maybe she wasn't pure. Maybe Noah fucked her and didn't admit to it..."

My ears begin to ring, a wall of alarms blaring in my mind. "*I carved and sacrificed that virgin.*"

I stare at her, the truth becoming clear. This was why Noah couldn't tell me. Rachel killed Georgia.

It had been her all along. The force of this terrible knowledge hits me like a physical blow, but I won't let it knock me down.

I force myself forward, ignoring the aches in my body and the rips in my soul. Killing Grace was self-defense. Killing Rachel will be vengeance.

"Take the shot!" she barks.

I pick up speed, aiming for her. I'll use my hands or whatever I can grab. My sister rots in the ground because of this woman, and I will make her pay. A strange sort of relief floods me as I push past the makeup chair. I have a target now. I know what I have to do. No more guesswork, no more investigation. It's just her and me.

"He's still in the fucking way!" Castro pulls my attention toward the stage. Adam stands with his back to us as he speaks to his father. The noise has grown so loud that I can't even get snippets anymore, but they're arguing.

Rachel groans. "It's all falling apart. He knew. Somehow Leon *knew*. He told the Cathedral to keep his bastard kids there. How did he know?" She's speaking quickly, as if to herself. "Leon has to die. Now." She scowls. "Shoot him even if it hits Adam. I don't care. Noah can take his place. Just shoot the Prophet *now!*"

I have to make a decision, and I only have a second. Save Adam or get justice for Georgia. It's not a choice. Not really. My body seems to make it for me before I even think it through. I throw myself at Castro, tackling him to the floor as he fires a single shot.

"*Puta!*" he yells as we fall, and I land on top of him, his gun skittering across the floor and hovering on the edge of the stage. It teeters there in slow motion, as if it can't decide whether gravity applies to it. I will it to fall, to get lost in the mayhem going on in the auditorium.

Castro shoves me off, and I turn to see Adam coming toward me, his limp slowing him down.

"Adam!" I scream and point at Castro who grabs the pistol before it falls over the edge.

He turns, but it's too late.

The shot is fired, a life taken.

CHAPTER 30

*N*oah runs down the center aisle toward me, a gun in his hand. Castro lurches sideways, a red burst blooming on his side.

The gun still in his hand, he steps toward me. "*Pendejo.*"

"I told you it would end this way, asshole." I raise my pistol and fire one shot. He falls with a hollow thump, his eyes open and vacant, blood flowing from his forehead. I've never had fewer fucks to give in my life.

I rush past him and drop to my knees next to Emily.

"Are you okay?" I lift her up.

She has blood on her white dress, and my hands go cold as I turn her over.

She winces. "My back. Grace cut me."

"Fuck." I sit her up and check the wound.

"Your hand." I pull it into my lap.

"There was a wire." Her lip trembles. "I had to."

I don't follow what she's saying, but it doesn't matter. Pulling her to my chest, I hold her. "We're getting out of here."

She nods, then looks behind her, her body going tense. "Where's your mother?"

"She took off when Castro fell."

"I have to find her." Her tone is flat, cold.

A sinking feeling rots my gut, and I turn her to face me. "You know, don't you?"

"I know it was her now." She nods. "How long have you known?"

Guilt adds to the sour tangle inside me. "A little while, but I didn't know Georgia was your sister until much later."

"I have to find her." She tries to get up, but I hold her close.

"We'll find her. Together. But I need to make sure you're safe first." I turn to find Noah standing with his back to me, staring down at my father who lies clutching his arm at center stage.

"Is he dead?" I call.

"No. Castro's bullet just winged him." He shakes his head as my father sits up. "That fucker always was useless."

Across the stage, the backgrounds billow, as if an outer door opened.

"Someone's coming." I point and move Emily so that she's behind me. The sanctuary has cleared out. Someone must have gotten the doors open. But we need to get out, too, before the whole place comes down around us. Dad isn't the bluffing sort. I have no doubt the sanctuary is rigged to blow.

My father groans and gets to his feet. Noah keeps his gun trained on him as he inspects the blood on his sleeve.

I squeeze Emily's good hand. "We need to go. You're hurt."

"I'm okay," she says, but the shake in her voice tells me otherwise. "I need to find your mother." Her voice is flat. "I'm sorry, Adam, but I'm going to kill her."

"Just wait—"

"He's mine." Jez emerges from across the stage, an automatic rifle in her hands. A dozen other women trail behind her, some from the Chapel and a couple of Maidens.

"Eve." Emily tries to rise.

I help her, but once she's up, she stands tall.

My father takes a step toward me, his hands outstretched. "Son, you need to get me out of here. The Protectors set dynamite, and if we don't—"

"Shut up." Jez jerks the barrel of her gun at him. "Girls, tie him up and gag him."

Noah turns to me. "Adam?"

I shake my head. We won't interfere. He walks over to me, standing at my side.

Our father's face crumples, tears in his eyes. "Boys, please. I'm your father."

I thought I'd feel at least some sort of grief when my father met his end. But all I feel is... nothing. Not a goddamn thing. Even when he starts cursing us in a language that's been dead for centuries, nothing changes in me. There is no remorse or regret. Just the finality of judgment. His is here, and I'm merely a witness. I squeeze Emily's hand in mine. She's the only one who creates emotion inside me, who makes my heart beat. Only for her.

"No!" The Prophet struggles as the women from the Chapel surround him, two of them grabbing his arms while a Maiden rips a piece from her dress and uses it to bind his hands.

"You left her blood on your floor." Jez circles the Prophet, her dark green eyes like glass. "My love. Her blood. All over your filthy floor. How could you do that?"

He opens his mouth, but the other Maiden shoves a wad of fabric in, gagging him.

"She was so beautiful. Did you know she could sing?" Jez presses the tip of her gun under his chin. "Like a song-bird. That's why I kept birds at the Chapel. They reminded me of her. And they would sing only for *me*." Her voice is loud in the empty space, no speakers neces-sary to get her point across. "You took that song away. You took so much away from all of us. Now it's time for you to pay."

My father cranes his neck to look at us, his eyes implor-ing. But once again, it doesn't move me. I am resigned, and if I could get through to him, I'd tell him to resign himself to his fate.

"Take him." Jez shoves him back, and the women grab hold of him and hustle him off the stage.

Jez walks over to us, her back stiff, her steps sure. "Do any of you have a problem with this?"

"Make him suffer." Emily's voice is stark, but true.

Jez locks gazes with her, then gives a short nod. With one more glance at Noah and me, she turns and strides out after her quarry. When the door shuts, the sanctuary goes silent.

"Holy shit." Noah drops to his haunches and dry heaves.

"Your mother." Emily's eyes rove the empty church. "I have to find her."

I don't want her to find Rachel. Simply because I want to shield Emily from any more death. But she deserves her revenge, and I can't keep her from it.

"Come on." I take her elbow and lead her away.

We're almost to the stage door when it bursts open and Zion rushes in with half a dozen men at his back.

"FBI, don't fucking move!" Zion aims his gun at my face, and I shove Emily behind me.

"Davis?" I peer at the man behind Zion. It's the same FBI agent I beat the shit out of a few months ago, the one who'd tried to infiltrate the compound.

"Yeah, it's me, motherfucker. Now, get on the ground, hands on your heads!"

I fight past the surprise and focus on Emily. "She's hurt. The woman behind me. She's lost a lot of blood. Please help her." I drop to my knees, my hands on my head, and Noah does the same.

"Ma'am, I'm going to have to ask you to get on the ground." Davis lowers his gun as another agent rushes forward and cuffs me.

"Yes, I—" Her voice cuts off as she falls forward.

Zion rushes forward and catches her. "Medic!" He scoops her up in his arms, her eyes closed, her face pale.

"Help her," I choke out. Emotion closes my throat, and I know right then and there that I'd happily die to save her. "Please."

Zion carries her toward the door, then pauses. "Where's the dynamite?"

"What?" Davis cuffs Noah.

"I hid it here behind this fucking makeup stand. A satchel full of dynamite. Fuck!" He kicks the makeup table onto its side, the light bulbs shattering. "Search this entire goddamn place. Don't stop till you've found it!"

When he carries Emily out of my sight, I sag, the events taking their toll on my still-healing body.

"Please save her," I whisper and clench my eyes shut, sending my prayer to anyone who's listening.

CHAPTER 31

DELILAH

*Z*ion lays me on a stretcher, the ambulance lights flashing red through the thin skin of my eyelids.

"What happened to this one?" A woman's voice, husky and sweet.

"Not sure. Just fix her. She's a witness. The others have run off, so we need her." Zion's voice is already distant. Good. I need him to be gone.

I peek for a split second. A line of men are on their knees nearby, their hands cuffed behind their backs. I close my eyes quickly, but I suspect Zion has rounded up all the Protectors.

The medic grabs my wrist and turns my hand over so she can inspect my palm. "Damn, honey. Going to need a lot of stitches here." Her hands gently probe the rest of my body as more sirens—some distant, some ear-splittingly close—rip through the day. "Rest of this looks okay. Let's see the back. Tommy, come over here and lift so I can check her."

Rougher hands grip my sides, but ease me gingerly over.

"Shit, would you look at this?" Her warm fingers spread the fabric at my back. "Cut clean across."

My impatience grows with each comment, each touch. I need them to scatter so I can go. From what I could tell when Zion carried me out, I'm at the back of the church in the wide parking lot. From here, if I can get to the gate —which I'm certain at this point is no longer manned—I can take one of the Prophet's golf carts or cars and follow Rachel. I know where she's going. Her depravity only leads to one place.

"We need to go ahead and take her in." A man, his voice a little wheezy as if he's been running. "There are some other injuries from the stampede, a few people trampled, but she's the worst we've seen by far."

"Come on. Let's get her in and light it up."

They lay me back down, slide on some shoulder straps, and lift me into the ambulance. Once the doors close, I open my eyes.

A woman with dark skin and her hair in tidy braids reaches for a blood pressure sleeve as the engine starts. "You know, I've always heard horror stories about this place, but I didn't know they were true."

"Yeah." The man in the front's voice is hard to hear over the blare of the horn. "My cousin went here for a while until it got too weird for him. That's saying a lot, especially since he married my other cousin."

She laughs, and wraps the cuff around my arm, then presses the stethoscope against me. I close my eyes before she busts me.

Squoosh, squoosh, squoosh. The cuff tightens, and I try to plot where we are now. The ambulance seems to have turned toward the front of the church, away from where I need to go. I sneak a glance at the back windows and see the church's façade, which verifies my hunch. *Shit.*

"Look at this." The ambulance halts as the horn blares again.

"What?" The medic lets the air out with a hiss.

"Fire trucks got this side blocked."

"I think I saw another way back—"

"Yeah, I'll head that way." The ambulance turns.

"Elevated blood pressure, sweetheart. Not good."

You have no idea. I lie still as she moves around some more, the crinkle and ripping sounds of unwrapping equipment up by my head. My mind follows the map of the church. We're almost at the very back, the closest you can get to the gate without actually heading down that short stretch of pavement.

"Yeah, we're clear through here." The ambulance speeds up.

No. I give up my charade and slide out of the shoulder straps. The ambulance stops quickly.

"Get out of the way, you dumbass!" the driver yells and lays on the horn. I slide down the stretcher and reach for the door.

"Honey, no." The medic reaches for me, but I push the handle and scoot off onto the floor.

"Grant, hold up. She's awake and trying to—"

I jump out of the ambulance. It's farther down than I thought, and my knees buckle. I hit the ground and roll, scraping my legs on the cold pavement. The momentum dissipates, and I stop, climb to my feet, and run. The gate beckons, and no one is there to stop me. Everyone is still at the church—the faithful and law enforcement.

"Girl, come back!" The kind medic yells after me, but I've already ducked under the gate arm and am speeding down the smooth road to the Prophet's house. The cold air stings against my face, and the wound on my back burns with each step, but I can't stop. This is for Georgia. And it's long past time I get it done.

The house looms ahead of me, its stoic brick face watching my approach with trepidation. I pass to the side of it and turn around the back. My lungs scream at each intake of cold air, but my steps are light. I'm going in the right direction. I can feel it.

Three white golf carts are parked along the back of the house. I hurry to the first one and look at the ignition. No key. Same for the other two. *Shit!* I try to lift the seats to search for a hidden compartment, but there's nothing there.

It'll take me longer, but I'm not going to let this stop me. I turn on my heel and stride away toward the heart of the compound.

The basement door opens behind me, the click familiar. I whirl.

Hannah stops, then rushes out to me. "Oh my God!" She hugs me, her hands on my back wrenching a cry from me.

She gasps and pulls away. "Oh shit. You're hurt bad." She points to the church. "Ambulances are up there. I'll get you—"

"No." I lean on her proffered arm. "I have unfinished business."

She blinks, then her concern hardens into resolve, matching my own. "So do I."

"I have to get to the Cathedral, but I can't find keys. Do you know if—"

She holds out her open palm. A silver key shines in the sun. "I found it inside. Busted through a window and got in easy. Come on. I'll chauffeur."

I sit on the passenger seat and glimpse a tendril of smoke floating through a broken window farther down the back of the house. "You?" I ask.

She doesn't even look. Just puts the cart in reverse, then guides it down the hill. "We're going to burn it all down. Jez told us, and we're doing it. My part is done. Now it's time for the spoils." Her smile is bright as she floors it. I grab the side rail with my good hand and hold on as the wind howls past my ears.

"Did everyone get out?" I try to yank at my sleeve to make a wrap for my hand.

"As far as I know." She reaches over and grabs the sleeve, then pulls hard enough to rip it at the seams. "About half of the girls ran into the crowd, but the ones who wanted to stay are still here."

"Thanks." I take the sleeve and wrap it around my palm. "Still here? You mean the ones—"

"The ones who want justice. They're still here. I want justice, too. For Sarah. For me." She takes a hard turn past the Chapel, flames already licking along the roof line from the busted out windows.

We're all owed something from this place. Justice is really the only word for it.

"I can't believe it's over." She shakes her head. "The FBI are crawling all over the church. Protectors and Heavenly PD in cuffs. It's done."

"It can't come back from this." I peer behind me, as if the church will be lurching after us like a villain in a horror movie. Nothing is there but empty road and a winter sky.

"It can't." She reaches over and squeezes my knee. "We won't let it."

We go deeper into the compound, passing the Rectory. To my shame, the first thought of my mother crosses my mind since this whole ordeal started in the church.

My stomach sinks. "My mom. Wait. We have to get her. She's—"

"We freed everyone. Your mom, too. She's still whacked out from withdrawal, but they took her to the Cloister. We're going to regroup there, then light it up."

"Thank you." I push my guilt down. "Thank you for helping her."

She just shrugs and gives one more glance to the Rectory as we pass. "Some of the girls have gone to the back of the property where they're doing all that construction. Going to burn all that shit down, then bring the bulldozers up this way. Jez thought of everything." She laughs. "I didn't even know that woman existed until an hour-and-a-half ago, but now she's like, my guru."

"She's been hurt. Just like us." I can't tell her how badly Jez is injured, can't speak about Chastity. Not yet. But I know the loss I feel is even deeper in Jez. The love they had defied this place, overcame the hell of the Prophet.

"They started without us." Hannah turns onto the road leading to the punishment circle. A group of women form a barrier around the center of the ring, and I can guess who's in the middle.

The Prophet's scream is thick, as if he's gargling blood. She pulls up next to a row of cars and golf carts.

She hops off, but leaves the key in the ignition. "Let's go."

"I can't. I have another—"

"You can't miss this." She takes my hand and pulls me with her.

I don't have time for this, but I let her lead me to the edge. She lets go and dives into the fray, hugging one of the women from the Chapel. The crowd opens enough for me to see the Prophet. He's been stripped and staked to the ground, his legs spread. The gag is gone, and Jez twirls one of the Spinners' black batons in her hand.

"Oh, Prophet, where is your Father of Fire now?" She swings, nailing him in the knee.

He howls, his bloody face contorting in even more pain. The women raided the Cloister's training room. All of them hold whips, batons, floggers—and from the looks of the Prophet's body, they haven't been holding back.

He spits blood. "If you release me now, the Lord will forgive you for—"

One of the Chapel women aims a kick to his side. He screeches, and she kneels down next to him. "Remember when you told me that I was a good girl if I didn't cry?" She pulls her shirt down to show scars along the tops of her breasts, as if someone cut her with a straight blade. "I remember every time you cut me. Every time you raped me. Every time you told me I was a good girl."

The women chant "punish him." I join in, the power flowing through all of us, connecting us in a sisterhood of vengeance.

She pulls a knife from her pocket and flips it open. "Now be a good boy for me." Dragging the blade across his chest, she leaves a deep crimson line.

Another woman kneels next to him, a gruesome story of torture and rape falling from her lips as she wraps a whip around her fist.

"No, please—"

"This is my perfect obedience." She punches him hard in the face, his lip splitting again and blood spurting from his nose.

I back away. Because I have somewhere to be... And also because I'm enjoying this so much it scares me.

"Emily," Jez points at me. "You're up."

The women whoop and I'm jostled forward, wincing against the pain in my back and hand.

I should go. They're handling what needs to be done. But I don't go. I can't. My soul breaks a little more when I accept that I have to do this, that the darkness the Prophet has created inside me means that I *need* this. To end some part of my own torment, I have to cause him pain. And what's worse, I want to.

I kneel down, looking at the man who seemed so large, so powerful. But he's neither of those things. He's only a man, stripped bare, and staring over the precipice at his death.

Looking him in the eye, I take a breath. "Remember when you told me I was a whore who ruined your son?" The words come easy from my lips as he shivers on the cold ground. I hold my hand out, waiting for someone to give me a weapon. Any will do. The hilt of a knife slides into my palm.

"Delilah, Adam wouldn't want you to—"

"Shh." I shake my head. "Remember my friend Sarah? You do. She was kind and strong, two things you hate. So you made your son cut her throat. I remember. You do, too." I start over his heart, carving an 's' as he screams and thrashes his head. Carving flesh is easy, far easier than I thought. The rest of Sarah's name materializes in blood, and I sit back. "You remember her now?"

"Yes!" he yells. "I remember. Please don't—"

"You hurt her, killed her, and did so much more. I'm sure you remember all of it. What you did to me, my friends, Adam, my mother, my sister." I stand and walk between his spread legs.

His eyes go even wider, the right one blotchy with blood. "D-Delilah."

"You named me well, did you know?"

The women around me start chanting "punish him," their voices low and strong.

"Deli—"

"In the Bible, Delilah takes Samson's strength, but God gives it back to him, and with it, he's able to destroy his enemies." I line up, my right foot back. "Our story is like that, but even better. I brought Adam to his knees, and *together*, we rose up and defeated you. All of us tore down your temple."

"No!" he screams as I rear back and kick him right between his legs.

The women around me yell with glee and pent-up fury. We are his fate, his justice. We are revenge for all those who have come before.

His chest convulses as he cries. I hope he drowns on his tears, drowns from the sorrows he's forced on so many others.

"That's nothing." Jez smiles down at him. "When they've all had their fill, I'm going to cut off that pathetic thing between your legs and shove it down your throat."

More raucous yells pierce the day as I back away. Jez gives me a quick nod as I turn and hurry to the golf cart.

My heart beats easier, my terrifying need for retribution temporarily sated.

Flooring the pedal, I race away and hope I'm not too late.

CHAPTER 32

DELILAH

I skid to a halt in front of the Cathedral. No guard on the front door, but the place seems locked up tight. I don't let relief in. Not yet. Not until I see the children and know they're safe.

Stepping off the golf cart, I hurry to the large double doors. They don't budge. Skirting around to the side, I try to find a window, but they're all high off the ground and barred. I suppose the Prophet wanted privacy for his personal harem.

A faint scream filters through the woods. I shiver. It's the Prophet. He's suffering. And I don't give a damn. I walk along the front, then turn the corner of the large building. A small lawn separates it from the woods all around. My steps are silent on the dormant grass. Up ahead, there's a door and small walkway that leads to a paved area with a dumpster.

I check the door. Locked. But there's a black button next to it that has to be a bell. Do I ring it? I scan down the long expanse of the stark building. I have to be midway along, likely at the kitchen. If anyone is inside, it would likely be a Spinner or a child. If it's a guard, I'm screwed. If it's Rachel... I'll deal with that.

Steeling myself, I press the button tentatively. After a few seconds, I remind myself that there are dozens of innocent children inside—children that Rachel wants to destroy. So I lay on the bell harder, pressing for a full minute before letting go. No one comes. I'll have to find another way in.

Returning to the grass, I move away from the kitchen entrance, but a squeak cuts through the quiet. The door is cracked open, a little boy of no more than five doing his best to keep the heavy metal panel from closing again.

I dash back and push it all the way open, ease in, then close it behind me. We're in a tiled kitchen, everything stainless steel and industrial, the scent of harsh dish soap and lingering onion on the air. I pull him behind a prep table and drop to my knees.

"Don't be scared. I won't hurt you." I put my fingers to my lips for a moment, then whisper, "Are you okay?"

He shakes his head, his dark eyes so like Adam's. "Mommy isn't here."

"Is someone else here?"

He nods. "A woman. The one with the sticks."

"Sticks?"

"*Dynamite,*" my mind chimes in.

"She told us all to stay in our rooms and that our mommies would be here soon. But I heard..." He looks back at the door and the bell above it. "Am I in trouble?" His eyes water.

"No." I pull him to me, wrapping his small frame in my arms. "You did good. So good! What's your name, sweetheart?"

"Ezekiel." He sniffs.

I know him. He's Ruth's son. God, I hope she made it out of the Prophet's house. Pulling him back to face me, I say, "I need you to do something for me, okay?"

"Okay."

"I'm going to open the door again. You run out to the woods and hide, okay? Don't come out until you see someone in a police uniform."

"Police?" He cocks his head.

I forget how stunted these children are, how sheltered. "Like the ones at the church who stand along the aisles. Blue uniforms and badges." I tap my chest, then reconsider. "But not them." I shake my head, because I know I'm confusing him, so I try something else. "Do you know your letters?"

303

He nods, a smile dawning on his face for the first time, his two top teeth missing. "Yes, I'm learning how to read. First one in my class."

"Good." I grab his arm. "That's great. When you see someone wearing a vest with the letters 'FBI' on it, you can come out. Or if they say 'FBI' then you can come out. It's like hide and seek, you know?"

"I'm the best at hide and seek." His smile grows bigger.

"I know you are." I turn him around and lead him to the door. "One more thing. I'll be sending more children out this door, okay? Make sure they hide with you. Like a big game. And none of you come out until the police arrive. FBI."

"F-B-I."

"That's right, Ezekiel. You got it. Go on, now, and watch for the other kids." I shoo him out the door and he runs over the grass and into the woods, then disappears behind a tree.

CHAPTER 33

ADAM

*Z*ion yanks me up and walks me to the outside of the church. Davis hustles Noah out behind me. Protectors and guards are lined up against the wall, all of them cuffed, all of them scowling. Church members stand next to their cars or sit inside them with the engines running, warming their children. No one has been allowed to leave.

I limp alongside Zion who shoves me into a black SUV. Davis does the same with Noah on the other side. They get into the front, and Davis grabs the radio handset off the dash.

"Once the wagon gets here for the assholes in cuffs, I want everyone to form up on the front entrance. Our warrant is good for the whole compound, but we need to be careful not to destroy any evidence. A controlled sweep." He replaces the radio and turns around to look at me. "It's all going down, fellas. Your little empire is crumbling."

Noah tries to pull his cuffed hands around to his side. "There are women and children inside. You know that, right? If your men go in guns blazing—"

"We know how to handle ourselves." Zion shoots him a nasty glare.

"All I've ever seen you do is kick a man while he's down and assault Maidens." Noah shrugs. "But what do I know?"

Zion slaps the metal cage that separates us. "I've been undercover in this fucking pit for years, asshole. Shut your fucking mouth."

"Oh, but I think you enjoyed it." Noah grins.

"Motherfucker, I'll—"

"Keep it cool," Davis intercedes.

"Where's Emily?" I keep my hands behind my back and pick at the stitches on my right palm.

"On her way to the hospital by now." Davis points to the modified bus approaching on the main road. "Paddy wagon is almost here."

"Agent Davis?" A voice comes through the radio.

He picks it up. "Speaking."

"We've got a problem, sir. The woman escaped from the ambulance and ran onto the property."

My heart leaps. Emily's run back to the compound. I pick harder at the stitches, gratified when the blood starts to ooze. I pull my hands as far around as possible, trying to get the blood to my wrists.

"The woman?" Davis slams his fist on the dash. "You mean our star fucking witness?" He starts the engine and pops the nearest curb, riding over landscaping toward the ambulance near the front gate of the restricted compound area. A paramedic stands outside the back doors and stares at the road leading to the Prophet's house.

Davis parks next to the ambulance and hops out, slamming his door behind him.

"You boys better get yourselves ready." Zion opens his door. "Because federal prison won't be a picnic for assholes like you." Another slam and Noah and I are alone.

"What's the plan?" He rattles his cuffs.

"Emily's gone to find Mom. We need to find her first."

"Mom?" He clears his throat. "What are we going to do when we find her?"

"I can't let Emily kill her. The guilt will eventually crush her. Maybe not today or tomorrow, but it'll come crashing down one day." I bow my back and bring my injured foot up to the bench seat. With a contortionist move, I slide my cuffed hands around my foot and up my leg.

"I can do that." Noah scoffs and pulls his leg up to the seat. His foot slides off when he tries to slide his hands beneath it.

"Yeah, good going." I bend my good leg and slide the cuffs around it. With my hands in front of me, I'm able to hold them up and pick more at the stitches. Every moment that passes is another moment Emily is in danger. I harbor no illusions that Mom won't kill her if she gets the chance. She's too far gone, too mired in the lies and delusions of Heavenly.

"The fuck are you doing?" He tries again and gets stuck with the cuffs wedged under his foot.

"What am I doing?" I shoot him a wry look. "If you can get your shit together, *we're* escaping."

"I got this." He arches and shakes the entire SUV with his efforts as I use my fingertip to spread blood along my wrist and the back of my hand.

With a grunt, he gets the cuffs looped over one leg. "Easy, see?"

"Do the second leg and get back to me."

The whine of a firetruck starts up, and I peer out the window toward the compound. Smoke rises from the Prophet's house, the dark tendrils blowing away in the cold breeze. The fire's just started.

Noah finally gets his hands in front of him, his red, sweaty face smiling. "Like I said, easy."

"Sure." I hold my hands out to him and jerk my chin at the wrist covered in blood. "Grab the cuff and pull."

CHAPTER 34

DELILAH

Once Ezekiel's disappeared into the trees, I snag the little brown plastic wedge from behind the door and shove it under the bottom, leaving it wide open. The door stays put, and I pull on it a little to make sure. It's stuck.

Creeping through the dark kitchen, I pass the wide stovetop and another prep table. The white tiles are quiet underfoot, and I open the door to the dining room. It only creaks a little, but it's loud in the still air. Nothing happens, so I pull it the rest of the way open and walk into the dining room. The lights are off, the high windows illuminating just enough for me to make my way through the tables and into the main hall.

A guard lies next to the doors leading to the children's rooms, his head a bloody mess, a splatter of crimson on the wall. I skirt around him and push through to the children's hall. Rachel isn't here, the rooms dark. A baby cries in the nursery, so I walk to the next set of double doors and open one just a hair.

Rachel stands in the center of the hall and pulls sticks of dynamite from the black satchel, lining them up and twisting their fuses together.

"Shut that baby up or I'll kill it right now!" she yells at someone I can't see.

I duck back in the door and close it quietly.

The children's rooms are silent, and I hope it's because they're gone. I go to the first room on my right and open it. Two little girls huddle between twin beds, their arms around each other, their eyes wide.

"Don't be scared." I drop to my haunches. "I'm Emily. We're going to play a game."

"But the mean lady said to stay here and don't move." The older girl's voice trembles.

"We don't listen to her. Come on with me." I hold my hand out.

The older girl eyes me warily, but the younger breaks free of their embrace and toddles over. She has blonde curls and deep brown eyes.

"Hello," she murmurs shyly and takes my hand.

When the older girl sees that nothing bad happens, she comes over, too.

"What's your name, sweetheart?"

"Nazareth."

"What a pretty name."

She blushes.

"Nazareth, can you take your friend to the kitchen for me? We're playing a little game. Ezekiel is hiding in the trees outside the kitchen door. I'm going to come try and find him in a little while. Would you like to play, too?"

Nazareth nods.

"Great. All you have to do is head out that kitchen door and hide with Ezekiel, okay? Can you do that?"

She takes the smaller girl's hand. "We'll hide, and then you come get us?"

"That's the plan." I smile.

"Okay."

I open their door and peek down the hall. It's clear, so I lead them out and into the main area, doing my best to put myself between them and the guard's body. Once they're through the dining room, I head back to the children's wing and go to the next room.

It's darker in here, the windows along the roofline not giving enough light to see.

I shut the door behind me. "Hello?" I scoot around the little bed toward the darkest corner of the room. "I'm not going to hurt you. I promise. Just come out."

"I can't make that same promise." Grace's voice stops me, and she rushes at me from the shadows, the Prophet's curved blade in her hand.

I leap backward, but the blade catches me on the arm and slices through my dress, leaving a shallow cut.

She lurches out, her face in shadow, the side of her dress dark with blood. "You're going to die here."

I dodge back as she swings again, but she seems to have used all her momentum on the first strike.

She staggers closer, one bloody hand at her side. "You ruined everything. Everything! You took him away," Her voice breaks on a sob. "He was supposed to be mine. All this was supposed to be *mine*. Not yours."

And, in her own mind, I think she's the hero of her tale. The put-upon woman who loved a man despite all else, who sacrificed everything just to be with him. As sick and twisted as it is, I remind myself that to her, she's a victim —of the Prophet, of Adam, of me.

But understanding isn't the same as sympathy.

I unwrap the binding on my hand enough to pull out the knife I stashed there after I used it on the Prophet. "Drop it, Grace. If you stop this now, you could live. You could be someone else."

Tears roll down her face, her eyes sparkling. "There is no one else but me. Just me. Weak, stupid Jenny who joined the Cloister and thought the Prophet was chosen by God. Dumb Jenny who followed every rule, did everything asked of her, but fell in love with the one man she shouldn't have. Jenny didn't deserve to live. She was a stupid bitch like all the other Maidens. So I killed Jenny." She thumps her chest with her palm. "She's dead in here. I don't want to be anyone but Grace. Grace is strong, smart. She fights for what she wants. She is no one's victim." Her back straightens for only a moment before she gasps and grabs at her side. "But you took all that from me."

I press my back into the corner as she shuffles closer. "Grace, listen to me. You can leave here. Start new. This is your chance. Forget about me. Forget about Adam." Even as I say the words, I know they're fruitless. She's destroyed herself—Jenny or Grace or whoever she is— there's nothing left.

She sways and holds the knife out as she approaches. "I won't let you have him. I can't."

"I'm sorry."

"Sorry?" She cocks her head to the side. "Sorry for being the thieving cunt who stole my man?"

"No." I take a deep breath. "Sorry for this." I propel myself off the wall and stab the knife deep into her chest.

Her eyes open wide, surprise turning her face into a caricature as she falls backward onto the child-sized bed. I follow her down, keeping the knife embedded.

She sputters and drops the curved blade to the floor with a clatter. "You—" A blood bubble pops on her lips.

Sorrow is a funny thing. You can feel it so deeply for someone you love, as if their tears are your own. But you can feel it for others, too. Your vilest enemy. I look down at her and remember my mother saying that the opposite of love isn't hate. It's indifference. That's one emotion I've never had toward Grace. I've hated her with the strength of a bursting star. Because she's horrible and cruel, and also because... under the right circumstances, I could have been her.

"I'm sorry," I whisper, my eyes surprisingly wet.

She grips my knife hand with her bloody one, her eyes closing. Her breath surges. "Hate you." With one more gasp, she stops moving, her chest going completely still.

I wait, but she never breathes again, and I know she's gone.

Smoothing her hair back, I kiss her forehead. "Burn in hell, bitch."

I hesitate over leaving the knife in her chest, but in the end I do and grab the curved one from the floor instead. Turning it over in my hands, I wonder if it's the one that took Georgia's life. The thought sends a rush of white hot anger through me. Grace is all paid up. Now it's Rachel's turn.

Easing from the door, I hurry to the room across the hall and round up the children in there. Taking them with me, I go room to room. The other kids are more accepting of my plan when they see their brothers and sisters in tow. Once they're rounded up, I send them all to the kitchen, herding them like precious lambs—hopefully not to slaughter. They run to the woods and hide. Ezekiel peeks out from behind his tree with a shy smile, and I give him a thumbs up.

It's time. I'm lucky Rachel hasn't finished her work yet. I race back down the hall and open the door to the nursery again. The stack of dynamite sits in the center of the hall, several of the sticks joined at the fuses. With no Rachel in sight, I push through the doors and hurry in. A baby hiccups and another cries. All of their cribs are placed in a half circle around the dynamite.

A Spinner lies dead in the corner, her throat slashed.

I grab the closest cribs and roll them back toward the children's area.

"I don't think so." Rachel bursts through the doors from the wives' dormitory area, a pistol in her hand. She fires a shot, and I have no choice but to backpedal through the double doors. Staying would risk the babies from either gunfire or explosion. She fires another shot that splinters the wood as I fall backward.

But I don't hit the ground. Someone grabs me and pulls me to the floor.

"Where do you think you're going, little lamb?"

CHAPTER 35

ADAM

*E*mily is finally in my arms where she belongs. Another bullet flies through the doors ahead of us.

"Who'd you piss off?" I pull her to the side, and we crawl through one of the side doors into a child's room.

She faces me and grips my shirt. "Your mom."

"I figured as much." I take her face in my mangled hands and kiss her.

She clutches me close, her mouth opening for me. I take and take as more shots reverberate through the hall. Pulling away, she says, "The babies are still in there. We have to—"

I kiss her again, unable to help myself, needing to feel her alive and warm.

When she melts for me, her body going lax, her breaths mingling with mine, I relinquish her mouth, but keep my hold on her.

"She's got a stack of dynamite." Her tongue darts out to her bruised lips, and it takes all I have to keep from claiming her mouth again. "She'll blow it any second and kill all of them. And us."

"Stay here." I stand and limp into the doorway. "She's my mom. Maybe she'll listen to me."

"Nothing's changed." She tightens the binding on her wounded hand. "I'm going to kill her."

I sigh. "I know." I shut her door and plaster myself against the wall. "Mom!" I call.

"Adam?" Her voice comes back, precariously close to the double doors. She must have been about to burst through, gun blazing.

"It's me. What are you doing?"

She opens the door with the barrel of her gun and peeks at me, then smiles. "It really is you. Good. You can help." A baby cries behind her, its wail high and piercing. She walks through the doors and lets them close.

"Help with?"

"I've got the dynamite set, but I can't figure out how to light it without being too close. I was trying to get some of the sheets off the whores' beds to use as a longer fuse, but then that—" She gestures down the hall with her gun. "Devil of a girl showed up." She walks to the nearest door and opens it. "She let them go. The children." Walking farther down, she opens another and gasps. I move up behind her, readying to take her down, when I see Grace lying inside, eyes closed, not moving. The knife in her chest is final.

"And she did this, too!" Mom slams the door and whirls on me. "Killed my Grace. Left her lying here like a piece of roadside trash. That whore you fucked is ruining everything! Where is she?" Her gun hasn't dropped, the barrel pointed at me the entire time. She's cagey.

"She doesn't matter. This is between us. What you're doing here, you—"

"She's still here, isn't she?" Her beady eyes dart to the dark doors on the left and right. "You're covering for her." She takes a step toward the nearest room, but breaking glass pulls her attention back to the wives' dormitory. "What was that?"

"I don't know." I gently take her elbow and turn her back around to me. "Mom, you can't kill these children. Let's get out of here and—"

"These bastards need to die. They're a threat to us, Adam." She adopts an imminently sensible tone. "Children grow up, then one day they'll all be challenging you for the throne. We can't have that." She pats my cheek.

A door opens slowly behind Mom, Emily's bloody white dress coming into view a few centimeters at a time.

Fuck.

"Let's just go." I put one hand on her shoulder and stare into her eyes, the ones that are still as sharp as they always were, even if I know in my heart they're clouded with madness. "The state will come in and take all of them. Put them in adoptive homes. They won't even know where they came from."

The door opens farther, and Emily steps through, the blade of sacrifice in her hand.

"They'll know. There's DNA and all sorts of devilry now. They'll find out. Besides, they need to be punished. Bastard children are filthy, unclean abominations. They have no place here."

Emily slinks closer, a cat stalking its prey. I can't let her do this to herself, and I hate to admit that some small part of me—the little boy that I used to be—wants to warn my mom, to save her. But she's long past that. No one can save her. And she needs to answer for Georgia's death.

There's no move I can make. "I know, Mom, and I agree. But you don't want blood on your hands. Living with it will break you." I'm not talking to my mother anymore. I'm talking to Emily, but I don't dare look at her.

My mom scoffs, her face contorting into the ugliness that now lives inside her. "You're weak. Just like your father."

She lifts the barrel higher and points it at my chest. "I was foolish to think you could ever be Prophet. You're too soft. You want to spare the bastard children that will one day destroy you. Idiot!" She presses the gun over my heart as the double doors from the dormitory open silently.

Noah creeps in, but Emily is blocking him. He raises a pistol and aims at Mom over Emily's shoulder.

Sirens blare, the sound growing louder by the second.

"I don't have time for this, Adam." She backs away from me. "I have one more son. He's even dumber than you, but he can be guided. He'll be the Prophet, but if he fails me, too, I'll find another. Blood doesn't mean as much as it used to." She puts her other hand on the gun, steadying it.

Emily is almost to her, the knife raised.

I break and look at her, then give a subtle shake of my head.

Mom squints. "What are you—"

"Emily, down!" I yell and drop at the same time.

The sound of gunfire deafens me, and scorching pain rips along my neck. I reach up to touch it, but my hand comes away wet.

I look over to see Mom lying on the ground, her eyes open, her mouth working silently, and a pool of blood spreading beneath her.

"Adam!" Emily runs to me and lifts my head into her lap. Her hand joins mine, pressing against the wound.

"Is he—" Noah drops next to me and his face blanches. "Oh fuck, she got him in the neck."

"That bad?" I try to say, but no sound comes out, and the ache in my throat intensifies.

"Don't try to talk." His words are warm, despite the starkness in his eyes. "I'm going to get help." Rising, he rushes out of the hall.

"It's going to be okay." Emily stares down at me and tries to smile despite the tears in her eyes. "You'll be just fine."

I love you. I can't say it, but I hope she can hear me anyway. *I will always love you.* I blink, but can't seem to open my eyes again. *You saved me.* I want to thank her, to throw myself on her mercy, to give her everything I am. But I can't form the words.

They fly away in my mind like a murder of crows scattering ahead of a harsh wind.

Somewhere, a baby cries. And then I'm gone too, blowing up into the darkening sky like a single black feather.

CHAPTER 36

EMILY

*N*oah pulls a flask from his pocket and turns it up. Frowning, he pulls it away from his face and holds it upside down. Not a single drop flows.

"Fuck." He stuffs it back into his pocket.

I reach out to him. He takes my good hand in his as the doctor stitches up the other one.

"Think he's out yet?" His palm is clammy.

Mine is too. "They would have said, right?" I look at the doorway leading into the bright white hallway. A nurse in light pink scrubs walks by.

"Right. They would have said." He nods but stares out the door all the same.

The scent of rubbing alcohol stings my nose as the doctor wipes down another part of my hand. "Can you feel this?" she asks.

I don't look. "I didn't feel anything, if you did anything."

"I pinched you, so we're good. I've got about a dozen more stitches to go, and then I'll start on your back."

She already put some sort of antiseptic compresses across my shoulder blades, but the stitches are next.

I stare out the door and spare a thought for my mother. She's sedated a few rooms away. The withdrawal wreaked havoc on her body, and they haven't assessed all the damage yet.

But I can't think about her for too long. Not when my heart is in an operating room three floors down.

"He's going to make it, right?" Noah taps his foot on the polished white tile, and scoots his gray hospital chair a little closer to my bed.

"He will. He's strong." I wince as a flash of pain shoots up my arm.

"She needs more pain stuff." Noah jerks his chin at the doctor.

"Thanks."

"No problem." He squeezes my hand and rests his head against the bed rail. "I fucked up. If I'd been quicker, he—"

"You killed your own mother to save him. To save me." I squeeze back. "There's nothing more you could have done. And I will *never* stop being grateful to you."

He shrugs. "I sort of... I don't know. It's like it wasn't me pulling the trigger. I had to do it. So I just... did."

"I'm sorry." I can't imagine what it took for him to put her down.

"Don't be." He sits up. "She killed Georgia. She was my mother, but Georgia was..."

"I know." I meet his sad eyes. "She was my everything, too."

A knock at the door pulls my attention away. Zion strides in. My stomach heaves when I recognize him, and Noah's grip on my hand tightens.

He walks up to my bedside, his FBI badge clipped to his waistband. "Emily." Turning to Noah, he says, "I'd prefer to speak to Miss Lanier alone."

I don't let go of Noah's hand. "He can stay."

"I'd prefer—"

"She said I can stay." Noah scoots even closer, as if he's guarding my side.

"Once you're done with your medical care, I'd like to get your statement."

I stare at him, trying to square the officer standing before me with the horrors he committed on the Prophet's orders.

"Do you think you'd be up to that?"

"Are you giving a statement, too?" I can't keep the note of challenge from my voice.

"Yes." He pulls up a chair.

"I didn't say you could sit."

Noah snorts.

Zion pushes the chair back and sighs. "I'm not the enemy here."

"You look like him, talk like him. You *are* him." I shake my head.

"I was undercover, Miss Lanier. Trying to bring down the entire organization from root to leaf."

"Are you going to tell everyone what you did? How you beat Noah and kicked him while you let Sarah bleed out? About how you did whatever the Prophet told you? About how you treated your Maiden?"

He puts his hands on his hips. "I did what I had to do."

"But yet you didn't bring it down. We did." I lift Noah's hand clasped with mine. "*We* brought it down."

"Charges are still pending against all guilty parties." His eyes flick to Noah.

"You can't be serious." I glare at him. "Noah killed his own mother to save a room full of infants!"

"She needs to stay calm." The doctor puts down her needle and removes her glasses with the sternness of an iron-willed schoolteacher. "Her system is too taxed right now. I've already ordered an IV for fluids. She's dehydrated, half starved, and she's lost blood."

"I understand, ma'am." He's apologetic.

It's a shock to see him defer to a woman. And that alone tells me that the doctor's right. My system is taxed, and I'm suffering from my time at Heavenly on all levels.

I lift my gaze to his again. "I'm not talking to you or anyone until I know that Adam and Noah aren't in any trouble."

"I can't promise—"

"I wasn't finished." I continue, "I want Jez and all the women who were on that compound given immunity, too. They didn't do anything wrong."

Zion clears his throat. "What you did with Grace—classic case of self-defense. But, well, those women tortured a man to death. Killed him by cutting off his..." He clears his throat again. "And ramming it down his throat until he choked on it. Not to mention what they shoved up his..." He swallows hard.

"They didn't kill a man. The Prophet was a monster! A serial rapist, abuser, murderer—you fucking name it. Don't you dare try to tell me what they did was wrong." My throat constricts with unshed tears. "Adam is in surgery. We don't know if he's going to live. And you have the nerve to come in here and tell me what you *prefer* I do and what you want from me." I lean forward, needing to lash out, to hurt this creep who now acts like he's some sort of savior. "Unless I know all my friends are safe, you can take your statement and shove it up your ass, you sick fuck!"

"Sir, I'm going to have to ask you to leave." The doctor puts down her needle again and stands. "She can't handle this kind of stress."

Zion backs up a few steps. "I'm going." He turns to Noah. "But I'd like a word, if I may, out in the hall." He walks out, but I can feel him hovering just outside the door.

"You don't have to talk to him." I take a deep breath and lean back, the stinging along my back subsiding.

"I know." He squeezes my hand, then lets go. "But I might as well see what he wants. Don't worry, I think he knows where we stand." He almost smiles. "Actually, I think the folks at the other end of the hospital know, too."

I would shrug, but it hurts too much.

"I'll be back." He follows Zion, and I'm left with the doctor who returns to her work.

I peer at my good hand, dark brown blood crusted beneath the nails. Is it mine? Grace's? Adam's?

"All done with the hand." The doctor pulls her steel tray away from the bed. "Go ahead and get on your stomach for me. I'll close your back."

She helps me turn in the bed and lie down, the back of my hospital gown open. "The cut on your arm will be fine without stitches, but you need to know it will scar."

"That's okay," I murmur. "I have a lot of those."

The room is dark when I wake, and for a moment, I'm back at the Cloister. Lying on my stomach, waiting for the next atrocity to happen to me or my friends.

"Adam?" I call out to the dark.

"It's me." Noah smooths my hair off my forehead. "Adam's awake. I came to get you."

"He is?" I try to sit up, but my back pulls, the stitches burning.

"Stay put." He gently presses on my shoulder. "They've got you hooked up to an IV and some other stuff."

"I fell asleep."

"I know. The doctor said you were exhausted."

"He's alive?" I seize on the fact that matters most.

Noah nods and sits next to me. "He's a tough bastard. Going to pull through. They gave him a lot of blood and repaired the damage in his neck."

"I have to see him." I try to push myself up.

"You can't."

"Noah, I am going to see him or I will scream this place down."

"Jeez." He stands. "Okay. Hang on. Just stay put and maybe I can wheel you to his room."

I collapse down to the bed, the ache in my back almost unbearable. "Yes."

He tinkers with the IV and gets it attached to the bed, then toggles the wheels. "I think this makes it go."

The bed glides across the floor, the tires whining a little as he turns me and pushes me into the hall.

He looks both ways. "If I get busted—"

"Don't be a ninny."

He laughs in the quiet corridor and picks up speed toward the elevators. After we get in and the doors close, he says softly, "You remind me of her sometimes, you know? She was brave like you."

"Georgia was a lot braver. The first kid in our neighborhood to use the diving board at Sissy Lee's house, the only girl who would play tackle football with the boys— she wasn't afraid of anything."

"She was still like that. The whole time she was with me. I wish..." His voice fades, and the elevator dings on the second floor.

"I know. I wish a lot, too."

He pushes me into the hallway. This floor is busier, and a few of the nurses raise a brow as he wheels me past, but they don't interfere.

The rooms are different, glass walls and more beeping machines. "Is this intensive care?"

"Yeah, post-op something or other. I'm pretty sure we aren't supposed to be here."

"Play it cool."

"I'm trying."

"Hey, what did Zion want?" I fell asleep before I could grill Noah.

"Nothing good. He thinks that Heavenly needs someone to transition. There are too many members who could be a danger. He wants to set something up so that I—"

"Am the new Prophet?" My skin goes cold.

"God, no. Just a preacher. Someone the people are familiar with. I'm supposed to defuse the whole situation, fill the power vacuum to prevent anyone else from trying to take my father's place and get things going again."

"What do you get in return?"

"Freedom. For me and Adam. And for the women."

I don't trust any deal offered by Zion, but if it keeps Adam and Noah out of prison, maybe it could work. "What are you going to do?"

"I'm going to think about it. He wants me to preach this coming Sunday. I don't know if I can."

"We'll talk about it. Once Adam is better."

"Yeah." He wheels me slowly toward the end of the hall, then stops in front of one of the rooms. "Hang on. Let me make sure he's decent."

That gets a real laugh out of me.

He disappears into the room with even more beeping machines than the others. "Emily is here to... what does that motion even mean... okay, I know what *that* motion means, and it's uncalled for, man. I'm bringing her. Hang on."

The sound of a chair scraping along the floor grates across my impatient nerves. Adam is only feet away. I need to see him, feel him, assure myself that he's going to be all right.

Noah finally emerges from the room and wheels me in head first. I roll over onto my side as Adam comes into view.

His face is swollen and white gauze is packed around the right side of his throat. He attempts a smile but it dies quickly.

"He can't talk yet." Noah scoots my bed until it clangs against Adam's.

He reaches for me. I leverage myself over despite the pain in my back and hand.

"Hang on. Give me a minute, you two!" Noah moves around behind me and lifts me until I'm right beside Adam.

I put my hand to his stubbled cheek and brush my lips across his. "I love you."

He grips my waist, love showing in his eyes as he stares at me as if there's nothing else in the world.

"I guess, um. I'll just... Yeah, I'm gone." Noah leaves and pulls the flimsy curtain to hide us from the rest of the ward.

"You're going to be okay." I kiss the tip of his nose.

He gently grabs my wrist and squeezes, then glances down my body and arches an eyebrow.

"I'm going to be fine. Don't worry. The hand will heal, and so will my back." I drop my gaze. "But I'll have scars."

He tilts my chin up until our eyes lock, then smiles a little and shakes his head.

"Oh, you don't care?"

He shakes his head again, then holds out his bandaged hands and wrinkles his nose.

"I guess you're scarred too, huh?"

He nods.

"And at least I have all my toes, right?"

He makes a low growly noise and pulls me tight to him, his hand easing beneath the hospital gown and caressing my hip. Goosebumps rise all over me, and I rest my head on his chest.

"I love you," I whisper again.

He squeezes my hip and kisses my forehead, his warm lips a balm on my heart.

His throat clicks, his body tensing with effort. "Never let you go, little lamb." The words are barely a rough whisper, but they send a tingle through me all the same.

I smile against his chest, safe in his arms, forever in his heart.

EPILOGUE

EMILY

*A*dam holds my hand tightly in his as we sit outside the church in a black limo, the back windows hiding us from the churchgoers brave enough to come back for this Sunday's service. Plainclothes officers stand in front of the main doors, and plenty are scattered throughout the sanctuary. But I don't feel safe here. I don't think I ever will.

Noah pulls his flask out, drains some of it, then offers it to Adam and me. We both shake our heads.

"I've been meaning to talk to you about that." Adam's voice is still coarse, as if there's glass in his throat. But the doctors say he'll heal. But, like me, there will be scars.

"Yeah, well, keep on meaning to, because today is not the day I stop drinking." He looks out the window and tugs at his collar. "Did I really have to wear a tie?"

"You're the preacher. You kind of have to. Besides, you both look so handsome." I try to force a smile.

Noah grimaces.

Adam grips my hand a little tighter.

"You know the plan. It's all been loaded onto the teleprompter. Easy." Zion is our driver for the day, though my mistrust still sends alarm bells ringing whenever I'm around him. "Just get it done, and the immunity is set. And, if you choose to stay on—"

"No." Noah shakes his head.

Zion straightens his sunglasses. "The federal government isn't in the habit of telling religious institutions how to conduct their business, but if you could just think about staying on for a little while longer, until things settle, that would—"

"He said no." I glare at Zion in the rearview mirror.

He nods and finally shuts his mouth.

Adam leans over and whispers in my ear, "You look beautiful."

He's only told me three times so far today, and I blush each time. He and Noah are wearing conservative suits, but Adam threw a growly fit when I tried to choose a simple navy blue dress for today.

"You can wear any color under the sun. No hiding. Shine like you're supposed to." His eyes light and send heat

338

rushing through me. I want to feel him so badly, but he still hasn't recovered enough for us to make love. We'll be there soon.

"Emily?" Noah's opened the car door and holds his hand out for me.

"I got it." Adam opens the door on his side and helps me up.

"Dick." Noah smirks over the roof of the car.

Adam wraps a protective arm around me as Zion and Davis walk us into the church. A host of media has set up on the grass to the right of the entrance, their cameras clicking and video rolling. A few journalists shout questions about the "atrocities" and "legacy of the Monroe family," but we keep our heads down and rush inside the church.

Zion, his sunglasses still on, leads us back into the hallway of classrooms and to the stage door. When he opens it, so much rushes back to me that I have to stop.

"It's okay." Adam pulls me in tight to his side. "If you can't do this, no one will blame you."

I take a deep breath and shake the ghosts away. They aren't here. No Prophet, no Rachel, no Grace. There's only a stage—wood floor, concrete walls, wide open space. I climb the stairs and look out toward the open where the stage lights shine brightest. No Maidens kneel along the front row, no children wearing white, no Heavenly PD officers. Only more plainclothes FBI agents directing people to their seats and standing across the way in the other wing.

"You're safe. I've got guys all over this place. No one is coming at you. And everyone was searched upon entry." Zion stands with his hands behind his back. Likely his best attempt at being reassuring—but it falls flat. I'll never see him as anything other than a Protector.

Adam turns me away from Zion, both of us facing the stage. "You really are safe. I won't let anyone hurt you. You know that, right?"

"I do." I take a deep breath as a recorded hymn, "Turn Your Eyes Upon Jesus," plays over the sound system. Noah mutters to himself, practicing despite the teleprompter, "Unity, love, acceptance, healing, compassion for others..."

Adam doesn't leave my side. "We can go anytime. The deal is for Noah. Not you. You don't have to speak if you don't want to."

I push up on my tiptoes and kiss his clean-shaven face. "I love you."

He closes his eyes, as if relishing the words. "Every time you say that, it's hard to believe. But, because you're the one saying it, I *always* believe." His dark eyes find me again, and just like that, he takes my breath away in a kiss. He slides his hands down to my waist as his tongue strokes mine, his mouth perfect against me.

Noah clears his throat.

We ignore him, and I rest my hands on Adam's shoulders as he pulls me tight to his chest. I could get lost in his kiss. Forget where we are, ignore the pain and the loss this place embodies, but he lets me go.

"I don't care what the doctors say, little lamb." He drops one more kiss on my lips. "Tonight, you're mine."

I tingle all over and drop back down to my heels.

"Get a room, sheesh." Noah shakes his head, but he can't hide his grin.

"Emily, whenever you're ready." Zion stands with his arms crossed and looks out at the audience. The church is half full, the rest possibly watching on the Heavenly channel from their homes. Or maybe they're shunning any association with the church, pretending that the Prophet never swayed their souls toward damnation.

"You can do this." Adam squeezes my hand one more time and steps back, his eyes never leaving me.

"Miss Lanier." An agent hands me a microphone and shows me how to turn it on.

I take a deep breath, then walk out onstage. The lights are blinding, and I can't see the crowd anymore. My remarks aren't scripted, so the teleprompter only shows the beginning of Noah's prepared speech. Looking up, I see myself on the huge screens along the upper auditorium. My dress—peacock blue with an empire waist and a hem that falls above my knee—flatters my too-thin frame and hides the bandages I still wear over my cuts.

Stopping on a black x toward the front, I flip on the microphone and bring it up. *Can I do this?* I take a deep breath and, to my surprise, the words flow.

"Once upon a time, I had a sister." My voice is loud and bright through the speakers. "Her name was Georgia. She was the most beautiful soul I've ever met. Smart, funny, brave. She was everything I wished I could be." Emotion threatens to stifle me, but I set it aside for now. For now, I have to speak my truth in a way that these people will hear it. "But then she joined the Cloister. And she died because of it. When I couldn't get answers, I joined the Cloister to find out why she was taken from me. Even though I knew exactly what the Cloister was. Some of you knew, too." I clear my throat. "But I'm not here to accuse or judge, I'm here to testify about what happened to Georgia, what happened to me, and how we can all change the future so as not to make the mistakes of the past."

I glance at Adam. He stands rapt, his gaze on me, pride in his eyes. And he gives me the strength to go on, to tell about the abuse, about the friends I made and lost, and above all, about the love I found and will keep in my heart for the rest of my life.

***

"I can say for a fact that was the best sermon I ever heard at Heavenly." Davis meets us in the lobby of our downtown Birmingham hotel. "And the improv parts, damn. You sure you can't be persuaded to stay—"

"I need a drink." Noah peels off and beelines for the hotel bar.

Davis curses under his breath.

"Lay off him." Adam keeps walking, his limp still there but less pronounced. He impatiently pulls me with him, and a shiver shoots to my toes because I know why.

The din outside wafts into the lobby whenever the door opens—media and zealots vying for attention in front of the hotel. We haven't given interviews, and we won't. Reliving it at the church was enough for me, and the nightmares haven't stopped. Maybe they never will.

Davis hurries to catch up. "We still need to talk about your plans. Where the two of you will go, what to do about Emily's mother. We'll need you to be available for the trials. There's planning that needs to—"

Adam jabs the elevator button and turns to Davis. "Step the fuck away."

Davis hesitates. "I—"

"Let me rephrase." Adam's voice, already hoarse, lowers to deadly levels. "Step the fuck away or I'll beat your ass the same way I did at the compound."

Davis glowers but moves away. "This conversation isn't over."

Adam turns his back on him. As in, the conversation is *definitely* over.

The elevator opens and we step on. Adam stabs the "door close" button until I think he may break a finger.

I slide my palm down the front of his suit. "We are going to have to talk to him at some point."

"Not now."

When the doors finally close, he backs me against the elevator's side wall. "Do you have any idea how proud I am of you?"

My heart falls all over itself, but I give a little shrug. "You told me a few times."

"Not enough." He runs a hand through my hair. "Not nearly enough." Though I expect it, his kiss still sends shockwaves through me. His mouth pressing against mine, his tongue tracing the seam of my lips. I open for him, and he groans, his hands tangled in my hair as the elevator slowly rises to our floor.

When the door opens, he pulls away and grabs my hand, hurrying to our room.

He reaches in his pocket for the key card, but his fine motor skills aren't there yet. I reach in and grab it for him, then swipe it through the lock. Anticipation buzzes through me like a drug.

When the light turns green and the lock clicks over, he shoves the door open and pulls me inside. He shoves me against the hotel room wall, his body pressing into mine as his mouth takes over again, kissing and caressing, his hands roving my body. I wrap my arms around his neck, standing on my tiptoes, my body lengthened and feeling every bit of contact from him.

He pushes his thigh between my legs, my skirt giving just enough for him to press against my most sensitive spot. I moan and my toes curl.

"Fuck." He breaks our kiss and scoops me up in his arms, though he's careful of the still-stitched area across my upper back.

Carrying me to the bed, he sets me on my feet and turns me around. Though it takes a few tries, he gets my dress unzipped. It pools around my ankles. His fingers start at my shoulders, touching every bit of bare skin with something verging on reverence. His lips follow, tracing a path that raises goosebumps and makes my stomach clench.

I want this. I want *him* so badly. But when I close my eyes, I see the walls of my room at the Cloister, hear the screams from the other Maidens. My breathing speeds up.

"Hey." He turns me around to face him, his dark eyes filled with concern. "What's going on up here?" He draws his fingertips along my temple.

Tears prickle behind my eyes. "I think maybe I'm messed up now. Because of what happened," I whisper my biggest fears, safe in the knowledge that he, above all others, will understand. "I don't want to think of that place when we're together. I want it to be new, clean. Just you and me."

He kisses me gently. "It's just you and me. No one but us. The door behind me? You can open it and leave whenever you want. You are *free*." He strokes my cheek. "Though I can't promise I won't follow. You may not have noticed, but I can't be without you. I love you."

I take a deep breath and let it out. He's telling the truth. I am free. There's no one watching, no ulterior motives at play. It's just us, and all those ghosts that still haunt me can't fit in the space between us. I won't let them.

It's a leap of faith—a sign of my trust—when I kiss him. He rests his hands at my waist, his thumbs teasing my hip bones. I swipe my tongue inside his mouth, and he lets me take the lead. My fingers go to the knot of his tie, undoing it and sliding it to the ground. Then I work on his buttons as his hands grip a little tighter, his heart beating faster against my hand. He's trying to keep himself reined in. I smile against him, enjoying what has turned into a wicked tease.

I strip his shirt off, my hands easing down his hard chest to his chiseled waist. When I grab his belt buckle, he groans into my mouth and smooths his hands up until he's unclasping my bra. The whole time, our tongues are seeking and caressing, our breaths coming faster and faster. The tightness in my stomach only increases, and I know my panties are wet.

He slides off my bra as I undo his pants and let them fall to the floor.

"No underwear?" I stare at his hard cock, the smooth skin and rounded tip.

He shrugs, then jerks as I run my finger along the side of it.

Breaking our kiss, he drops to his knees and presses his nose against my mound. Looking up, his eyes half-lidded, he asks, "May I?"

My nipples ache, and I think I might combust, but I nod.

He pulls my panties down, then spreads his palm across my stomach, gently pushing me back until I'm sitting on the bed. Spreading my legs, he nuzzles against my soft flesh, and tingles shoot through me.

"I want to please you, little lamb. To show you I'm worthy." He kisses me, his tongue darting against my clit.

I grip the bedspread.

He presses his mouth against me, opening wide as his tongue sweeps from bottom to top. I moan and spread my legs wider.

He takes the invitation and presses his tongue inside me, his palms pushing my legs open as he devours me. I stare down at him, his dark hair falling across his forehead, his strong back tense as he pleasures me with his tongue. I run one hand through his hair, pulling him closer, guiding him to my clit. He flicks his tongue across it, and my legs shake. Then he seizes on it, pinching it lightly between his teeth before running the broad side of his tongue against it again and again. He speeds his pace, each lick a flame adding to the fire burning inside me.

Sliding one hand up my thigh, he presses a finger inside me.

I arch, my head thrown back as my hips move against him, following his rhythm. He adds another finger, pulsing them inside me, stroking me in tandem with his tongue. My legs begin to shake, my hips seizing. I'm on the edge, ready to fall over, to give myself to the pleasure only Adam can provide.

He curls his fingers inside me, and I fall. He licks the orgasm out of me, my body seizing around his fingers, squeezing and shooting sparks of release all over my body. I moan low and deep, relishing in each wave of delicious bliss. He groans against me, his low rumble sending me into another series of crashing pleasure. I fall backwards, my body limp, the last aftershocks making my legs jerk as he licks me a few more times.

"Adam," I breathe out. "I need you."

He kisses me, giving me one more long sweep with his tongue, then crawls up my body, kicking his shoes and pants off.

Lifting me with one arm, he lays me gently in the center of the bed. "Are you okay?" The genuine care in his tone makes my heart ache, and I wrap my arms around him and kiss him again.

His cock presses against my wet skin, and I spread wide for him.

He tenses. "Are you ready? I don't want to—"

"I'm ready." The heat is already building inside me, and I need him. He's the only one who can put me back together, can join our broken pieces and make us whole.

"Your back. Will it hurt?"

"I'm fine." I rock my hips up, and his cock head rubs against my clit. I bite my lip at the sizzling sensation.

He keeps his gaze locked with mine and positions himself at my entrance. With a steady push, he groans and seats himself inside me. There's only a little sting this time that fades quickly.

"I don't want to hurt you." He pulls back and thrusts again, as if he can't help it.

"You won't." I nip at his bottom lip. "Not until I ask nicely."

His wolfish smirk appears, and my heart purrs. Another, harder thrust follows.

I dig my nails into his shoulder. "You're so cute when you're trying to be gentle."

He kisses down my throat and bites. "Don't get used to it."

God, yes. I hold onto him as he thrusts harder and faster, his cock pounding me as he bites down my neck and to my shoulder. I tangle my good hand in his dark hair as he kisses to my breasts. Running one arm beneath me, he lifts my chest to his mouth. He bites my nipple gently, then sucks it in, his tongue working it as he pounds into me. Each stroke sends a jolt of pleasure through my clit, and the way he's holding me, I'm at his mercy. Completely exposed and safe in his arms.

He moves to the other breast and wraps one hand around my shoulder, leveraging me down onto his thick cock. I spread my heels wider, getting every bit of contact between us, so filled with him it almost hurts. When he bites my breast, I moan, and yank his hair. He just bites the other breast harder, then moves one hand to my clit.

"Adam," I gasp as he lays me back down and claims my mouth again in a rough kiss. It's messy—teeth and lips and tongues—and everything I need. The swirling pool of need inside me coalesces on the spot where his fingers stroke me, and I feel the sharp edge of release approaching. My movements grow more erratic, my hips on the verge of locking. When they do, I come on a long moan. He swallows it, still pounding inside me as my orgasm turns me inside out, wringing the pleasure from me.

"Fuck, little lamb." He thrusts deep, his length growing harder as he groans. His cock kicks inside me as he comes, and I pull him close, biting his neck as the tension dissipates, our bodies sated, our souls entwined. He relaxes on top of me.

"I love you so much." He presses his forehead to mine. "I can't make up for my past, for my mistakes. But with you, I'll work every goddamn day to make you happy. I swear it."

I smile, my heart fluttering like a contented bird. "I love you, too."

He closes his eyes. "Say it again."

I laugh and kiss the tip of his nose. "I love you."

"That's all I need." He opens his eyes and peers into the deepest part of me, the part where he's reflected. "You're all I've ever needed."

ACKNOWLEDGMENTS

Thank you, as always, to Mr. Aaron for alpha reading and encouraging me and watching me fall apart and putting me back together and listening to me say "I can't do this" and telling me "you can do this" and letting me have the comfy spot on the couch and always being there for me (even when I can't remember the last time I showered because I'm too busy trying to get my words).

To the girls for forcing me to play dolls or watch a mind-numbing Youtube video about My Little Pony, or making me go outside and watch you in our #economypools (it's baby pools, folks, along with a sprinkler, but they think it's pretty fancy, so we go with it) to get me out of my own head a bit.

To Viv, who hounded the ever-loving fuck out of me about Grace. Look, Viv, for the last time, Grace is a VICTIM! (And also, not breathing, so it's a win-win, eh?)

To Trish Mint for begging me for darkness, even though she's a fairy of goodness and light.

To my Rabid Readers for helping me with reviews and getting the word out. To my Acquisitions for enduring all my posts about cheese. You gals rock.

To Stacey and Trina for catching my grammar and continuity booboos. Y'all are the shit.

To my readers who have loved this series as much as I have, or maybe even more. You've given me room to run, and I've taken it [too far, as usual]. Thanks for supporting me when I go super duper dark.

And, finally, to any women out there who have lived in a backwards, misogynist culture and survived. And if you've thrived? You are a badass, and I bow down to your perseverance and strength. Like I said in the Author's Note at the end of The Maiden, my dark books are, at their very core, a feminist scream. This series is no different. These happy endings are for you, to prove that love can change everything.

Thank you for reading.

Xx,

Celia

PS Just as a side note, my mantra for this book—from outline to last word—has been "All are punished," which is a line from the Prince at the end of *Romeo & Juliet*. I feel like it's a fitting for the end to this series.

ALSO BY CELIA AARON

Dark Romance

Devil's Captive

I'm to be married. It should be a time of joy, but all I feel is dread as I walk down the aisle toward a man who only wants me for my family ties. But my walk is cut short when Mateo Milani enters the cathedral, murders my groom, and takes me for himself.
Mateo is cold, violent, and vicious beyond anything I've ever experienced. The devil with a handsome face and eyes that haunt my dreaming and waking moments.
There's no escaping his grasp, and even if I could run, Mateo would find me and drag me right back to hell. He wants to possess me, stealing pieces of my soul with his cruel words and heated touches.
His motives are sinister, his methods calculated.

I hate him in ways I've never hated anyone in my life. But the part of this nightmare that scares me the most is the way he makes me forget my hatred, the way he commands my pleasure, and the way I crave him when I should want him dead.

The Bad Guy

She was a damsel, one who already had her white knight. But every fairy tale has a villain, someone waiting in the wings to rip it all down. A scoundrel who will set the world on fire if that means he gets what he wants.
That's me.
I'm the bad guy.

The Acquisition Series

Darkness lurks in the heart of the Louisiana elite, and only one will be able to rule them as Sovereign. Sinclair Vinemont will compete for the title, and has acquired Stella Rousseau for that very purpose. Breaking her is part of the game. Loving her is the most dangerous play of all.

Blackwood

I dig. It's what I do. I'll literally use a shovel to answer a question. Some answers, though, have been buried too deep for too long. But I'll find those, too. And I know where to dig—the Blackwood Estate on the edge of the Mississippi Delta. Garrett Blackwood is the only thing standing between me and the truth. A broken man—one with desires that dance in the darkest part of my soul— he's either my savior or my enemy. I'll dig until I find all his secrets. Then I'll run so he never finds mine. The only problem? He likes it when I run.

Dark Protector

From the moment I saw her through the window of her flower shop, something other than darkness took root inside me. Charlie shone like a beacon in a world that had long since lost any light. But she was never meant for me, a man that killed without remorse and collected bounties drenched in blood.

I thought staying away would keep her safe, would shield her from me. I was wrong. Danger followed in my wake like death at a slaughter house. I protected her from the threats that circled like black buzzards, kept her safe with kill after kill.

But everything comes with a price, especially second chances for a man like me.

Killing for her was easy. It was living for her that turned out to be the hard part.

Nate

I rescued Sabrina from a mafia bloodbath when she was

13. As the new head of the Philly syndicate, I sent her to the best schools to keep her as far away from the life--and me--as possible. It worked perfectly. Until she turned 18. Until she came home. Until I realized that the timid girl was gone and in her place lived a smart mouth and a body that demanded my attention. I promised myself I'd resist her, for her own good.

I lied.

Mississippi King

In Azalea, Mississippi, the only thing hotter than the summer days are the men of the King family. When the patriarch Randall King is found dead, Detective Arabella Matthews will race the clock to stop the killer from striking again. Benton, the eldest of the King siblings, has to decide if he wants to cooperate with the feisty detective or conduct his own investigation. The more he finds out about his father--and the closer he gets to Arabella--the more he wants to keep her safe. But the killer has different plans . . .

ABOUT THE AUTHOR

Celia Aaron

Celia Aaron is a recovering attorney and USA Today bestselling author who loves romance and erotic fiction. Dark to light, angsty to funny, real to fantasy—if it's hot and strikes her fancy, she writes it. Thanks for reading.

Sign up for my newsletter at celiaaaron.com to get information on new releases. (I would never spam you or sell your info, just send you book news and goodies sometimes). ;)

Newsletter Sign Up

Stalk me:
www.celiaaaron.com

Made in United States
Troutdale, OR
09/21/2023

13099250R00204